PAM CLARKE

ROSEMARY REMEMBER

ROSEMARY REMEMBER

ISBN O 9537058 2 X

First Published in 2001 Prism Press Cheshire

E/Mail address prismpress@talk 21.co.uk

Printed in England by Redwood Books Ltd.

Other Titles by Pam Clarke.

Winds of Despair.
The first in the Rosie trilogy.

Cover Illustration
Graham Kennedy.

ONE

Yelling as he ran, Samuel squealed. 'Mummy, mummy.'

Wobbling on her stubby little legs and chasing after her beloved brother, Emily cried. 'Daddy, daddy.'

Emerging from the kitchen busy wiping her hands on her soiled apron Molly smiled fondly at her children's clamour, this roly-poly, tubby little girl, and her wonderful son. Considering the circumstances of his birth, the trauma of her pregnancy, she marvelled daily that he has turned out such a fine sturdy boy.

Pushing with her finger at the wayward curl on his blonde head she waited for him to collected his breath and tell her what the noise was about.

'There's a stranger asking for you,' he informed her seriously.

'A stranger? The Refuge is always full of strangers,' she smiled with motherly concern as she reminded him. 'They've never bothered you before.'

'I think he means me.' The deep voice said, it belonged to a tall, slim, elegantly dressed male with a pleasing smile. He held out a firm hand asking in a cultured tone. 'Are you Molly Ebson?'

Bobbing her head in salute Molly confirmed her name a tremor of apprehension making her shiver.

'I'm Simon Saunderman,' he said softly, his gaze travelling her face watching for a sign of recognition.

Her legs refusing to hold her weight Molly slumped into the nearest chair, mouth agape she stared at him foolishly. Emily, frightened by her mothers reaction scuttled to her knee, her tiny hands gripping at the screwed up apron being twisted in Molly's lap.

Absently taking her small daughter onto her knee they watched the stranger place his hat and cane on the table beside him. Molly lowered her head and nuzzled her child's neck, collecting her emotions as she breathed the baby smell.

'Please sit down, Mr Saunderman,' she requested quietly. Then turning to her son she instructed. 'Samuel run and find your father.'

Sammy stole a brief look at their visitor before he inclined his head towards his mother and fled the room.

Mentally shaking herself, Molly absently smoothed Emily's baby fine curls, vivid pictures of a past she had hoped would never return to torment them flashed through her brain with lightning speed.

'Molly, Molly,' Jake's anxious tones preceded him into the room as he rushed to his wife's side. He stopped short at the sight of the stranger and looked in bewilderment from one to the other, his face telling of his wary instincts.

'I am Simon Saunderman, Edwards younger brother,' the stranger held out a hand of friendship. 'I take it you are Jake?'

'Edwards younger brother,' Molly whispered in confirmation of her worst fears, her voice barely audible, her face blanched white she stared at her husband.

Taking the proffered hand, his stance still wary and protective of his wife and family, Jake asked. 'What can we do for you?'

'I feel duty bound to come and speak to you,' Simon said, he cleared his throat before continuing. 'In the light of what I wish to do now, my Father the Earl,' he took a deep breath about to launch into a long speech. 'My father died two weeks ago.'

2

Holding up his hand to stop the discussion going any further, Jake spoke firmly, 'if, this is about Rosie. There are others who should be privy to this conversation.' Acknowledging Simon's slight bow of agreement, he went on. 'Then I suggest we delay it until I have notified them.'

'You have taken me a little off balance,' Simon admitted. 'I had assumed you, and your good wife here, were the only people involved. That is why I came to Battersea. Now you are telling me there are others?' His eyes opened wide in amazement. 'I was led to believe you were her designated parents.'

'Rosie was a popular young lady,' Jake replied, an edge of misery in his tone, his hand going to Molly and gripping her shoulder. 'There are a number of people who felt close enough to her to suffer guilt and remorse at her abduction. Two in particular that would wish to be included.' His tone indicated clearly he would not be swayed on the matter.

'Whatever you say,' Simon responded politely.

'In the meantime, Molly,' Jake said smiling at his wife. 'Perhaps our guest could be persuaded to join us for a meal.' His words were more a statement than a request. He looked directly at the younger man. 'Allow me to show you around our humble premises.

'I...I don't wish to put you out,' Simon shuffled uneasily, his eyes casting about the large, communal dining room in which they stood. 'Perhaps I should return later.'

Stepping up beside him Jake clapped him on the back. 'Not at all,' he admonished firmly. 'Under the circumstances I feel it may help you to see the home Rosie had here, she was part of The Refuge, *Home for the Homeless*, whatever you want to call it. She helped to build it. Not physically,' he joked. 'But it was Rosie and Molly that persuaded me to accept my inheritance and use it for the good of others. She helped plan it in the beginning and was part of the team that ran it when we opened. This place,' he waved an expansive arm about him with pride. 'Is as much, Rosie as any of us here.'

Visibly putting his discomfort to one side, Simon accepted his tour of the building. 'Tell me about, Rosie as a child,' he requested. 'I know little about her past, only what detail I had been able to glean at the time when she, and Edward disappeared, and that was very sketchy.'

Jake rested his thigh against the window in the empty bedroom that had once been Rosie's, not looking at his guest he gazed out at the sky, allowing his mind to travel backwards in time.

'Once upon a time there was a waif,' he began, 'a pretty, delicate child who, found herself sitting on the workhouse steps. I took her home with me. I couldn't give you a reason why I did such a thing, not then, nor now. In those days I was a vagrant,' Jake smirked at his visitor, 'not exactly what you'd expected?' he asked, not waiting for a response. 'Then I found another treasure and added her to my life. Molly. It's a long story, but in short Molly and Rosie had known each other in the past. We became a family, a happy family. Then your brother came along and destroyed us all.'

'Rosie's mother?' Simon queried.

'The child had been born in the workhouse her mother died there. Later she was sold, with a young woman, Nancy, to a whore house.' Jake shrugged. 'That's another story. Suffice to say that Nancy rescued her from a future of depravity but was forced to return the child, for her own safety, to the workhouse.' Jake turned and rested his buttock against the wall his arms folded across his middle. 'Before she reached the age of five years, Rosie knew more about hardship and turmoil than a lot of people experience in a lifetime,' he added vehemently.

'What about Molly? Am I correct in saying she was imprisoned for murder?' Simon raised an inquisitive eyebrow that questioned his bristling companion.

'Yes. Again the blame lay at your brother's door,' Jake replied tersely. 'Not that she didn't commit the crime. She did, under great provocation. She suffered terribly in prison

4

and almost died from the injuries inflicted upon her. Later it was confirmed another inmate was paid, by a 'toff' to do the work' Jake's tone softened. 'But you don't need to know about all that.'

'My brother,' Simon replied with resignation. 'That part of it I already know.' he confessed. 'I have acquainted myself with as much detail as I possible could. How old was Rosie when Edward abducted her?'

Shocked at the question, Jake stood upright with a start shaking his head regretfully. 'We were never exactly sure of her age, eleven, twelve, maybe a little older,' he shrugged. 'We were never able to establish any genuine facts.'

'So, she would be what? Sixteen or so now.' Simon asked thoughtfully. 'A lot may have happened to her in the last four years. Would you recognise her if you found her?'

'She may have matured,' Jake growled, turning aside and walking out of the room the conversation clearly at an end. 'She may have changed facially, but love never changes. I would know her instantly,' he threw the words over his shoulder as he led the way back to the dining room.

Later in the Ebson's private quarters, Jake passed round generous sized glasses of port before formally introducing the gathering to Simon.

'This is Lewis Maxwell, a lawyer, retired now,' he recited the details bluntly. 'Our Lewis I'm afraid is more eaten up with guilt over Rosie than any of us.' Jake threw the elderly man a respectful glance. 'Not that he need be, he played no greater part in the girl's disappearance than any of us.'

Jake waited whilst the two men shook hands and exchanged brief words of greeting, before turning to a figure sat quietly in a corner.

'This is Ninny,' he said placing a protective arm on the back of the old woman's chair, looking down fondly at the tired black face and head of tight curls, more grey now, than black. 'Don't be fooled by her frail state of health, there is a strong spirit and a good brain still functioning in this woman,' he joked lovingly and she turned rheumy old eyes up to his.

Again Simon shook hands politely, he smiled at the black woman whose eyes suddenly twinkled delightedly at his discomfort.

Moving to the centre of the room Simon coughed to clear his throat then, began.

'As I have already said my Father died recently. He ailed for years,' there was a defensive edge on his voice as he relayed the details. 'I believe strongly that the hope of finding my brother, Edward and clearing his name of the many charges against him increased his time on this earth. We had expected his demise for a very long time.'

'I'm sorry,' Lewis murmured, his expression puzzled. 'What has this got to do with us?'

'Whilst my father was alive,' Simon began, picking his words carefully. 'I was never able to follow my own instincts.' His tongue popped out and licked nervously at his lips, a flush touched his cheek he looked cautiously from one to the other. 'I think I had better state my case bluntly. I wish to attempt to trace my brother.' He paused again when a murmur rippled through the room.

'In the last years,' he continued almost apologetically. 'Edward's name was never mentioned in front of my Father. He hoped, wished, his son would miraculously return and everything would be made right all sins forgiven, and forgotten.'

Jake jumped to his feet, the dark liquid in his glass slopped dangerously as he waved his arm in violent motions. 'If you have come here to plead your brother's innocence of the crimes levelled against him,' he spluttered, beside himself with rage. 'Then leave now. What about my Molly?' he yelled. 'What about Rosie?' he added in quieter desperation. 'Abduction of our little girl is the least serious of the crimes against him.'

6

Lewis rose and took hold of Jake's still outstretched arm in an effort to restrain him.

'Never mind the brutal murders your brother committed.' The words continued to pour from Jake's mouth he ignored all Lewis's efforts. 'He took our Rosie, Molly almost died, and we are sure he was responsible for the death of Dirty Sam,' spittle sprayed from Jakes lips when he shouted. His eyes bulged and his face grew crimson. 'For any or all of these things we can never forgive him. What we want is justice. To see him hang.'

'I have no wish to argue with you,' Molly interjected, rising to assist Lewis in calming her husband. 'But Jake is correct, we have no reason to want to help you clear your brother's name.'

Holding up his hands to ward off any further verbal attacks, Simon cried, 'no. No, you misunderstand. I wish to see justice done. That's why I want to take up the search myself,' he turned his head to encompass them all. 'I apologise for my cowardice in not having done so whilst my Father lived. Now he is gone.'

'Then you would be the next Earl? Entitled to take up the rich trappings of such a life!' The words dropped into the silence. Surprisingly strong they came from Ninny, the old woman wrapped under the blanket.

Uncomfortable at the directness of the question Simon replied with all the honesty he could muster. 'No, not entirely officially my brother is the new Earl. Until we find him and he comes to trial the family can do very little. There have been no legal provisions made for dealing with the estate in his absence. My Father was always convinced of his son's innocence.' He concluded lamely.

'Bought…you mean,' Jake snarled.

Lewis stepped forward. 'Ill feeling will get us nowhere,' he said firmly, taking charge of the situation. 'I want to see this fellow caught as much as anyone, so lets hear Simon out without the animosity.'

7

Jake stabbed a finger in Lewis's direction. 'This man spent six months trailing your brother.' With effort his tone more reasonable, he went on. 'The search was fruitless. He ran into nothing but dead ends and at that time the trail was still fresh.' He looked Lewis's aging figure up and down with sympathy before turning directly to Simon. 'What makes you think four years on, you could find what he couldn't?'

'Unless?' Lewis intervened, a light of hope springing to his eyes. 'You believe your father knew where his son went. Perhaps you have information we are not aware of.' He gazed questioningly at Simon, anticipation on his features. 'I retired from my business when all this happened four, long years ago. It was me, after all, that gave Edward the right to collect Rosie, expecting him to bring her to the bedside of Molly here, who was dying.' He sighed audibly, his sagging jowls shaking with emotion. 'I, we, did not know who he was then. We had no idea he was already acquainted with the child, known to her as Raymond.' He stopped speaking to listen to himself it was all so complicated. 'But I have never given up following any line of investigation however meagre, that has come my way.'

'Your brother abused my trust by running off with a precious member of this extended family,' Lewis stated with more resolve. 'If you have knowledge of his whereabouts, we have a right to be informed.'

Simon clenched and unclenched his fists, the knuckles gleaming whitely under the pressure he exerted on them.

'In the beginning,' he said evenly. 'I too was sure my Father knew. We received periodic visits from a very unsavoury character. Conversations were carried out in whispers. Later I was less sure. Somehow the door I thought linked them, closed. I am sure my Father went to his maker without the knowledge we all seek.

'Where does Rosie come into this picture?' Jake asked quietly, his brow furrowed by concern.

'I still think if I find Edward, I find Rosie,' Simon replied.

8

Shaking with memories which stirred her inners like a witches brew, Molly whispered. 'You, think she is still alive?'

'In truth, I don't know,' Simon shrugged helplessly. ' Just a feeling, I make no promises, but I must try.' He sat down at last. Perching on the edge of his seat his body pushed forward, elbows digging heavily into the flesh above his knees he asked earnestly. 'Please tell me all you can about the child...and my brother.'

They all began to speak at once. It took Lewis to monitor the conversation and put the information thrown at him into some semblance of order, for Simon to understand. It took several hours to tell all they knew. Stunned speechless Simon listened patiently.

'You are right,' his words whistled through his clenched teeth, his head nodding. 'My Father would have given any amount to clear his favourite son's name. With a background like that, the girl would have become the guilty party, my Father would have achieved his aim.'

He studied the occupants of the room one by one, his head shook sorrowfully at what he could only imagine this family had endured.

'Edward,' he went on, 'was a great one for acting out the many fantasies that made up his world. I strongly believe Rosie is still alive. I also believe in his own way, Edward loved her.'

'That's a crazy thing to say,' the words exploded from Jake's lips, he would have said more but the others hushed him immediately.

Simon chewed on his lip as he continued. 'He, Edward, was capable of all consuming love. A love that was almost evil. He was obsessive about things that belonged to him and I think he would consider, Rosie belonged to him, nobody else. If I'm correct about his feelings he won't let go of her, his all consuming love won't die, not until he does.' He sat back in his chair digesting all that had been said.

The room fell silent Molly's whispered, 'oh, My God,' the only sound.

Lewis stood again. Placing his hands under the lapels of his coat he took an unconscious legal stance. 'I would not wish to raise anyone's hopes. If, and I repeat if, Rosie were found alive, she would no longer be the child we knew and loved.' He bowed his head. 'She may be much changed. But I admire this young man for the effort he wishes to make. Therefore Simon I offer my services. Whatever you wish to do I will do it with you. Wherever you wish to go I will go with you. If you'll allow me.'

Jumping to his feet Simon grasped Lewis's hand and pumped it up and down heartily. 'This is more than I could have hoped for,' he cried with delight and beamed about the room, personally acknowledging the message in each pair of eyes that stared back at him.

Battle plans were being drawn up. It had taken a day or two, and a great deal of organisation and restraint. Now Simon and Lewis sat in the sunniest corner of the garden, stacks of paperwork in front of them, much of it held in place against the playful breeze by stones rummaged from beneath the flowering bushes surrounding them.

Beside the table in a softly padded chair Ninny dozed fitfully in the warmth of the afternoon.

'There is eight years and two months in age, between Edward and me,' Simon explained quietly. 'Edwards mother died not long after his birth, he was brought up by hired hands,' he confided. 'My Father married again, and I arrived.' His face saddened at the tale. 'My mother ended her days living a lonely life in the west wing of our home. She was surrounded by luxury, waited on by servants,' he paused before adding. 'Loved only by me.'

'Edward was paranoid about cleanliness he hated being dirty.' He went on softly, a down turned smile twisting his mouth. 'I remember once he physically attacked the chimney sweep with fire irons. Our boot boy led a most miserable existence.' Simon tapped his chin as he recalled his memories. 'Edward used every excuse possible to cause the boy trouble.'

'When I was very young,' he confided with a little embarrassment. 'I worshipped my brother, even tried to be like him. Then as the years went by, Edward's liking for powdered and perfumed atmosphere's cut him more and more away from the general activities of the house.'

Lewis was puzzled. 'Did you continue to grow up admiring him?'

'No...I became the subject of Edwards cruelties. There were always well planned and discreet. He never received any blame. For instance, I gave up keeping pet animals they always met violent deaths.' Simon's tone dropped low as he enlarged on his tale. 'My toys were always miraculously destroyed. In the end I refused to make any friends for fear it would happen to them.'

'You seem to be describing two people, not one,' Lewis said thoughtfully, 'the first, a perfumed, dandyish, type of fellow, the other, a near monster. Do you believe him capable of the crimes laid at his door?'

His gaze fixed firmly on the papers in front of him Simon nodded dumbly, his acquiescence speaking volumes.

'But could he live without finances?' Lewis pushed his point.

'That is another matter,' Simon replied with a sigh. 'The amounts Edward spent on clothing.' He lifted an arm in a hopeless gesture. 'I have never known him wear a garment more than once. How he would be managing now! I cannot imagine.'

Shuffling papers Lewis studied his young friend from beneath lowered lids. 'I have the feeling you are still a little mixed up emotionally about your brother. Although your adult senses tell you how evil he could be, there is still a tiny corner of your heart that loves that brother you knew as a small child.' He touched Simon's arm and look directly at

11

him. 'There is no shame in that,' he concluded, before he changed the subject completely.

'The police, and other authorities are being very helpful,' he mumbled. 'Despite the time lapse, I feel hopeful.'

Looking sideways with admiration at his newfound comrade, Simon grinned. 'Aided by a few of your old acquaintances,' he said with a chuckle.

'Being an almost heir to an Earldom helps,' Lewis affirmed. 'Together we seem to be making progress.'

Ninny stirred in her dozing as Lewis absently stretched out a hand and patted her arm. 'She's dying I'm afraid,' he remarked sadly. 'She's lived longer than her due, that heart of hers should have given out a long time ago.'

'I can see you're very attached to each other,' Simon murmured. 'Do you wish to wait until,' he left his sentence unfinished. 'Join me later, maybe?'

'No,' Lewis replied sharply. 'I don't wish to lose her, neither do I wish to prolong her agony. We understand each other.' Stating the facts unemotionally, he picked up the latest documents and returned to discussing their plan of action.

'I feel sure they are still in England,' he said, examining a document closely. 'I don't feel they took ship at all, what say, you?' Lewis turned his head to wait for his companions reply.

'I agree,' Simon nodded vigorously. 'Four years ago when you followed them to Plymouth, the authorities were certain they had taken ship and left the country. But knowing Edward of old, I would say he did that to put anyone following off his trail.' He studied the notes of Lewis's first attempts to find his brother. 'I can't blame you for believing he had done so,' he acknowledged. 'Edward would have made his plans very carefully.'

'But,' Lewis said thoughtfully. 'He wouldn't have had a lot of time to think these things through.'

'Several days,' Simon reminded him. 'All the time it took for his carriage to travel from London, to the West Country, time enough for a brain like Edwards.'

'These banking notes were a find,' Lewis perused the paperwork with pleasure. 'Payments made to Raymond Jenkins; that was the name Rosie knew him by. Collected at regular intervals by an agent, pity his identity remains unknown,' he added with disappointment. 'Why do you think they came to such an abrupt end?'

'Almost two years ago,' Simon confirmed. 'My Father suffered a seizure it left him unable to conduct his own affairs, other people had to deal with his documentation for him. It drove him mad, more so than I would have thought necessary. Now I know why.'

'The final withdrawal from the agents account was some sixteen month's ago,' Lewis tapped the page with his pen then spoke again. 'It is almost two years since any money was paid to the agent on behalf of this young man. I doubt Edward would work for a living. So, how would you imagine him to be surviving?'

'Off Rosie,' Simon replied flatly, his face mirroring his thoughts.

'Dreadful.' A shudder passed through Lewis at his own thoughts on the situation. 'Now are you sure no other unusual things happened during your father's illness?'

Simon pondered the question, his long sensitive fingers stroking his chin in an absent gesture. 'I'm sorry no, my Father's affairs were dealt with very strictly by his man, Henry he would have known I'm sure, but I'm equally sure his lips would have been sealed. He was devoted to my father.'

'Where will we find him?' Lewis asked eagerly.

'I let him go,' Simon replied. 'He was elderly. He expressed a wish to have time to himself after years of servitude. There was a home available to him on the estate, he refused to stay.'

'He could have gone straight to Edward,' Lewis shouted, his violent gesture as he spun round on his companion, almost knocking the table over.

'Oh,' Simon groaned. 'I'm so sorry, I didn't think. How stupid of me.' He slumped backwards in his seat, the slap as his palm hit his temple ringing in the air. 'How could I have let him go like that, why did it not occur to me?'

'It can't be helped,' Lewis replied, deflation in his tone. 'I feel it may well confirm what we already believe. Edward, and hopefully Rosie, are both still in this country. They never took ship anywhere. So,' he said, standing and rubbing his hands together with more enthusiasm. 'The sooner we start for Plymouth, the better.'

Rosemary

TWO

The sea stretched as far as her eye could see. The tide in full flow lapped beneath her against the foot of the retaining wall. Droplets of salty water sprayed upwards occasionally some unseen force carrying a wave before it. Breaking against the stonework it wet her cotton dress and she chuckled.

The sun, a deep orange ball, hung on the edge of the sky barely touching the watery horizon, it darkened the light above whilst setting fire to the sea below.

Could some invisible hand hold it in place? She wondered, the late summer dusk slipping about her. The orange, yellow rays danced on the wavelets and she hugged her knees to her chest. Her long hair, darker than its usual golden brown in the twilight, lifted from her neck in the playful wind. Turning her face into the light warm breeze she allowed the caressing sighs to push the curling tendrils away from her tanned face. Laughing aloud she gazed up at the antics of the home going gulls, whooping and wheeling above her.

'Rosemary, Rosemary, supper's ready,' a voice called from the cottage doorway behind her.

Turning reluctantly from the water she made her way to the long, low building she thought of as home. The tiled roof showed green in patches from the wear and tear of the rough elements. The walls, a dirty yellow, were scaled in places the colour bleached by sun and wind. She had been told it had once been the colour of bright sand. Now it looked moss covered, neglected and unloved.

Heavy wooden shutters hung either side of each of the low windows they kept out the strong winter winds. Stout wooden boarding against the lower portion of the door made you step high to get inside. It kept water out when gales caused the sea to rise over the low, protecting wall, which happened at least twice each winter.

'Come along, Rosemary. We are all waiting.' The voice had taken on an urgent impatience.

Rosemary hated winters. She did not remember always hating winters. Then she did not remember much at all. She was a person without a past. Placing her small hands on her temples she tried to remember how long they had lived here. They had arrived at the end of winter, her and her brother Robert. Everyone had told her the worst of the winter was over. Then had come summer, she had enjoyed the summer.

Followed by winter, it must have been. She did remember the bad weather, the storms and bitter cold. She had spent most of it inside by the big fire in the comfortable kitchen with Mrs Gee and Abel. She thought of the homely soul like a mother, yet not her mother. Funny, she thought as she dawdled, she did not even know the woman's first name. In all the time they had been living in the cottage she had never heard her referred to in any other way than Mrs Gee, or 'woman' in Abel's case.

Robert told her their mother was dead. Things never seemed quite what they should be.

Arms folded across her breast in a severe manner, Mrs Gee stood in the hallway watching the child amble across the grassland. 'Come on slow coach,' she called, her face cracking into a smile. The love she felt for the child written on her features.

'Your daydreaming will be the death of you, my girl,' she said softly, pushing Rosemary gently towards the kitchen door.

Laughing, Rosemary hugged the bony figure accepting the small gesture to hurry her. Making her way to her place

17

at the long table, that groaned with home cooked fare. She grinned cheekily at Abel, Mr Gimlet where he sat stiffly at the head of the table, knife ready in hand, waiting for her to settle.

'Hello,' she said quietly to the assembled gathering, then turning to her brother added. 'I'm sorry to have kept you waiting Robert.' Thankfully he chose to ignore her.

Beside Robert sat Mr Timpson. A humble little man, modest in both build and manner. He had confided in Mrs Gimlet, he never called her Mrs Gee like everyone else. How much he had wanted to follow a calling to the church. Unfortunately the thought of standing up and addressing a congregation had proved too daunting a task, and monk hood had not appealed to him. Rosemary knew the poor man was the butt of every cruel joke possible. She felt sorry for the way he scuttled about, bible clutched to his chest. Her own brother regularly taunted the man to tears.

In their time at the cottage Rosemary had never been able to make friends with Mr Timpson, much as she had tried. He only appeared at meal times then hurried away again.

My, she thought as she studied the two men, her brother and Mr Timpson, from beneath lowered lids. Robert looks so large beside him. Broader and more muscular, yet he was not the tallest man she had ever met. In fact Abel, an ex seafarer, old and wrinkled as he was, could make any man seem small and weedy.

'How was your day, Robert?' Mrs Gee asked pleasantly, making polite conversation.

Robert grunted without replying. Rosemary piped up for him. 'Oh just as usual.' She could not possibly know what usual was for her brother. He kept himself very much to himself, professing to hate everyone in the place, except her: A feeling that was mutually upheld by the rest of the household.

'Eat now,' Abel instructed, his clear green eyes circling the table, his arm waving fingers still curled about his knife.

Summer and winter the sleeves of Abel's rough shirt would be rolled in a ridge above his knobbly elbows The thin skin of his arms beginning to wrinkle and sag with lack of energetic exercise.

'This house is a cage to me,' he told her regularly with a sigh. 'I need to feel the rolling sea beneath my feet. To see the empty landscape, it's like no other you could ever imagine. All the hard work.' It had been tales of his seafaring days that had passed the long winter nights in front of the fire.

'We'll be going to town tomorrow,' Mrs Gee informed Rosemary with a smile. 'Is there, anything I can get the child?' she asked Robert politely.

He shrugged, only looking up briefly from his meal. 'Whatever you think,' he replied carelessly.

The kindly woman always brought Rosemary her clothing they enjoyed their trips to town, together.

'You can't trust a man with personal requirements,' she stated bluntly. 'And I can't trust my Abel with store cupboard shopping either,' she laughed.

Rosemary knew that was not strictly true. Store cupboard goods were supplied by the local farmstead, eked out by they're own, few hens and rabbits. Together with Abel's vegetable patch, they ate extremely well. Shopping trips were purely pleasure, Mrs Gee just had to make excuses.

The day dawned bright and sunny. The short trip to town an enjoyable anticipation of the pleasure to come. Arms linked they walked the narrow cobbled streets, peering in the low, often lopsided windows of the hotchpotch of traders that made up the shopping area.

Owners called a cheery 'hello,' from doorways, before crying their wares in a hope of attracting their custom.

'Can we go to the tea shop?' Rosemary asked, squeezing affectionately at the older woman's arm, 'please.'

'We always do,' she smiled her reply. 'First you need some dresses, and new underwear.'

Laughing, their arms laden with parcels, they entered the little teashop, finding a table by the window they settled for a well, deserved rest. Rosemary liked the crisp, white table covers, the big black kettle that sang on the shiny, black range. She liked the delicate cups and saucers and the matching plates full of scones and jam. She felt she had known this place all of her life.

'Tell me how you met Abel?' she begged as she spooned jam on to her plate.

'Again,' Mrs Gee laughed. 'You must know the story better than I do. If I've told it to you once it must be a hundred times.'

Rosemary knew that, none the less she loved listening to it. Mrs Gee had been born in the far north of England, and still retained some of her lilting accent. Her father had brought his young family south, to London, to search for work. Work had not proved so much more plentiful, but the children, Mrs Gee, her two brothers and two sisters, had all grown strong and healthy.

'He was a seaman,' Mrs Gee sighed. 'Just docked in the Port of London. Oh, he was so handsome.'

'Why didn't you stay in London?' she asked thoughtfully. 'I was born in London, so Robert says, but I can't remember any of it. I often wonder what its like.'

The older woman smiled at the child. 'I know dear,' she replied softly. 'Abel's family lived here, in the cottage. His parents greeted me like a daughter. Our home had been their home.'

Rosemary knew that too. Abel had told her stories of his childhood, and his son's childhood before the boy had been lost at sea, as a young sailor. Abel had left the sea then, allowing his wife to re-model her life on looking after him and taking in paying guests for a livelihood.

'Did you love him?' Rosemary asked dreamily.

'You wee minx,' her companion chuckled. 'I loved my man then and I love him now. One day I hope you will meet someone who will make you as happy.'

The day ended all too quickly, they were back in the cottage taking they're evening meal and re-living the highlights when Robert spoke. 'I may not be back tonight, no need to leave a lamp burning.'

He scraped his chair back noisily across the stone flagging on the floor making his way to the door that led to the side of the building. On his way he reached up and pulled a lightweight cloak from a hook, shrugging it about his shoulders before slamming the door behind him.

'Manners,' Mr Timpson muttered before excusing himself from the table.

The pots banged together in the chipped sink and Mrs Gee mumbled. 'Sinful, that's what it is, sinful, what he gets up too,' she tutted, peering over her shoulder at her husband and the girl. 'And her such a good, wee mite.'

'What's the matter with you woman,' Abel cried, winking at his young companion. 'Live and let live,' he laughed. 'What say you, Rosemary?'

Joining in the fun, she helped with the clearing and the cleaning. What Robert did with his time was not for her to question.

'How old do you think I really am?' she asked when the three of them settled for their evening chat. 'That assistant in the dress shop said I must be small for my age. Robert says I'm sixteen, do you think he's right?'

'Aye lass, I know what he says. An' well you might be that old. But I would say more like thirteen or fourteen,' Mrs Gee shrugged. 'Who can say?'

Rosemary puzzling on her problem did not fail to catch the strange look that passed between husband and wife.

THREE

Robert froze where he lay in the semi darkness, something had woken him…what? His gaze travelled about the unfamiliar room, his eyes adjusting rapidly to the half-light. Sniffing disgustedly he smelled stale body odour, and more, much more, that hung redolently in the air.

'Oh no, dear God, not again,' he groaned peering at the sleeping woman by his side, her mouth open, her breath rattling in her throat.

Straggled hair splayed out over the filthy pillow. The early rays of daylight gave it a multi coloured hue. Dark brown where the tips were in shadow, orange red along the centre and black close to her head. He shuddered when he recalled, he had stroked those tresses and called them beautiful. 'Soft and silky,' he had told her he could hear his own voice ringing in his head.

Now he was awake next to her! How did he find himself in this situation so often? Licking at his lips he tasted his own sour breath. His furred tongue felt too large for his mouth swallowing to clear his sandy throat his saliva reminded him of dank water.

How could it all have tasted so exquisite last night? He asked himself. How could he be allowing his life to sink this low?

The noise came again, a scratching at the doorway. Turning his attention from the dirty face of the woman in the bed he allowed his eyes to travel slowly along the wall. The child stood in the doorway, three or maybe four years of age. Wisps of pale, frizzy hair framed her sleepy face, she stared at him. A thumb was stuck deep in her mouth, a grubby piece of rag clutched tightly in the fingers of the same hand it dangled across the front of her torn night shift. Her small feet were bare.

Easing himself up in the bed, the framework creaking with each movement, he lifted his legs gingerly and placed his feet on the floor, careful not to wake the sleeping woman.

At his movements the child retreated, pulling the door almost closed she slunk backwards into the darkness of the hallway.

Padding in his stocking feet, Robert followed her the smell of rotten cabbage assailing his nostrils when he passed through the doorway.

'Hello,' he whispered, swallowing the bile that rose unbidden into his mouth.

His eyes adjusting to the dimmer light he saw her clearly. The sound from her mouth as she sucked on her thumb, grating on his strung out nerves. Her small back was to the wall, her eyes fixed on him. With her free hand she was feeling her way along, searching for the open door to her own sleeping quarters.

'Wait, don't be afraid,' Robert called softly, increasing the size of his steps.

Falling backwards at the opening the child grabbed at the door of the walk in cupboard that held her mattress. Robert jumped, silent as a panther. He pushed the small body into the confined space, a tiny skylight relieving the darkness and he closed the door behind him.

It was still early morning when Robert left the scruffy little terraced house, one of a row of equally dingy homes. The low sun of a dawning day struggled to break through a white, sea mist rolling at the water's edge.

He walked jauntily along the sea front. He saw not a soul, no early workers, no curtain peepers, and felt satisfied that nobody saw him. He felt better having washed in the cold water left in the basin on a stand by the bed he had vacated.

His mouth he had swilled in the fountain in the square. 'Yes,' he said happily. 'This day promises to be a good one.'

There were things he wished to do, things so far not done. A cruel smile swiped across his lips, he allowed himself to get sidetracked so easily, he decided. It was time to travel again. Not across the sea, never across water. The fish would not have chance to feed off his bones. He remembered a tutor from his childhood, telling him grisly tales of pillage and plunder, swordfight and cannon fire. Those old fools the Gimlets, they had lost they're only offspring to the sea, had they not?

Making his way over the grassy headland, Robert congratulated himself on finding such isolated quarters. 'The old woman could do with some decent cooking lesson's,' he muttered. 'She had no idea how to feed a gentleman.' He laughed aloud. If only they knew who they were housing in their home.

He whistled to himself whilst he walked. It was time to be moving on. He had worked well on the girl once before. He could do it again. Two years he had given sufficient time to complete her memory change. She had been muddled and confused at the beginning, now she was clear and lucid.

'It's because we have recently lost our parents in a tragic accident,' he had told the Gimlets. 'The doctors tell me she will recover, she needs rest and love,' he said with his most appealing air. 'Who else can give that to her than her big brother,' he had simpered at the stupid old fools. 'That's why we came to the sea.'

'People will believe anything if you give them enough money,' he told a swooping gull with a laugh. 'And I have plenty of money,' he shouted into the wind.

There had been a small hiccup, money wise at first. Then he had found silly Billy. A daft lad with a background as rough as the earth he was treading. Destined to end up swinging from a gibbet, that was Billy. Just as his father before him.

Robert had offered him what must have seemed like a king's ransom, plus a horse, for a messenger to London. Billy had been willing. After a week of worry in case the lad realised what he was carrying, he had returned and Robert's money problems had been over. From then on he had made arrangements for his finances only using Billy as a periodic go between, travelling the country between him and his Father, the Earl.

Over the weeks and months he had stripped away his so-called little sister's memory, replacing it with his own version of their childhood. She loved him so, no, adored him, he knew that. She would do anything to please him.

Hands deep in his pockets he raised his head and looked about. The sea did not inspire him. He was tired of this place it bored him. It was time for another memory lapse he was sure he could do it safely. Then again he reminded himself, there was not much to lose if it failed. The girl was expendable if she had to be. A shudder went through him when he thought about that. Rosemary, as she was now known, was the only secure thing he had to hold on to. What would he do if he were alone?

The Gimlet's would surely be willing helpers in his new plan, wouldn't they? They loved the girl with a passion verging on pathetic. If they believed he was leaving to take his sick sister back to the family doctor, they would do whatever he told them.

FOUR

The first person Rosemary saw each morning was Robert. Waking from her troubled sleep he was always there hovering, an anxious look on his face. Today was no different.

'What's happening to me?' she asked, she struggled to sit up, bending her head against the pain shooting through it when she moved 'My head feels funny, all muzzy, and my body's heavy,' she moaned.

Robert perched on the side of her bed and took her hand in his. 'Don't worry,' his tone was reassuring. 'I'm here.'

His assurances were all very well, but she still needed to know. 'Am I ill?' she persisted, 'I haven't felt well for days.' She could not remember when she had started to feel off colour. 'Tell me?' she implored plaintively, stretching an arm out to touch him.

'You were calling in your sleep, that's all,' he reassured her tenderly. ' I brought you a drink of water,' Robert reached for the tumbler and held the glass to her parched lips.

'Did I drink some?' she asked, tasting her still furry mouth with dismay.

Holding up the glass he showed her how little of the liquid remained. 'Yes dear, you have drunk all this.' He sat more comfortably on the edge of the high bed, his manner full of concern.

Rubbing her eyes, Rosemary took the glass and drank some more. 'I feel so muddled,' she moaned sleepily. 'My head has stopped working. It aches so.'

26

Dear, dear,' Robert clucked with concern. He walked to the door and called loudly for Mrs Gee, she appeared as he had expected, immediately. No doubt hovering in the hallway to eavesdrop. 'I'm worried,' he whispered, putting on an elaborate show of emotion. 'Please take a look and give me your opinion. I feel she is having a relapse.'

'Oh, please God, no.' Mrs Gee clapped her hand to her mouth. 'The poor bairn.' She pushed past him ignoring his distress, not in the least bit happy at the state of her patient and placed a cool hand on Rosemary's burning brow.

Hardly had the hand touched the girl's skin before Rosemary leaned forward and was violently sick. Dismayed at what was happening to her, and distraught at her own actions, she burst into tears.

'There there,' Mrs Gee crooned, trying to make light of the incident, at the same time whipping away the soiled bedding. Turning to Robert she directed sternly, 'find Abel. Send him for a doctor without delay. Trust my husband to have gone early to town when he is needed.'

'I will not have a country doctor looking at my sister,' Robert blazed defiantly at her, taking her by surprise. 'The only doctor my sister requires is our family doctor. He knows of her background and will no doubt know how to treat her instantly. I will ask Abel's help though,' he added thoughtfully, refusing to look at the woman's wide-eyed disbelief. 'I need to make arrangements to take her back to London, at once.'

Turning he left the room ignoring the woman's protests. She stood staring after him, mouth opening and closing, so beside herself at his high-handed attitude, the twitch of a grin at the corners of his mouth had gone completely unnoticed, by her.

Fighting back her tears, Mrs Gee ministered to the girl, bathing and changing her visions of the pathetic child who had first arrived at their door returning with force.

They had arrived in a big fancy carriage, Robert and Rosemary, big brother and little sister, as unalike as two people could be. Him, his dark brooding eyes set in sallow coloured skin. Her, a fair skinned waif like creature with pale brown hair and eyes that matched. Not a scrape of baggage between them. Her face so pale, her wide frightened eyes, dark circled, fear oozing from every pore.

Spine chilling screams had rent the night air, as the child tossed and turned in her nightmare world. Weeks of patient, loving care it had taken simply to stop her being scared of every movement about her. Weeks during which, Robert had sold the fancy carriage, an action which Abel had never been able to understand.

'Them only being here on holiday, like,' he had said, scratching his head over the problem. She, herself, had never been able to form an opinion that satisfied her.

Abel, she recalled, had spent the most time with the child, talking endlessly to the bowed head. It had been Abel who finally convinced the wee mite she should stop trying so hard to remember the past. He understood better than most, from his own terrible loss, how the mind longed to forget.

'Love,' he insisted. 'Love is all she needs.' And that was what he had given her, in abundance.

In the end Rosemary had rewarded him, she had stopped sitting day long, shivering in the kitchen, finally she had begun to live again. Now it looked as though she was back where she started.

The heavy kitchen door banged open and Abel charged inside, the sea breeze rushing in with him slamming the wooden structure against the wall. His arms full, he pushed the door closed with the heel of his foot and shouted. 'Woman, woman, you should hear what they're saying in town.'

The appearance of his wife with her finger to her lips shushing his noise stopped him in his tracks.

'I know that look, woman. What's the matter?' He sniffed the air like an animal that knew danger lurked.

'It's Rosemary, she's worse?' he cried, dropping his purchases on the corner of the table and struggling out of his course jacket.

'Hush now,' Mrs Gee soothed going to his side and sorting out the muddle he was getting himself into. 'The bairn is poorly. Robert,' she informed him softly. 'Is going to take her to London, to their own doctor.'

'What's wrong with the town doctor?' Abel fumed angrily, seeing Robert loom in the doorway. 'He's a fine man, as good as any from London.'

Robert turned and stomped from the room a loud rasp in his throat the only reply.

'He thinks it's a relapse,' she whispered, guiding her husband to his favourite chair. ''Tis maybe for the best if she sees a body that knows of her past problems,' she stated unconvincingly. 'There is little we can do anyway, she's his flesh and blood, not ours,' she added sadly.

Abel slumped the life leaving him. 'So he says. I have tried to like the man,' he admitted, more to himself than his wife. 'But I don't trust him. This cottage will be empty without the child.' He looked up at her, his face mirroring her thoughts.

'They will come back,' she said defiantly, patting his old arm. 'Robert has promised.'

Abel snorted. 'It's a long journey, they won't return. She shouldn't be made to travel if she's ill.' His lips set in a firm line he watched his wife put the big kettle on the range.

Turning to him, her heart full of sorrow for both of them, Abel and Rosemary, she asked lightly. 'So what was all that clatter when you came in. What did you hear in town?'

'There's been a murder,' he stated flatly, no interest in the gossip now. 'Not just one, two.' He had been so full of the news all the way home, anxious to tell all before he forgot any details.

Mrs Gee gasped she could never recall a murder in the town, not in all her years of living here. There were stories of dire deeds in the long distant past, but mostly she thought them exaggerated nonsense; family feuds hundreds of years ago, that sort of thing. Seating herself on a hard chair pulled up beside her husband, she encouraged him to tell her the facts.

'A mother and her child, still in their beds, it seems,' Abel's voice was low and husky, he hated violence. 'Mind, she was a loose woman by all accounts,' he could only repeat what he had been told. 'Not fussy who shared her bed.' He wrinkled his nose. 'In all my years at sea I have never found a need for such a woman,' he assured his wife.

His wife smiled fondly, he did not have to tell her that, she knew what a faithful man she had as a husband.

'Strangled they say,' he continued. 'No sign of any fight, must have gone easy.' His dour face added solemnity to his words.

'A child you said? Would I be knowing them?' Mrs Gee questioned, she mentally ticked off the children of her acquaintance in the town. 'Girl or boy?'

'A girl,' Abel replied, nodding. He was no good with names, so he endeavoured to explain where she lived instead.

'Oh her, she's known for her lack of morals,' Mrs Gee, clicked her tongue before adding. 'But she was pleasant enough mind. Needs must when the devil drives she used to say to anyone who commented on her way of life. But, by heck, she loved that wee lass. Never entertained in the daytime, she told me that herself.'

'The child was suffocated, had a dirty piece of rag stuffed right down her throat.' Abel's voice shook shudders made his body tremble, he looked pityingly at her.

'And,' she prompted, knowing instinctively there was more.

'Used,' he stated bluntly, his eyes shifting from her face. 'You know what I mean.' His head bounced as he tried to indicate without words. 'Torn, so I was told. She was most likely dead before the worst happened. Before he satisfied himself like.' Tears swam in his eyes a sob choked him as he listened to his wife's low moan.

'How could, anyone,' she wailed. 'When, when did it happen?'

'Four, five, nights ago,' Abel shrugged. He had not asked and could not remember if he had been told exactly.

'She weren't the worse woman in town,' Mrs Gee said softly, a tear sliding down her face. 'I've seen that little lass with her bitty cloth. Pretty little thing, she wasn't more than four years old.'

'I can't recall anything that dreadful happening around here before, hanging's too good for a crime like this,' Abel muttered in response.

'We're getting too old for this world,' she stated, wiping the back of her hand across her eyes. 'It's getting too evil for the likes of us.'

The departure to London was delayed for three more days, as Rosemary began to suffer regular, severe bouts of sickness.

'She's far too weak to travel,' Abel insisted, beside himself with worry, surprised when Robert agreed with him.

'Her eyes have gone vacant, I don't think she recognises me any more,' Mrs Gee cried against her husbands shoulder when they were alone in the kitchen. He smoothed her grey hair allowing her tears to wet the front of his shirt.

'He should let us call a doctor,' he moaned. 'This sickness has come on too fast for my liking. I don't understand anything about the mind,' he confessed. 'But I'm sure it shouldn't be like this.'

Stepping back and turning her red ringed eyes on him, she mumbled. 'Maybe he's right, their own doctor is best, but I'm frightened for her.'

'Well I've done all I can,' Abel told her, in despair. 'I've arranged for the hire of a carriage. But I'll be blessed if I know why he insists on driving it himself. I've offered to accompany him meself,' he informed her quietly.

'What if she needs attention on the journey,' he had levelled at Robert. 'You can't drive and attend to her.' His protests had been in vain. Robert was determined.

'If she gets sick, I will stop,' he insisted. 'There is always a good hostelry to be found in all the towns we will pass through.'

'He's insisted on paying several weeks rental in advance,' Mrs Gee reminded her husband. 'Say's he will return the carriage himself, when she's better, and they come back.' The hollow words of comfort did not help the way either of them felt.

'How could he ever come back, after what happened in town?' Abel scoffed, his pitiful face turned on his wife.

'You think... no, surely not,' she cried in dismay. 'I know he's an objectionable fellow, but a murderer, and worse.'

'Think what you like, woman, but these things never happened before he came.' Abel stated flatly.

'Well you can stop thinking like that,' his wife reprimanded sternly. 'Unpleasant he may be, but a killer, never. Let's put all that to the back of our minds and get on with making the most of the time she is still here, with us.' Mrs Gee turned her back on her husband and got on with her normal daily tasks. There was no way she could entertain her husbands suggestion, it would destroy her. She had to believe that Rosemary was leaving in the care of someone who loved her, who would one day bring her back to them.

'Now be sure to stop often. See you make her eat a little,' Mrs Gee beseeched Robert, before she loaded a basket of snacks inside the carriage next to Rosemary. He ignored her completely, tapping an impatient foot at being kept waiting.

Abel, busy wrapping a fine blanket around his favourite guest propped in the corner of the carriage seat, motioned fondly to his wife. 'Don't get upset now,' he warned. 'She needs to take away memories of happy faces, not tears.' He

32

smiled lovingly at Rosemary, receiving a bemused look in return.

Covering the child's small, pinched face with kisses, Abel pulled his wife away from the carriage door, Robert, had made it clear he would wait no longer.

'Goodbye,' he shouted, he cracked the whip, snapping it in the air to hurry the horse and they lurched away.

'I will miss her,' the timid voice of Mr Timpson took them both by surprise he stepped to their side and watched the carriage draw away.

'This house will never be the same again,' Abel agreed. They all stared along the wet and empty road. Each equally convinced that they would never see the child again.

Rosemary lay on the uncomfortable carriage seat, the continuous rocking movement and the sonorous rumble of the wheels along the uneven road, adding to her malaise. Her head ached from her efforts to make sense of all that was happening.

Though she found herself unable to recognise the people making such a fuss of her when they left, she was fully aware they all knew her well, and loved her greatly.

Yet she recognised her brother with no difficulty. The only sure thing in her mind being how dear he was to her.

She had heard him telling the kindly old lady they would be travelling inland to London. The old man had picked out details from a map in his hand. Robert had agreed they would be turning away from the sea as soon as they passed the town. Raising herself on her elbow she squinted out of the window she could see water stretching away in the distance, yet they seemed to have been travelling a long time. Could she be wrong, had it only been a few minutes, she was so confused. How far was this town he had referred to? She could not remember any town, how could that be?

Rosemary had no reason to believe she knew London. Despite that a little voice in her head was nagging that

33

London was where she belonged, and she was prepared to put up with any discomfort on the journey, if she could get there. There she would be safe, somehow she knew that as a certainty.

A sudden overwhelming sense of loss filled up inside her, she slumped back on the seat, but try as she might, she could not understand why.

FIVE

Rosemary gagged on the pungent smell of raw fish. Muddled about what was happening to her the nausea did not help her to make sense of it. Happy that the movement of the carriage had ceased at last, she stared out of the window, trying hard to understand why they were here.

'Well how are you feeling now?' Robert asked cheerily pulling open the carriage door and making her jump violently. He grinned widely at her, rubbing a hand over his unshaven face.

She reached out and touched his cheek. 'You look different,' she said, feeling foolish. They had been travelling almost none stop for two days how would she expect him to look? 'You look tired,' she murmured gazing at his red veined eyes.

'I know,' he answered ruefully. 'You've been so ill I've forgotten my ablutions.' He looked across the roadway at a black beamed, inn front. 'I have secured rooms for us here, let me help you down.' He reached in and gently lifted her from the carriage placing her gently on her feet, one arm around her middle to steady her.

'It looks lopsided,' she said in a small voice. 'It's tired. Like me,' she added plaintively looking at the row of huddled buildings opposite.

Slamming the carriage door, he gave orders to a scruffy boy holding the head of the shivering, sweating horse, then led her slowly inside, whilst the lad, the horse and the rumbling carriage vacated the narrow roadway.

Later, resting on her lumpy bed, still trying to piece together the events that had overtaken her, Rosemary responded to a gentle rapping at the door, surprised when the transformed face of Robert peered into the room.

'What have you done?' she cried staring at his new look.

'Don't you like it?' he asked petulantly, a sulky little boy look springing to his features.

She nodded slowly acknowledging. 'It's a surprise, I don't recall you ever having a beard before.' She watched him stroke the tiny square of dark hair on his chin. Under his nose he had left a pencil line moustache and he had shaped his lengthy hair around his ears so that the sides grew further down his face. 'You look very handsome,' she told him with feeling.

He smiled and preened himself then he paraded around the room.

'Where are we, Robert?' she asked. 'I thought we were going to London.' She studied him quietly surely those were new clothes he was wearing? She could not recall seeing them before.

'Oh,' he cried, waving his arm in a careless gesture. 'I didn't want to impose such a long journey on you. I thought we would travel just a little, for your recuperation,' a smile softened his words he avoided her gaze.

Rosemary bit her tongue on the remark that sprung to her lips. She was sure she had heard them saying it would take but three or four days hard riding to get to London. Surely they had been travelling two days already and were still beside the sea. They could have been half way to London by now. Her heart sank with a kind of despair as she realised he had never meant for them to go there at all.

'Could we please go somewhere that does not smell of fish,' she asked, slumping back on her pillows exhausted, her nose wrinkled against the persuasive aroma.

'See,' he cried with delight. 'You feel better already.' Laughing he took a lungful of air as he finished speaking. 'It smells fine to me. But if you wish we will leave tomorrow, after a good night's rest.' Still laughing he turned and left the room.

Rosemary struggled to a sitting position she was bemused. Suddenly nothing made any sense at all, except Robert. In him she knew she trusted implicitly.

They travelled at a much slower speed for almost a week, stopping each night in pretty little villages. Rosemary's health improved rapidly and her appetite returned. She was enjoying her time in her brother's company enormously.

'You were quite right, the travelling is doing me good,' she confided in him over an evening meal, her worries about her memory fading into the background whist they chatted and laughed together.

'Do you feel fit enough for a walk before retiring?' Robert asked, reaching to help her move away from the table, accepting her nod of agreement as a reply.

They strolled arm in arm stopping at the edge of a small pond.

'How would it be if we find a bigger town, one where we can go shopping, maybe look for somewhere to settle for a while?' he asked quietly, shuffling his feet where the water met the grassy surround.

Rosemary pondered his question. 'Are we not expected somewhere?' she felt sure they were. A frown creased her brow she watched a pair of playful ducks dodging in and out of a nearby reed bed.

'Who would be expecting us?' he queried, turning to stare directly into her eyes whilst she thought about it.

'I don't know,' she replied, clearly confused. 'I was sure, but I must be mistaken.' She chewed on her lower lip as she struggled with her thoughts. Pictures flashed across her memory, but she could put no substance to them. 'No-one,' she admitted at last, then put her head to one side and returned his stare. 'What about the sumptuous mansion waiting back in London for us?'

Robert's body jerked. 'What mansion,' he snapped.

'The one you told me about,' she said softly. 'I'm sure I didn't dream it. You sat on my bed, somewhere,' she screwed up her face trying to remember the location, then she shrugged, that part did not matter. 'You described it in detail, it sounded wonderful.'

Robert visibly relaxed as he listened. 'That's our home,' he told her. 'The one waiting for our return when you feel well enough to go there.'

'But I'm much better now,' she argued enthusiastically. 'You've just agreed with that opinion. Don't you want to go home?'

Robert answered with more feeling than she had ever heard before. 'Very much, but you are not yet fully recovered. You may feel better, but once the terrible memories returned, and they might if we go home too soon, you would slip backwards and be ill again.'

He pulled her small hand more tightly through his crooked arm and patted her fingers turning their steps away from the pond. Smiling proudly Rosemary gripped onto her brother. She was not blind to the gazes of the passing ladies. She knew he was the best looking man in the world.

'The first big town we come to tomorrow,' he promised. 'That's were we will stay.'

SIX

They ran from shop to shop giggling foolishly like a pair of naughty children, trying on outfit after outfit, their purchases mounting up at an alarming rate. Robert had everything they bought sent to the largest hotel the town boasted. That was where he has decided they would stay until he found a more permanent home to his choice.

For two weeks they visited every premises the town had to offer for rent, finally deciding on a set of neatly furnished rooms above a delightful parade of shops. A scrolled, wrought iron balustrade and walkway surrounded the group of buildings, turning them from ordinary, to special.

The area on the edge of the town was quiet and refined. It had wide streets and neatly cared for open spaces, well-tended flowerbeds and grassland with wooden benches. It was exactly what they had been looking for.

The large window of the main living room looked out over sloping rooftops, showing just a thin glinting line on the horizon.

'That must be the sea,' Robert remarked, laughing. 'Is it far enough away for you, little sister?'

'I don't dislike the sea at all. Merely the small of rotting fish,' Rosemary replied with a dignified toss of her head. 'But,' she went on to confess. 'I do feel happier in a town.'

The shops beneath their new home were charming an expensive, exclusive dressmakers, took up most of the row, the showroom at the front obscuring the workrooms behind. Next to that was a milliner. A pretty, pink-framed mirror on the rear wall threw her own reflection back at her, when

39

Rosemary pressed her nose against the window. Hanging next to the mirror was a wide brimmed straw bonnet with a blue band and matching ribbons trailing down the wall. Her stomach lurched at the sight of it, her eyes refusing to be torn away. A vague memory stirred in her mind as she saw a child, a girl, twirling beside water, not sea water, brown water, the girl was laughing and dancing. The memory hurt, with a gasp, she turned her steps and hurried to the next window. A toyshop completed the row. Rosemary studied its contents allowing her heart to return to its normal pace.

'At nearly fourteen, you are a little old for toys I would have thought,' Robert remarked pompously.

'Am I nearly fourteen?' she asked turning her head and looking at her brother in surprise. 'When is my birthday?'

'What,' cried Robert, 'you can't even remember your own birthday,' He laughed loudly, then said in a confidential whisper, 'it's next week. So, you can stop pretending in case I have forgotten. We will celebrate on the day. Now,' he said, taking her by the arm. ' Let's get back inside and start making ourselves comfortable in our new home.'

Rosemary giggled as she hung on to him. She could not remember ever being so happy in her life before. They had everything they could wish for.

Unfortunately the euphoric mood only lasted a day or two before things began to change. Robert began to stay away from home and Rosemary found herself alone for long periods. Their rooms stretched the length and breadth of the block, not enormous, but sizeable, certainly far too big for one lonely young lady to occupy alone.

The days crawled into weeks, with no promised birthday celebration, she was not even sure of what date it should have been celebrated on. Finally threatened with a depression of the mind that worried her she confronted her brother on one of his brief visits.

'Can you not stay home this evening?' she begged following him from room to room, picking up his clothing as he casually discarded it.

'Don't pester me,' he growled, entering his own room and closing the door firmly against her.

'But, Robert,' she cried, leaning her head against the woodwork. 'You are always going out and leaving me. I get so lonely.'

Reappearing, resplendent in new clothing, he pushed past her and stomped from their home, the outer door closing with a resounding thud behind him.

Tears tripped from her lashes and she rushed to the window to see him leave. How could he be so cruel, surely he knew how much she loved and missed him?

Only minutes later the door re-opened heralding Robert's stormy return.

'You won't be left alone any longer,' he yelled at her, his cheeks pink with anger. 'I have secured you a position with the dressmaker below. You start at seven thirty in the morning.' He thumped the heavy cabinet that stood against the wall, making the china it contained rattle. 'Make sure you are not late,' he commanded.

'I know nothing about dressmaking,' Rosemary said in a strangled voice, her skin turning an ashen colour her mouth gaping in disbelief at him.

'Well,' he replied with an evil chuckle. 'You had better learn quickly.' He sneered, bringing his face close to hers. 'Otherwise you will find yourself lonely again, won't you? You make me tired with your whining and moaning. It's no wonder I don't come home to your company very often.' He shoved past her making for the direction of his room once again.

'Don't wake me when you leave in the morning,' he growled harshly.

'I...I thought you were going out this evening, you changed your clothing,' she waved an arm helplessly in his direction.

'I was,' he hissed. 'But you have spoiled my mood. Anyway, what I do and don't do, is none of your affair,' he concluded angrily, before turning his back on her and marching to his own quarters.

Curled tightly into the armchair that sat by the fire which she lit daily, Rosemary sobbed quietly, not wanting to make matters worse by disturbing him. Unable to fathom what was wrong with her brother, she accepted that his solution to her loneliness was the only one available to her.

Shuffling her feet she waited with all the patience she could muster for her new employer, Madame Mildred to appear. Rosemary looked about her. A tapestry bearing a script, *'Gowns sort after by the rich and famous'* hung on the wall of the small receiving area she had been directed to. Madame Mildred's strident tones could be heard issuing the days orders to her seamstresses.

Twisting her body Rosemary could glimpse the work area. Her stomach churned as she thought how she barely knew one end of a sewing needle from the other.

'You must be the new girl,' the staccato voice made Rosemary jump and she stared upwards at a tall, thin woman. The woman's back was so ramrod straight it made her seem more like a stone statue than a human being.

Beckoning with her finger, Madame Mildred indicated that Rosemary should follow her. With hesitant steps she did as instructed.

The view of her new employer from the rear was no less imposing than the front. The woman's close fitting dress, with its unfashionable bustle and high, ruffled neckline, held her head so upright it only added to her height. Rosemary wondered a little unkindly, if this stiff woman tried to bend, would she simply snap in two pieces.

'I'm pleased to meet you, Madame,' she offered hesitantly when her employer came to a stop and turned her attention to her as a person. 'My name is Rosemary,' she added quietly, unsure whether she should proffer her hand.

Smiling, the action lightening the otherwise plain face, Madame Mildred responded in equally quiet tones. 'I know,' she looked almost tenderly down at the young figure. 'Your brother told me.'

Panic seized Rosemary, how much had Robert told her? Had he said she was ill, that her mind sometimes made her crazy? Despite his claims that she was better now and her health was perfect, he had told her never to tell anyone about her problems.

'They will lock you away in an Asylum if you do,' he warned regularly.

'I hope you will be happy in your position with us,' Madame said, raising eyeglasses that hung on a thin cord about her stiff neck and placing them on the bridge of her nose to peer closely at Rosemary's face. 'You are very pretty,' she murmured stroking a light finger down the side of the girl's loose hair as she spoke. 'I like to think of my girls as an extended family,' she said softly.

Her employer's action adding to her nervousness, Rosemary licked at her dry lips, unable to think of anything to say in response, she watched the stern face break into a smile once more. If she wore her hair longer, instead of scraped back into such a tightly twisted bun, she thought, Madame Mildred would not look half as frightening.

'I have built a reputation on first class, workmanship. Nothing less than excellence will do here,' Madame went on with more severity. 'I am told you have no experience. Is that correct?' She placed an arm across Rosemary's shoulders, softening the sharpness of her words.

'If you please, Madame, I know nothing about sewing,' she answered honestly, her eyes travelling over the girls sat

43

around the long table, each pair of hands diligently plying they're needle in a different manner.

'Then my dear, you will have to start at the bottom. It will be hard work at first but I'm sue you will learn fast. Then when you learn more you will move on to finer work.' She smiled again, concern playing around her eyes. 'The more enjoyable aspects of dressmaking,' she added by way of encouragement. 'I am a hard taskmaster at times I know, but never be afraid to talk to me if you have a problem,' she said, beaming around at the faces looking up at her. 'I won't ask more of you than you can give, will I ladies?'

'No, Madame,' the chorus of voices politely responded in unison, each face smiling back at their employer.

Relaxing a little, Rosemary unbuttoned her cloak maybe this would not be so bad after all. The girls looking at her with interest all seemed friendly and welcoming.

The ages of her new companions seemed wide ranging, the youngest a child, younger than herself, was busy handing out threads from a wide, heavy basket that she carried over her arm.

'This is our little Fanny, she will keep you supplied with all you need to carry out your work,' Madame said, she patted the child's arm as she passed. 'You have no need to rise from your seat, Fanny will fetch and carry, she will also pick up the thread ends which are dropped on the floor. It is essential to keep everywhere as tidy as we can.' Fanny bobbed a curtsy then continued with her task.

Seven other women sat on the stools placed around the table. The table itself contained quantities of different coloured materials, the women having no difficulty in determining their own piece of work. Rosemary was introduced to each one in turn. They all seemed so much older than her. Then, guiding her through an annexe into a separate room with a small window that looked out on the side of the building, Madame introduced Rosemary to a girl not much older than she was. The girl stood respectfully as Madame entered.

'Tildy, this is Rosemary,' Madame said softly, smiling. 'I want you to teach her all you know.' Then looking down at Rosemary she added quietly. 'Tildy is one of my fastest learners, I'm sure you will get on well together.'

Coming round the side of the table Tildy pulled forward another stool, taking the cloak held across Rosemary's arm, she hung it on a peg, then smiled at her new work mate and said a simple 'hello.'

Taller than Rosemary, Tildy was very pretty in a china doll sort of fashion. Her long fair hair, high boned, pale pink cheeks and clear blue eyes, gave her a delicate air that no doubt belied her true strength of character.

SEVEN

Those early days at Madame Mildred's emporium, had proved hard and long, but had brought their own rewards. Rosemary found herself so tired from her day's exertion, hunched over a sewing needle for hours on end, she was glad to take her aching back and crawl into an early bed each night. She hardly noticed the emptiness of the apartment, or the absence of her brother. Her eye's too tired to consider any other activity than closing.

An adequate daily meal was provided at mid-day, for her workers, by Madame Mildred, it was by no means lavish, but for some it was the only meal of the day.

'Is it usual for an employer to furnish their workers with food?' Rosemary asked Tildy on her second day at work.

Tildy shook her head. 'Madame is one of the better employers,' she confided with pride. 'She says it ensures her workers won't fall ill from starvation. She says, it would cost her more in time and trouble than feeding us does. Mind you we pay part of it ourselves,' she grinned. 'She stops us a penny a week from our wages, I don't think anyone minds, really.' Turning her attention back to her work, Tildy smiled at Rosemary's naivety.

It only occurred to Rosemary at that point, she had no idea what her wages would be, or who they would be paid too. Having seen the look on the older girl's face, she hesitated before admitting. 'My brother made the arrangements for me to work here I don't even know how much I will be paid,' her confession made she looked hurriedly back to her needle.

'Only half of what you earn,' Tildy replied bluntly. 'I heard your brother discussing it with Madame. She is to pay you half of your earnings, the rest he will collect once a month himself.' She clicked her tongue on the roof of her mouth, but refrained from adding how disgusting she thought the arrangement. She had already said that to the other female workers around her.

'He's so oily, he makes me cringe to look at him,' one of the women had remarked. They had all been privy to Robert's demands. He, on the other hand, had appeared totally un-ashamed of his unusual request.

'He is a rather slimy character,' Madame Mildred had agreed, readily.

Rosemary had determined that she would ask Robert about this arrangement at the very first opportunity. Unfortunately it had never arrived and weeks later she had become used to the situation dwelling on it no more. Robert was the one who paid the bills, she told herself, and it was reasonable and fair for her to help him do so.

Tildy she learned, came from a large, happy family that lived further out of town on Canny's Hill. She was the youngest of the children who were extremely close and protective of one another. Her constant chatter about her relatives, and their exploits, made Rosemary more than a little envious. She wished she too had a host of brothers and sisters to laugh and argue with, as Tildy described so vividly.

'My fingers are so sore,' Rosemary complained, sticking each finger in her mouth in turn and sucking on them. 'Don't yours get sore?' she asked her companion.

'They did when I was sewing the Fustian fringes, as you are,' Tildy answered with a laugh. 'Now they are hardened to the work, yours will be soon.'

'What is Fustian? And why do we need to put it inside the dresses?' Rosemary questioned holding up a length of the stiff webbing, eager to learn as much as possible about the art of dressmaking.

47

'The fringe sweeps the dust from the roadways as the ladies walk. It helps to stop the gown getting so dirty around the bottom.' Tildy explained patiently.

'But I've never had any of this in my dresses.' Rosemary exclaimed, feeling she had missed out on something.

Tildy laughed aloud. 'Neither have I, but then I would not spend a years wages on one dress, the ladies that shop here do.'

Rosemary gasped, how could anyone justify spending a whole years wages on one gown? 'Well I hate it,' she grumbled laying aside a finished article. 'I would never make someone sew this dreadful stuff in my gowns, however much I paid for them,' she stated with authority.

'I felt exactly the same when I first started here and had to do what you are doing.' Tildy agreed. 'I was so glad when I could move on to the next, and easier stage.'

Rosemary sucked at a spot of blood on her finger, she was forever pricking her skin and fearful of staining her work. 'When will that be?' she asked between administering to her sore hands.

'When a new apprentice starts,' Tildy told her. 'Madame will probably take on someone new in about a month.'

Rosemary pondered her companion's words. 'In a month! Surely, if Madame takes on a new person each month, there won't be room for everyone?'

'Madame's reputation is growing rapidly,' Tildy assured her. 'We always have more work to do than we can fit in. So don't worry about it.'

In less than a month, Tildy's words had proved correct and a new girl took Rosemary's place, allowing her to move up the ladder. In that time her friendship with the girl from Canny's Hill had also grown, the two females becoming inseparable, daytime companions.

'My mother wants to know if you'll come home for your evening meal with us?' Tildy asked one morning as they settled to the day's tasks. 'I've told her so much about our friendship she can't wait to meet you.' She turned beseeching baby blue eyes on her friend. 'You will come, won't you?'

Overjoyed at the invitation, Rosemary was about to say, yes, when thoughts of Robert, and his temper flashed into her mind. 'I should ask my brother first,' she confessed with disappointment.

'Rubbish,' Tildy cried, anger at her friend's subservience to a horror like Robert, making her tone sharp. 'You probably won't see him for days. Anyway you can go to tea with a friend once in a while, surely?'

Never having had a friend that she remembered she was not as confident as Tildy on that point, but anxious not to jeopardise the relationship, she made up her mind quickly and answered. 'I'd love to come, thank you.'

That evening found them giggling as they walked together up Canny's hill to the higgledy-piggledy, house that the Sharp family called home. Mr Sharp, who had died some years ago, had built the original structure in the early days of his marriage, adding to it over the years wherever possible when the new arrivals kept coming.

The house had been extended on each side and upwards, giving it a strange appearance. The work had often depended on the material available and therefore could not always be carried out in the same style.

'How many children are there in your family?' Rosemary asked, nervous at the thought of having to meet so many people.

'Nine,' Tildy replied with a grin. 'I'm the youngest. Only three of my brothers are at home now, my three sisters are married and have families of their own. Don't worry, it isn't that crowded.'

'I can't imagine anyone having all those children,' Rosemary gasped in astonishment. She had known her friend came from a large family but had not realised the true extent.

'Oh, my ma had more than that, they didn't all live,' Tildy laughed. 'Anyway she loves babies, and all the children

49

helped with the work. It's not so hard. Here we are,' she said stopping beside a gate. 'Welcome to the nightmare.'

Her words did not worry Rosemary she had learned early in their relationship that 'The Nightmare' was how the family affectionately referred to their home. She also knew that each and every one of them loved it dearly.

That first visit soon turned into a regular weekly affair, and she found herself being drawn into the Sharp family as though she belonged there. With the deepening of the friendship she also found herself confiding her personal problems to Tildy.

'So I often think that is why my brother stays away from home so much. He is frightened I will suddenly get ill, and he will have to nurse me again.' She concluded after telling her story to the best of her ability, nervous at the reception it would receive.

Putting her arms about her friend and hugging her close, Tildy sympathised. 'Oh you poor thing fancy not knowing what had happened to you in the past. I have always led such a happy life. I would hate to forget my childhood. In future we will spend part of every day trying to bring your memory back. Together, we will make you better,' she promised.

True to her word, each day as they ate their lunch they discussed Rosemary's life, trying to unlock any detail, the tiniest glimmer of a memory delighting them. Many times Rosemary found herself on the edge of remembrance, only to have it slip away again. It proved such a frustrating experience.

'It's always so tantalisingly out of reach,' Tildy sighed, 'but we won't give up.'

Christmas came and went with little input from Robert, who seemed to be living an entirely different life from his sister.

'Go to that friend of yours,' he told her when she asked what he wanted her to prepare for Christmas day meals. 'I won't be home, so don't expect me.'

50

At first she had gone to the Sharp's home to join in their family celebrations with reluctance, wishing she could be in her own home, spending the time with her brother. Only after a splendid meal, when they sat around a blazing fire singing carols and toasting chestnuts, had she realised how much more enjoyable it was in this comfortable, humble house than it would have been with Robert. Finally she had been glad he was away.

'I'm sorry I can't return your hospitality,' Rosemary said sadly to her friend as they sat, at the end of the working day, in the sitting room above the workshop. 'I would love to ask you to stay, but if Robert came home.' She did not need to finish her sentence she knew how Tildy felt about her brother. The girl had been unfortunate enough to witness his return, and his bad temper on several occasions. - - -

'I miss him and I worry about him,' Rosemary confided. 'When he does come home sometimes he is so dishevelled, almost fearful in the way he acts.'

'Why don't you ask him where he goes, and what he does,' Tildy suggested bluntly, her manner showing how tired she was of the man's tantrums. 'That's what I would do.'

'I dare not he gets into such dreadful rages.' Rosemary cried in horror. 'The other evening when he returned his shirt was so badly torn it can't be repaired. I will have to dispose of it,' she stated flatly chewing on her lip as she considered the situation. 'He's growing his beard again,' the words were an after thought. 'He doesn't seem to care what he looks like anymore.'

At a loss for what to say, Tildy did not answer immediately. 'Nothing like this has ever happened to me,' she said slowly. 'But if one of my brother's acts badly the others gang up on him until he tells them his troubles.'

'It's lucky for you,' Rosemary replied unhappily. 'I'm on my own and Robert can be very difficult, she bent her head to hide the tears glistening in her eyes.

51

'He's the lucky one,' Tildy cried, upset for her friend. 'He should appreciate having someone like you to love him. He doesn't deserve you,' she added vehemently. 'You should hear my mother and what she says about a man who abandons his sister at Christmas.'

'That was a long time ago,' Rosemary cried in her brother's defence. 'Anyway, he did remember in the end,' she sniffled. 'He brought me that bonnet.' Several weeks after Christmas had passed, Robert had returned home in an excellent mood and presented her with a large hatbox.

'You should have received this before Christmas,' he told her apologetically. 'Unfortunately, you were out when the shop tried to deliver it and this is the first I have known of it.'

She had accepted his apology and pulled open the box in anticipation, it had contained the straw bonnet from the milliners below, she had tried manfully to hide her surge of emotional confusion from him, placing her arms about his neck and kissing his cheek dutifully.

'Yes, two weeks late and it made you cry,' Tildy answered her cheeks red with anger.

'He was not to know how it would affect me. He knew nothing about my vision of the girl in a bonnet like it. I only told you, I didn't tell him.' Rosemary countered. Although she, herself often complained of Roberts behaviour, she hated hearing other people talk about him in such a manner.

The two girls had spent many days discussing the bonnet with the long blue ribbons after Robert had given it to her, but failed miserably to unlock the door to the memory.

Later that night, after Tildy left, Rosemary had looked at the bonnet again, taking it from its ornate box and placing it on her bed. She sat before the fire thinking, trying to recall the connection and was startled by Robert's unexpected return, his mood unpredictable as he slumped beside her.

'Robert, I'm so worried about you,' she said timidly, trying to take Tildy's advice. 'Won't you tell me what troubles you?'

Leaning forward and resting his elbows on his knees, his head falling in his hands, Robert mumbled about his problems, not making any sense to his sister.

'Is it home?' she queried laying a hand on his back. 'Do you need to go back to London?'

'Yes. No.' he said aggressively, shaking her hand from him with a shrug of his shoulders. 'It's nothing for you to worry about. We can't go back,' he stated almost petulantly. 'It might make you ill again. I'll sort it from a distance.'

'I will go if we have to,' she offered quietly, careful not to upset him. 'I will manage,' she promised. 'I'm sure I will. I won't get ill again.' Falling on her knees in front of him she reached up to touch his face in an effort to comfort him, anxious to do the right thing, desperate to help her wonderful brother.

Pushing her away, a grimace of distaste on his features, he stood up and reached to retrieve his hat and cane. 'I'll let you know,' he said sharply, leaving again without any further goodbye.

'I'll go anywhere you want to go,' she cried after his retreating back. He must know she would do anything to please him, she thought as she rose slowly from her knees. Why did he constantly push her help aside?

For the next hour, curled in her favourite chair, unable to help herself, Rosemary cried bitter tears. Her love for her brother so mixed up with other, stranger feelings, she was, she knew, no longer capable of sorting the good from the bad.

Rising she went to her bedroom and retrieved the bonnet with the long blue ribbons from where she had left it. She twisted it this way and that in her hands. It was such an ordinary thing to have such a strange affect on her. Lifting it gently she placed it on her head and stood before the mirror to study her own reflection.

Little by little, the mirror misted before her eyes, the small girl dancing in the bonnet returning. A girl that looked remarkably like her, she stared delightedly, and was only half aware of the thought as she watched new faces swirl on the scene. Male faces, young and old, grinned and laughed lovingly at her. A toothless female head floated towards her, she could almost hear her own name being called, Rose, Rosie she studied the strange face.

A younger, female figure beckoned her into the mirror's surface her arm's open wide in welcome. Confusion began to cloud her mind as she watched. Suddenly she knew she must go to London, these people belonged to her. She had no idea who they were or how, her, and her brother would be so closely linked to these unusual visions, but she was certain that each and every one of them were important to her. She must convince Robert of that fact she had to get to London at once. These people were waiting for her there. They loved her, wanted her. She stretched a hand forward to touch the faces and they disappeared fading slowly into the distance, leaving her with only her own image and a sense of desolation so deep it was like a knife carving pieces from her soul.

A heavy blackness crept up Rosemary's body, gradually engulfing her as she slipped to the ground in a heavy faint.

EIGHT

In the early morning light of a new, spring day, Rosemary was rudely awoken by the noise of the apartment door.

The door slammed so hard it reverberated through the building. Rushing from her room, her heart hammering with fright at what she might encounter, she almost fell headlong across Robert. He half knelt, half sat on the floor his arms clasped across his stomach, his body doubled over as though in terrific pain. He rocked backwards and forwards, moaning softly to himself.

'Pack your things together,' he rasped, his breath coming in short, harsh pants, as though he had run many miles.

'Robert,' she cried, ignoring his orders, kneeling at his side heedless of the fact she was still in her flimsy night shift and peering into her brother's face. There was blood trickling down his left cheek, raising a tentative finger to his skin she whispered with concern. 'What has happened to you?'

Knocking her arm away with unnecessary force, toppling her backwards on her heels, he shouted. 'I said, pack your things together. Hurry!'

Rosemary remained rooted to the spot staring at him wordlessly, a multitude of reasons for his condition chasing through her brain. His hair was wild parts of it matted with dried blood she noticed. Stupidly, she questioned. 'Have you been in an accident?'

Placing his hand heavily on the top of a solid wooden cupboard, he heaved himself painfully to his feet. Taking a minute to catch his breath he waited for the pain of the movement to settle again. Turning towards her, his face livid with anger he yelled. 'Do as I say, now!'

Rosemary was incapable of movement, the shock of his appearance robbing her of the ability. She was standing before him, though she could not remember rising from her knees. More blood came into view as Robert straightened. The front of his shirt was torn and the elegant silk waistcoat that she had never seen before was partially undone, the fastening missing, both were soaked bright red. A livid, swollen scratch reaching from his ear to beneath the neckline of his clothing, oozed droplets of blood down his neck. If he had not been in an accident then a fight, she thought, he must have been fighting. Had he lost his temper with the wrong person? She had always known something dreadful would happen to him, one day.

'Move,' he hissed through clenched teeth, raising a threatening arm high in the air, she stood rooted to the spot. He brought it down heavily on the side of her face knocking her motionless body across the room.

'Robert,' she screamed, her hand flying to her stinging cheek. She hardly recognised the person in front of her. Seeing his arm raise again, despite the fresh, blood, stains the last exertion had caused, she scrambled into her room, closing the door before he stepped towards her.

Pushing her feet into lightweight leather slippers and grabbing a long cloak from where it lay on the back of a chair, she flung it about her shoulders. Clutching the cloak closely to her, and wrenched open the door she ran. Darting around the hunched figure of her brother, still leaning heavily on the cupboard for support, she fled out of the apartment before he could realise exactly what she was doing.

Running as she had never run before, her heart pounding, the cold air of the early morning stinging her skin, hot tears flying from her face in the cutting breeze, she forced her limbs not to slacken the cruel pace. Uncaring of her attire, gathering the folds of her cloak to a bunch in her arms she gave her legs the space to move. Pushing her limbs ever onward, ignoring the crippling pains seizing her body. Her mind raced feverishly through all the reasons she could think of to excuse her brother's behaviour. Panting, her breath rasping in her chest, her feet sore in their inadequate coverage, she rushed up Canny's Hill. Grateful for the emptiness of the early morning streets, she ran pell-mell to the only shelter she could think of, the Sharp's family home.

'My God, child,' Martha Sharp, cried peering out of the doorway to see who had come through her gate at this hour of the day. Used to rising with the dawn, Martha usually relied on several hours of peace and solitude before the rest of her family stirred.

'Tildy, Tildy,' she yelled as she rushed to help the fleeing figure in a state of near collapse at her door.

In minutes the whole of the family crowded into the tiny kitchen, each person in a different state of undress had scrambled to answer the desperate call.

'Rosemary, what on earth has happened,' Tildy squealed with concern, rushing up to hug her friend, immediately seeing the raw red mark, thickening and darkening on her face. 'Who did this?' she demanded, cupping the girl's chin between her hands. 'Robert?'

Staring from one concerned face to another Rosemary nodded dumbly. She hated saying anything bad about him, but she was incapable of telling a lie.

Dipping a cloth in the cold water waiting in a basin at the sink Martha placed it gently on the child's swollen face. Water trickled down the front of Rosemary's cloak, only then, when she reached to wipe away the drips did Martha realise the girl was still in her nightclothes. 'My God,' she roared, her face showing a myriad of unsavoury thoughts that flashed across her mind. 'He ought to be horse whipped. What has he done to you child? What has he done?'

The veiled suggestion behind her words taking time to sink into Rosemary's brain, she merely looked from one face

57

to the other in silence failing to deny their thoughts and adding fuel to the rising tempers about her.

Embarrassment at their visitors attire, made the males of the household suddenly self-conscious. They all begin to move at once, either to complete their own dressing, or to prepare the family's breakfast, leaving Martha and Tildy alone to comfort the distraught girl.

'I've raised a brood of boys,' Martha muttered, rubbing a soothing lotion on Rosemary's face. 'And they scraped plenty, but none of them ever marked one another like this. They would have me to deal with if they had.'

Tildy gently led her shaking friend to a chair and sat her down. 'Stay here, have something warm to eat, then we'll go back and get your things,' she told her. 'You can come and live with us. Can't she?' she added looking up at her mother questioningly.

'Of course,' Martha agreed readily. If she thought it was an imposition her face did not betray it. 'She can't go back to that brute, not ever,' she added forcibly.

'Thank you, 'Rosemary gulped, clasping her friend's hands in her own, realisation of how these wonderful people were prepared to take her into their lives so easily, making her want to cry again. Knowing it could never happen, Robert would never allow it, she said between dry sobs. 'I don't want to be a burden to you.' She had raced here in such haste it had not occurred to her that anyone would want her to leave her brother. 'If I can just stay until Robert's temper dies down, that's all I need,' she begged. She had no wish for good people to get in the middle of a silly row between her and her brother. She had fled in panic, now, the kindness they were showing her made her regret her actions.

She had seen Robert in a temper many times, but never as bad as this morning. Never before had he raised a hand to her in anger, that act was what had frightened her more than anything else, she realised. She should have stayed with him, not left, stood up to him, found out what was wrong and helped him, she knew that now.

'He was hurt, I upset him,' she stammered. ' He didn't mean to hit me. There was blood, blood all over him, he must have been in some sort of fight,' she concluded lamely.

'I'll fight him if he comes near you here,' Martha growled. 'Cowardly, that's what it is. Hitting a woman.'

The noise of a carriage rumbling to a halt outside, told them all who had arrived.

'Rosemary,' the strident yell, broke the silence that had fallen. 'I'm waiting for you, get outside, now.' The sound of his voice carried on the playful breeze seemed magnified at this early hour. Peeping through the window they saw him, balancing, feet apart, on the drivers bench his face like thunder.

Moving like a sleepwalker Rosemary disentangled herself from Tildy's arms and turned towards the doorway. Robert did not sound in a mood to be disobeyed again. She had barely taken one full step before Tildy and two of her burly brothers had barred her way.

'You can't go out there, look at him,' Tildy cried, she extended her arm and pointed at the window. 'He's in a fighting mood he may kill you this time,' she warned in an urgent whisper.

Pushing unkindly at her friend, unreasonable panic once again rising inside her Rosemary answered tearfully, 'I must go. He won't hurt me.' She struggled against their restraining arms her fear for them over riding her manners. 'I'm sorry to have brought my troubles to your door,' she pleaded for understanding as she pulled away from them

'Oh,' scoffed Saul, the eldest of the two brothers hanging onto her arm. 'So what do you call what he's done to your face then?'

Looking away to the doorway where Robert continued to yell, Rosemary's eyes beseeched them. 'Something bad has happened to him,' she begged. 'You must let me go.' She had foolishly fled to them in blind panic. Now if they tried to protect her she would only bring more trouble on their heads. 'I'm very grateful for your help, I should never have come,' she cried helplessly. 'You have all been so kind to me.'

Robert's fists were pounding on the door of the house adding to his shouted curses. Eventually someone, Rosemary did not know who, opened the door. He stood, dishevelled, his bloodstained clothing covered by a heavy cloak. Extending his arm he stabbed a finger viciously at the people surrounding his sister.

'Get away from her,' his words were low and full of menace. 'She is coming with me.' He left them in no doubt he meant every word he was saying.

The restraining hands dropped from her and slowly, slowly, Rosemary walked forward. Turning his body sideways he allowed her to pass him and walk on down the short, garden path.

Ignoring the move that Robert made to stop her, Tildy ran past him and caught up with her friend bringing her to a halt. Grabbing the girl's shoulders she embraced her and they clung together for several seconds.

Pulling them roughly apart in his agitation Robert flung Tildy to the floor, forcing Rosemary forward to the carriage. Numb with events she dutifully raised her foot to step inside the open carriage door then, screamed as her head was yanked backwards by the hair, her hands flying to her head, the pain almost obliterating his contemptuous words.

'Don't you ever disobey me again, do you hear me?' he growled in her ear menacingly.

Involuntarily turning her head into the grip to ease the pain, Rosemary saw Tildy hunched against the earth, she sobbed broken-heartedly at the pain she had caused for her only true friend. Then, Robert let go of her hair with such suddenness she was propelled into the interior of the carriage, letting out another involuntary yell and stumbling heavily against the seating.

At that moment Saul launched himself at Robert wrestling him to the ground. The fight was short and painful. Robert unexpectedly produced a short horsewhip from somewhere beneath his cloak and cracked it on the ground beside their struggling bodies. Lifting Saul's weight from him with one arm, he brought the whip down again, this time across the man's back. Knowing of his previous injuries her brother's strength amazed Rosemary. The howl of pain from Saul caused the members of the Sharp family, and the curious group of onlookers that had been roused by the noise, to step back instantly. Saul was grabbed by his loose shirt-tails and quickly dragged to safety by his brother's, Robert seemingly possessed by demons, whip raised again, looked set to kill him.

Leaping into the drivers seat he turned his attention to escape and wasted no time whipping the horses into full trot. Rosemary was left to kneel on the seat and gaze tearfully out of the window at her friends. Saul stood, his family gathered about him. She could just glimpse his bloodied face from where Robert had dug his fingers to force him upwards, how badly he was injured elsewhere, she would never know.

The carriage raced away. Robert's shout and the crack of his whip ringing in her ears. It lurched and swayed dangerously. Bounced about inside the run away vehicle she stared at the array of clothing littering the floor. Both Robert's and her own and personal items too, all thrown inside without benefit of bag, or box.

Broken ornaments scattered the interior, thrown in without regard She knew from the amount that she had inadvertently trampled on Robert had not stopped to collect everything they owned. What was missing she could not tell but this probably did not amount to half of their wardrobes.

She bent and picked up a broken figurine. 'A lady with dog' it had been labelled in the shop. She balanced it in the palm of her hand, the lady in her elegant pink dress now headless, the dog with only three legs. Scalding tears burned her lids as she recalled the love with which she had purchased the ornament; the first she had ever been able to buy with money earned by her own efforts. Surely a brother should realise how much these things would mean to her. These home making items that spelled love. The love she had for both her brother, and her friends.

Her head ached and her jaw hurt, leaning back on her seat she crossed her arms about her middle, cuddling herself for what little comfort she could achieve. Finally giving way to her emotions, she turned her face into the corner and wept herself into a fitful doze.

NINE

The carriage slowed to a sliding halt. Rosemary was still huddled in her corner shivering from fear and cold. Her doze had lasted only minutes, she was sure. The journey had taken on nightmare proportions as they rocketed along, jolting and swaying over every loose stone and rut in the road. The breakneck speed with which Robert was driving grated on her nerves.

Dread had filled the empty space in the pit of her stomach. Her tears had ceased to flow a long time ago they had left her with a raw throat and swollen eyes. Dry sobs racked her body from time to time, like hiccups. Maybe it was Robert who was mad, she thought, reliving again the morning's events, not her. Maybe that was why he would not go back to London. Maybe Tildy was correct perhaps he would end up killing her, or someone else.

She hitched forward in the seat to peer cautiously out of the window. The sound of trickling water invaded her senses as her eyes searched for Robert. Stepping gingerly down from the carriage she found him knelt before a fast flowing, clear stream, washing his face in the water that tumbled over the rocky bed.

Cupping his hands in the water he drank liberally from them. Then pulling handfuls of long grass from the water's edge he rubbed at the heaving flanks of the poor horse. Its harsh, rasping breath showing how ill-treated it had been. Releasing the beast from its prison he allowed it to rest and graze for a while.

Following his example Rosemary knelt by the waterside and dipped her hands in the gurgling stream, gasping at the icy feel of the water. Cupping her hands and scooping the liquid into them the way she had seen him do, she brought them to her lips. Most of it trickled through her fingers but what she tasted felt good. She dipped some more until she began to feel better. Splashing water on her tired eyes she wiped at her face with the hem of her night shift. It was no wonder she was so cold and shivery, she acknowledged, she was barely wearing any clothing.

'Sort out something to put on,' Robert snapped returning to the water's edge.

'Where have you been?' she asked fearfully, only now realising he had been gone for some minutes.

He did not reply, merely nodded across the narrow road at the thickly wooded area beyond. Rosemary felt her cheeks flush and turned her attention to the task he had given her.

Seconds later she heard the resounding splash when Robert dunked himself bodily in the water. Her breath caught in her throat at the thought of the icy temperature of the stream. The breath turned to a gasp as she watched the water change from clear to red, the rapid flow rushing the stain over the stones and boulders and carrying it quickly out of sight.

'You're badly hurt,' she cried viewing the slashes on her brother's chest. 'How did it happen?' she queried, her fear of his temper forgotten in her anxiety over his wounds. 'They need treatment,' she said loudly casting helplessly about her, searching uselessly for some way of ministering to him. He was still wearing his lower underwear, so she had no idea if these wounds on his chest and neck were his only injuries.

'Get dressed,' he commanded harshly. 'I can take care of myself I don't need any help from you.' With that he rose from the water and began to dry himself on his torn, stained clothing.

64

Striding past her immobile figure Robert reached inside the carriage and grabbed at a handful of clothing. Turning his back on her he returned to the trees.

'Be properly dressed when I get back,' he shouted before disappearing from her sight.

Taking her time Rosemary began to sort the disrupted bundles of clothing, putting hers to one side and Roberts to the other. Robert now attired in clean clothing was stretched out on the grassy bank sleeping. Unable to find suitable items of under clothing for herself and only miss-matched outer clothing, she began to feel like crying once more. Using the carriage as a screen in case of any passing travellers, she dressed as best she could. Her much loved silver backed hand mirror had proved to be one of Roberts casualties, only one jagged piece still clung to the frame. With difficulty she used it to help her brush the tangles from her hair. The deep rumbles coming from Roberts prone figure telling her he had fallen into a deep sleep, and would probably not wake for a long time.

Following his lead, she climbed back inside the carriage and settled herself for a nap the day had already been a long one it had started so early. Closing her eyes to encourage rest, she thought of how much she had grown up since going to work at Madame Mildred's emporium, she now worried about her appearance, actively enjoying the planning of her wardrobe each day. What would Madame say about her leaving this way, she wondered. Tildy would have no choice but to tell her of all the terrible things that had happened.

The day was closing when Robert woke up. Rising stiffly from the ground he went in search of the horse, returning minutes later to harness it.

'Where are we going?' Rosemary asked, sure he would not answer home, as she hoped.

He shrugged. 'I have no idea,' he muttered wincing and climbing awkwardly back into his drivers seat.

'I'm hungry,' she said petulantly to his back.

'We'll stop for something to eat,' he promised in a mumble as he flicked his whip over the horse's head to re-start their journey.

The days rolled into one another as they travelled. There were no more glimpses of the sea now, only rolling hills and woodland. They stopped from time to time to eat and change horses. Robert refused to let her minister to his wounds, or to stay in the comfort of Inn or Hotel. They slept in the carriage, her on the seat him on the floor. The level of conversation between them reduced to the minimum necessary.

'We don't want to bring any attention to ourselves,' he told her whenever she asked why?

At each sizeable town Robert sought out a land agent. Commanding her to stay in the carriage he went to find out what accommodation was available to them. On each return the look on his face grew more sour and his temper blacker.

Rosemary would have loved to get out of her prison and wander around the shops. To walk in the fresh air and stretch her cramped limbs. Instead she sat quietly doing as she was told.

On the fifth day a trace of a smile played on Roberts lips when he returned.

'Have you found somewhere?' she asked enthusiastically. Robert had barely spoken to her in days, she felt so alone and isolated, despite his nearness.

'I hope so,' he replied his voice almost cheerful.

Turning the horse away from the town he steered them along a narrow lane that led through sparse woodland, emerging on the open moors.

At first Rosemary thought the extended vista was awesomely beautiful. She delighted in the heathers, the hues of purples and white, that filled her vision. After an hour or more travelling with no change she decided it was bleak and unfriendly. Her stomach began to lurch with a panic that was slowly gripping her mind. Where was Robert going, and why? His behaviour was not normal, even for him. She did not understand what they were doing on the moor; towns with entertainment were her brother's style. He hated isolation.

Finally, the carriage crested a rise and below them in a hollow nestled a homestead, surrounded by low walls and fencing.

Robert pulled the carriage to a stop and studied the sight before him. The two-storey building had a wide brimmed roof casting deep shadow over the small windows and the stonework of its walls. The house stood squarely in the centre of the plot. Dry stone walling enclosing it and several out-houses at the rear on all four sides, with just one broken gate for entry. Then, the whole area had a further width of scrubland on all sides, which was enclosed again, this time by a wooden post fence.

Rosemary stared at the building from this distance she could see no detail of the house, but the ground around it looked parched and neglected. Movement caught her eye at the back of the building, animals, she thought, whether domestic or wild, remained to be seen. Robert she knew would not want to live here. He liked life about him he was never home after all. He required company to exist. He could no more live in the middle of nowhere, than she could.

Urging the horse carefully on he made his slow way down the incline and through the broken gate, reigning in and dismounting. He extended his hand to her, clearly expecting her to alight also, with his help.

'Dearest, ' he said, his arm going about her shoulder in a show of affection that took her by surprise. 'I would like you to meet Mr Garth. He will be showing us over our new home.' He beamed falsely at her showing more teeth than a genuine smile would be expected to do.

Jumping, her heart pounding, Rosemary looked at the man who in her mind appeared from nowhere, she shivered icy drips of fear trickling down her spine. Could he have been following them all the time she wondered foolishly, had she looked out of the back window she thought not, everywhere else but not behind.

'Robert, we can't live here,' she cried in dismay. On closer inspection she could see how run down the building was. Even the weak sunshine finally breaking through the clouds could not dispel its gloom.

'We can, darling, and we will,' Robert responded his voice taking on a note of steel the glint in his eye telling her not to argue. His arm pulled her closer to his body in a most unnatural manner.

The man, in his middle years, stepped forward. 'I am Henry Garth pleased to meet you Madame,' he murmured. He leaned forward and graciously took Rosemary's hand lifting it to his wet lips. 'Welcome to your first home Mrs Saunders,' he simpered, looking her up and down in a vaguely embarrassing way, the dimple in his chin almost cutting the lower portion of his face in two.

About to correct his mistake in her name, she caught Robert's eye, and closed her mouth. Where did he get the name Saunders from, and why? She fretted over this strange behaviour had this man mistaken them for another couple?

'My wife and I have been searching for just such a place as this,' Robert said, nuzzling at her ear. 'We are so in love, ' he murmured. 'We need no other company.' He dropped an affectionate kiss on Rosemary's cheek causing her to blush deeply red in her abject embarrassment.

Whatever game Robert was playing she knew she should put an end to it immediately. She felt disgusted by it. Humiliated by the way he was acting. Only the thought of his instant temper and the recall of his raised hand stopped her. Instead she stood silently, head lowered, looking at the ground.

Mr Garth shrugged still looking at her from beneath his dark, bushy eyebrows, a sardonic leer creeping across his face. She cringed inwardly at the thought of what he must be imagining.

Turning he marched to the front door, which to his chagrin, he had to shoulder open before he could lead them into a leaf and twig littered hallway. The dirt of ages it seemed had blown against its ill-fitting base and trapped it shut. A musty, dusty, dryness assailed Rosemary's senses making her cough. She was sure the place had not been occupied for years.

The interior of the house proved much smaller than expected, the rooms low and poorly lit by the tiny windows. A rough set of broken steps leaned against the corner of the room leading to the upper floor, which had two crudely partitioned bedrooms. She listened as Mr Garth extolled its sumptuous virtues.

'The views from these windows are one of natures marvels,' he crowed as he pulled her, none to gently, to his side to look out with him.

'What's that?' Rosemary asked, pointing to a blackened ruin standing a short way off. She had not noticed it from the rise when they had been looking down. So the ground must rise again at the rear of the house obscuring it.

'Oh that,' Mr Garth scoffed. 'It was once an abbey, burned down many years ago. Don't worry about it, look at the view around it.'

Rosemary did, she saw nothing but scrubland and the odd bowed tree that struggled against the prevailing wind to stay upright. She looked back at the room, the furniture she supposed, could just about be called adequate.

Mr Garth noting where her gaze was falling hurried to bounce on the edge of the bed. 'Sturdy stuff,' he quipped, ignoring the clouds of dust his activity produced.

'You love birds will have all the time you want to yourselves out here,' he laughed as he dusted at his trousers.

Those were the first words he had spoken that Rosemary could agree with. She imagined they would never see a soul from one years end to another. What was Robert thinking of? She was desperate to question him.

'Robert,' she turned to her brother, insistent on attracting his attention when she tired of listening to the boring Mr Garth complimenting the stone flagged lean to that he passed off as a kitchen. 'What about London?' she said softly, tugging at her brother's arm.

'One day,' he said, beaming a wide smile at her. 'My little woman is dying to see London,' he told the land agent in a confidential manner. Turning again to Rosemary he added indulgently treating her like a favoured child. 'I've promised to take you there and one day I will.' His eyes bore into her with force. She knew better than to argue any more.

Clapping the agent on his back and steering him towards the front door of the hovel, Robert said loudly by way of dismissal.

'Mr Garth this far outweighs our expectations. We are both so grateful.' He turned his head over his shoulder looking at Rosemary, 'are we not dear?'

Nodding dumbly she raised the brave smile, which was expected of her.

'Thank you so much for your help.' Robert continued, he grabbed the man's hand and shook it heartily up and down, making it clear it was time for him to take his leave. 'Say goodbye to Mr Garth, my dear,' he called as he pushed the man out into the daylight.

The Chase

TEN

Leaning back in his chair in appreciation of a very fine dinner, Lewis asked his companion. 'Why, in your opinion, would he choose to come to Plymouth. There are many closer ports?'

Simon smiled, the dark liquid of his after dinner port swirling in his glass. 'It goes back to our tutors,' he replied.

'It seems to me these tutors of yours have a lot to answer for,' Lewis retorted. He smacked his lips together savouring the heady wine.

'There were many of them,' Simon agreed with a nod. 'Because of the age difference between myself, and Edward, we often had more than one at a time. One in particular I recall, claimed to have seafaring ancestors. He told many fine tales of the sea also a good few less reputable ones. After embarking on many of them, he would break off and send me away. Edward always professed to love the tales, but it's my belief that they were the cause of many of his nightmares. In truth, I think they scared him as much as they scared me. Most of the tales began, or ended in Plymouth.'

Lewis did not reply, instead he raised a quizzical eyebrow.

'I spent many years believing that Plymouth was England's only sea port,' Simon responded to the silent query. 'I can fully understand why Edward would come here.'

'Well, it has been a tedious journey from London let's hope this time it bears fruit,' Lewis replied wearily. He was tired but happy that they had arrived. The journey had been less palatable than he would have wished because they had chosen to stay en-route wherever available. Not to waste time seeking out quality accommodation. 'We certainly chose some seedy lodgings on the way,' he chuckled, knowing his companion well enough by now to feel they shared a similar sense of humour.

Simon laughed with him helping himself to a refill from the decanter. 'We can't complain at this hostelry,' he concluded.

'Was Edward fond of the sea? When he heard these stories did he talk about taking ship when he grew up?' Lewis asked settling back to the business in hand.

'No, I think I've said before,' Simon replied with feeling. 'He hates the thought of crossing water. Edward you must remember is at heart a craven coward. He loathes hardship of any kind, life aboard ship, for however short a time, would be abhorrent to him. I'm sure he never left dry land.'

Wind rattled the tightly closed windows and the two men sank into a mellow mood, their last chance to relax before their enquiries began in earnest the next day.

Both men had been disappointed when the Plymouth authorities told them categorically no crimes of the type they were enquiring about, had occurred during the time period they had requested. It was Lewis's conviction that Edward was responsible for several unexplained murders in and around Battersea prior to Rosie's abduction. He felt sure that Edward would not give up on his life of crime. He would not be able too. Therefore they're best hope was to find a similar pattern in this part of the country.

'The authorities are going to pass our request around the area,' Lewis had assured Simon in an effort to blunt the edge of the disappointment. 'I told them to take a wide sweep. I have also told our host why we are here,' he continued. 'I'm a great believer in local gossip. It's amazing what people know that they aren't aware of knowing,' he added with a wink.

'This Inn has been in the family for decades,' was what the Landlord told him. 'Unfortunately I have only been here three years, but I'll ask around for you,' he promised.

'Anything to keep good paying guests under his roof for a day or two more,' Simon responded with a smirk.

'Well it's not proved a wasted move,' Lewis answered, tapping a pile of papers in front of him. 'He has supplied us with some very useful local mapping.'

'Which way do you think they would have gone?' Simon asked, reaching out and unfolding one of the neatly penned maps of the local coastline.

'I was rather hoping you would have some suggestions to make on that question.' Lewis admitted. He believed in the unseen bond between blood relatives, which often made them follow the same path without realisation.

'Well,' Simon chewed thoughtfully on his lip. 'If he goes further westward he will effectively find himself retracing his steps.' He ran a finger along the coastline to the end, which doubled back on itself as it climbed in a northerly direction. 'If it were me I would strike out the other way. That would eventually take me back to London. I feel sure my brother would one day wish to return and take up the lavish lifestyle he was used to.'

Lewis nodded his agreement, on this they were of the same mind. However long it took he was convinced they would one day achieve their goal.

So the weeks sailed by all too rapidly. Daily Simon rode to outlaying villages following up each detail relayed to him from local gossip, to officialdom, often stopping to make his own futile enquiries along the way.

They laughed heartily at many of the tales, real and imaginary, that led them up one blind track after another, steadfastly refusing to lose faith in their quest.

Lewis had placed himself in charge of documenting the details that found the way to them. 'I think I'm drowning in paperwork,' he confided to their trusty host, as he completed yet another statement, from yet another of the landlords many relatives.

Then one day travelling further than usual, lulled by the warmth of the afternoon, Simon found himself in a small coastal town. Staring at the semi circle of coastland in front of him he thought it a perfect haven for someone seeking a quiet, secluded life. Something about it drew him on, could it be that invisible bond Lewis was always talking about, he wondered. Hoping his friend would not worry at his absence, he decided on a whim to stay the night.

Seeking out a tavern and ordering a well-earned meal, which he enjoyed, Simon wandered to the bar. This was where Lewis would tell him to go if he wanted to hear the local gossip. He stood allowing his eyes to rove about the half filled room before attracting the landlord's attention.

'I suggest a gentleman like you should return to the other room,' the landlord said with deference. 'It can get rowdy in here, and you a gentleman,' he emphasized, his unease at Simon mixing with the common folk written all over his features. 'I'll be happy to bring your drinks to you,' he offered.

'Not at all my man, ' Simon cried expansively. ' On the contrary, I would like to buy every man here a drink.' He spoke loud enough for the occupants of the room to hear.

'You're mad sir, if you don't mind me saying so,' the uneasy landlord replied, a glower on his face no doubt thinking of the trouble it could cause.

Simon turned to face the room. 'I offer these drinks with an ulterior motive,' he admitted, figuring Lewis's belief in honesty at all times was the best way. 'I am seeking information.' He gave a potted version of what he wanted to hear and waited for the stampede.

Various people stepped forward and regaled him with stories that were of no interest at all. It must have been a full hour later when an old man sat in the corner spoke up.

'Ere' what about them as stayed at the Gimlet's?' It was more a statement than a question. 'He was a rum 'un an no mistake,' the old man said with satisfaction.

Ordering more drinks, Simon moved to sit at the old man's table. He was joined there by another, equally aged resident who was not to be outdone when it came to gossip.

'Now 'e was a strange fellow,' the second man said, accepting the proffered drink. 'Had a sister, pretty little thing. Mrs Gimlet took to her like a daughter, always seen together they were. Broke the old man's heart when they left, it did.'

'What did this young man look like?' Simon asked, his heart pitter-pattering with excitement.

'Dark,' the first old man replied. 'Black hair, tallish, slim a bit above 'imself.'

Simon groaned inwardly not exactly the description he had hoped for.

'Surly,' the other one added. 'Sour faced, bad mannered, treated you as though he were better'n anyone. Left about the time of those murder's,' he nodded to himself his old eyes glazing as he drifted back in his memory.

Suddenly Simon did not wish to hear anymore. He wanted to get to bed so the morning would come quickly, he could not wait to get back to Lewis. This was it, what they had been waiting all this time for, he knew it.

'Slow down, slow down,' Lewis commanded. 'I'm getting confused by what you are saying.'

Simon had rushed to the Inn in the early morning, banging on Lewis's door and rousing him from his relaxation as he gabbled his news.

'Well,' Simon began again. 'It seems at the time Edward and Rosie disappeared, a young man and a girl, he called his sister, were in the town looking for lodgings.' He paused pulling out a map and pointing to the town. 'It's a good days carriage drive from here, quicker on horse. Normally I would not have gone so far... but it was a lovely afternoon and the countryside was so attractive.'

76

Lewis clucked his tongue the boy was inclined to be a romantic. 'What about them,' he asked impatiently.

'The fellow called himself Robert,' Simon rushed on. 'He couldn't remember the child's name, and at the same time the child was murdered.'

'Who are we talking about,' Lewis raged, holding up a hand. 'Who's Robert the man in the bar?'

'No, the young man at the Gimlet's.'

'Then what child was murdered? Not Rosie?' Lewis's hand flew to his throat in horror.

'No, the child in the town.' Simon sighed in agitation and began once more.

'So the Gimlet's took in this Robert and his sister, they stayed about two years,' Lewis finally grasped the story. 'They left at the same time as a murder in the town?'

'Yes. A mother and her child. The mother was a known prostitute she was strangled. The child, a girl about four years old was brutalised.' Simon added quietly.

'So we can assume the murderer had been visiting the woman for his own pleasure, the child was an extra,' Lewis stated bluntly. 'It sound's like Edward.' He pressed his lips together running a hand over his head and through his grey hair as he pondered the news.

'How would he have known she had a child?' Simon queried. 'The old men were at pains to say she adored the little girl and kept her well away from the seedy side of her life.'

'She probably interrupted, may have felt ill or something,' Lewis mused 'Then Edward would have seen the way to a better game than the one he was already playing. My boy, you have found us our first lead, and after only three months, congratulations.' He clapped Simon on the back heartily.

'We had better send word to Jake and Molly,' Simon responded a little less enthusiastically.

'Did you make contact with the Gimlet's?' Lewis asked, beginning to collect together his papers, which had begun to litter every corner of the Inn.

Simon shook his head. 'I wouldn't dream of doing so until you were with me,' he admitted with amazement.

Collecting their baggage had taken an interminable time, taking their leave of a landlord who had begun to think of them as permanent guests had also delayed them. In the end it had been well into the evening before they arrived at the hostelry Simon had used before. The landlord rushed to welcome not one, but two gentleman visitors, to his establishment.

Late though the hour was, he willingly bustled about supplying their every need.

Taking their time over breakfast, pushing food around their plates, neither Lewis nor Simon would admit to their inner tension. This could be the day they found Rosie.

'I think our first stop is the police authority,' Lewis said as they prepared to depart the Inn and make the enquiries they had come for. 'We need to know the real facts of these murders, not fairy tales. Then on to the Gimlet's and lets hope we are on the right trail at last.'

ELEVEN

The Gimlet's cottage lived up to expectations. It was way out of town across the headland, by the edge of the shimmering water. By mid afternoon they were sitting at the same kitchen table that has served Rosie for two long years.

'I can't believe it,' Lewis almost whispered his eyes roved about the room. 'At last we have proof they did not leave the country.' He mentally drank in every detail of the homely room. He wanted to be able to talk to Rosie about it one day in the future.

'She was a lovely, wee bairn,' Mrs Gimlet said, she sat before them her hands wringing together, twisting the apron in her lap. She spoke in disjointed sentences. 'My Abel, he loved her. We both disliked him, Robert he called himself, Robert and Rosemary.' She reached up and brushed at a tear trickling down the side of her face. 'She had no memory, cause she had lost her parents in a nasty accident. Now you say that weren't true.'

'What sort of accident did he say?' Lewis asked. His initial disappointment at hearing the Gimlets had no more knowledge of where he could find Rosie than he had, softening as he listened to news of her. He knew the story was a fabrication but the answer, he hoped, might help him to understand the workings of Edward's mind.

'I don't know he never said, he wasn't one you could question' she replied, her eyes fixed on Simon. 'Is he really your brother?' she asked with quiet curiosity. 'You are not alike.'

79

'I'm sorry to say there are similarities,' Simon replied unhappily. 'Hopefully not many, and nothing detrimental,' he added.

The woman leaned to one side and patted the shoulder of her husband sat in a chair by the window. His shrunken figure huddled in a soft, wool blanket his frigid face staring along the roadside beside the sea wall.

The man did not turn her way, simply kept on staring, she looked tenderly at him. 'I don't think he ever gave any details, ' she said with mild surprise. 'In fact he never told us anything of consequence,' she admitted a little shocked at her late realisation.

'Abel,' she said softly her eyes misting. 'He spends his day watching for her to come back. He misses the bairn greatly, don't you Abel?' She received no reply. Both men watching knew she had not expected one. 'You see she took the place of our dead son in his heart. Abel blamed himself for that loss also, he it was, encouraged the lad to go to sea. Now he blames himself for the wee girl.' The tears ran freely down her face as she spoke the barely audible words, her hands clenching and unclenching in her lap. 'He knew Robert would never bring her back and he feels he should have stopped her being taken.' She sniffed loudly and shook her head sadly. 'I'm sure you see, that in his old heart he is convinced Robert killed that woman and the little girl in the town.' A sob stopped her words. 'He will never forgive himself for possibly sending his beloved child to her death.'

'We don't know that Rosie is dead,' Lewis cried, her words mirroring his most dreaded thought.

'Did he do it, do you think?' She asked, ignoring Lewis's remark and searching each face in turn.

Neither man replied their silence telling her more than any words would be able.

'Edward loves her,' Simon added quickly in hopes of comforting her. 'I don't think he will do Rosie any harm.'

On the way to the cottage, Lewis and Simon had fabricated a tale to tell the Gimlets, not wanting to burden them with more detail than necessary. But in the light of the unhappiness tangible in the air they had relented and told the woman all they knew of Rosie's life history.

'I knew the bitty mite wasn't the spoiled brat of any gentry,' Mrs Gimlet replied with conviction. 'Him though, he was different. I can understand everything you say about him. There was something almost evil in his makeup.'

'We are very hopeful of finding her,' Lewis told her in gentle tones.

'But she won't know you,' Mrs Gee cried horrified. 'She has no memory. She didn't know where she had come from when she arrived here, and she had no idea who we were when she left.' Her eyes goggled at her visitor's. Her face told them she thought the suggestion incredibly stupid. 'However much you all loved her, it won't matter, he has destroyed her mind,' she moaned brokenly.

'Tell me,' Simon encouraged. 'All you can about this strange memory loss. How long before they left did she started not remembering. I'm no doctor, but there are doctors who specialise in these things. The more they know the better chance of being able to help her when we find her.'

Patiently they gleaned what information they could, prompting the woman's memory at each pause.

'We will get her the very best doctor's,' Lewis promised.

'I hopes you do find her and no permanent harm has come to her,' she said dubiously, smiling weakly for the first time since they arrived. 'And I hope you hang him,' she added bitterly, her eyes straying to her husband. 'And make it soon.'

Back at what had become known as Simon's Inn, Lewis paced the floor in anger, unable to contain his feelings whilst Simon arranged for a messenger to be despatched to Jake and Molly.

'They must be told that at last there is a glimmer of hope,' he had insisted when Lewis had suggested it would only add to their worry.

'We promised to keep them informed, good or bad, every step of the way,' he reminded him gently. He knew the older man was suffering more from his own fears of what had happened to the child, than how Jake and Molly would react to the news.

During the days that followed both men were surprised at how word of their quest had travelled. People came from far and wide with tales of dark deeds. Only one attracted their attention, that of a murdered vagrant. It bore such similarity to the Battersea killings that it could not be ignored. They mentally added it to Edwards list of crimes though all enquiries led them no further along the road.

Maybe, because it helped ease his own pain, Lewis paid two more visits to the Gimlet's. He felt sorry for Abel and was anxious to let them know he laid no blame for anything that had happened to Rosie at their door. On the contrary, he would be eternally grateful for the love and care they had given her.

'Whatever Edward wanted, he got,' he assured her. 'He would have achieved his desire in the end. Abel would never have been able to stand in his way,'

'Unfortunately guilt is a very heavy cross to carry,' she countered. 'It is too late to bring Abel back to me now, all my hopes are on Rosemary, Rosie,' she corrected.

Lewis took out his pocket watch and looked at it. 'Time to go,' he sighed, standing and straightening his silk waistcoat over his ample girth. 'Whatever news we get of Rosie, good or bad,' he promised. 'You will be one of the first to know. I will keep you informed of our progress every step of the way. When we find Rosie I will send and tell you,' he vowed, bending to kiss her cheek, then lay a sympathetic hand on Abel's shoulder. 'I wish there was something I could do for you,' he murmured, his eyes fixed on the old man. 'To say my

82

own personal, thank you for loving someone I cherish so dearly.'

Mrs Gimlet rose and stood by him. 'She loved him in return, he wouldn't want more thanks than that,' she assured him, smiling as she opened the door and said. 'Goodbye.'

Later he questioned Simon on aspects of his childhood to the point of exhaustion. 'There must be something you can remember that would have encouraged Edwards interest in hypnotism.' He badgered relentlessly.

'Edward did once befriend a man who purported to hypnotise people, but I've already told you that, 'Simon answered tiredly. 'I never met him and know nothing about him.'

'Was he in private practice, or did he do it as an entertainment?' Lewis pushed his point.

Simon shrugged. 'All I remember is the rows. My mother and father shouting at each other, her saying that his eldest son was bringing disrepute on the house. It was that sort of contradiction of his eldest son that turned my father against her. Other than that I know nothing.' He sighed, genuinely sorry for his unhelpfulness.

'And I know nothing about the brain bending business,' Lewis raged. 'But I do know he's playing a dangerous game if he's tampering with Rosie's mind.'

Finally, reluctantly, they took their leave of the sleepy township. They had exhausted all they could do in this area. There was nothing left to do now but start again further up the coastline.

'I don't feel like I thought I would,' Simon remark quietly as they climbed into their carriage.

'I know what you mean,' Lewis agreed despondently, sniffing at the thin white, sea mist swirling above his head in the cool morning air. 'When we discussed the theory of all this it seemed an easy task, find the information, follow it up, move on wherever necessary. Now it feels as though we're deserting people, people that have loved and cared for the child as much as, us, her family did.'

'Unfortunately we cannot collect them together and take them with us,' Simon grinned wickedly. 'This carriage isn't large enough.'

TWELVE

They spent their days travelling slowly back along the coastline spending time in each town they reached, asking endless questions, getting ever more tired and dispirited.

Simon made regular forays alone on horseback, leaving Lewis to rest every few days. He was worried about his companion, not only because he was aging and tired easily. He was getting worried about his state of mind. Somehow, well meaning soul that she was, Mrs Gimlet had managed to plant the first small seeds of real doubt, in the old mans brain and they were growing daily.

'We could be passing her in the street,' Lewis repeated constantly. 'We have no idea what she looks like now and she wouldn't know me if I stood next to her.'

'What happened to your conviction that your love would recognise her,' Simon reminded him each time. Lewis never replied, simply continued to worry and fret about his own insecurities.

'I'm sure when we find her. You will recognise her,' Simon responded with equal conviction, it was almost becoming a battle of wills.

Weeks rolled into months and they were no nearer picking up the trail again. The boost they had received when they found the Gimlets long since faded. Their quest as far away as it had been in the beginning.

Still their notoriety continued to follow them along the way.

85

'I can't tell these days,' Lewis said dispiritedly, on Simon's return one late autumn afternoon. 'Whether any of these tales are really true or if they are telling them in hopes of a payment.' He jiggled lose coins in his pocket to emphasise his meaning.

Simon rubbed his hands together to revitalise them, then stretched them to the warmth of the fire blazing in the hearth. He half smiled, his mind preoccupied. On his return he had been met by a messenger from London, the man had wordlessly thrust a sealed package into his hand then turned tail and ridden off. Now opening the package he laid its contents on the table.

Apart from a lengthy letter from Jake, the only other object, wrapped tightly in a piece of cloth, was a small, gold pin.

'I gave this to Ninny the first Christmas after I found her, when Molly was still in prison.' Lewis said sadly, picking up the pin and weighing it in his hand, sorrow etched on his features. 'She promised she would give it back to me, with all her love and fond memories, when she died.'

Simon looked up from the letter he was reading. 'She went quietly in her sleep,' he said softly. 'The last remarks she made were about you and me. It says here, she said she had great faith that we would be successful.'

Lewis nodded. 'She had tremendous faith and something else,' he added, an awesome note in his voice. 'Something that you and I would never understand, something known only to those that had suffered as she had. She came to this country on a slave ship, you know,' he went on as though he had never told his companion the story before.

Simon listened quietly, he reasoned it would be better for his friend to talk his grief away than hold it inside himself.

Later, after a light meal, Simon silently handed Lewis a different batch of papers, ones he had collected from the authorities earlier in the day. These he had held back, giving the older man time to digest his unwelcome bad news.

'I've sorted these into order of likelihood,' he told his companion. 'If you want to leave them until tomorrow?'

Lewis smiled and shook his head. 'Not at all,' he replied taking the much, thumbed batch and clearing a space on the table to accommodate them. 'Ninny would have been the first to tell us to get on with things. What am I looking at?'

Not waiting for an answer he perused each sheet carefully. 'They are all killings of vagrants,' he said sharply, looking up in surprise as he read though the pages, turning back and re-reading several of them.

'Very like the Battersea murders,' Simon agreed, prepared to wait patiently for as long as it took his companion to make the necessary connections.

'Hit from behind, battered beyond recognition after death occurred,' Lewis read with enthusiasm. ' This one, attacked from behind, witness talks about a huge, inhuman shadow. And another, hit over the back of the head, possibly with a heavy knobbed cane.' Lewis was becoming more excited with each page he read. 'Where did you get these my boy,' he cried with jubilation.

'The Police, they've been collecting them from around the county. Our fame has spread, our requests anticipated,' Simon replied smugly, he had enjoyed his little bit of notoriety that day.

'None of them are young, again same as Battersea,' the old man mused. 'This one,' he tapped at a dog-eared scrap of paper, 'energetic enough to walk the country, not local, in his middle years. Not the same hand do you think, huh?'

'What about this one a month later,' Simon said, hitching himself closer to peer over Lewis's shoulder pointing at another, well thumbed page. 'This one was found by the river Ashburn, just outside the village. The incidents are very close together.' Searching for one of his well, used maps he traced a rough circle around the area that contained many of the killings listed. Then pushing a hand in his pocket he pulled forth another paper and held it out to his friend. 'This is the one that interests me most,' he said with a controlled air of excitement. 'Take a look and see what you think.'

Lewis studied the writing then, turned a quizzical face at the younger man. 'Edward had a vendetta against older vagrants this is a young man, what makes you think this, or those other two, would be his?'

'Opportunity maybe,' Simon replied philosophically with a shrug. 'Just a feeling I suppose,' he added. 'This fellow seemed to have fallen on very hard times, failed business. Left his wife and small child because he couldn't face a penniless future.'

'The wife went back to her family,' Lewis read from the script. 'The family welcomed her back into the fold and left him to fend for himself.' His tongue clicked in contempt. 'These well placed parents often have a lot to answer for.'

'The poor fellow seems to have sunk lower and lower,' Simon answered with compassion. 'They think he was huddled by the river, could have been asleep. Viewed from the back, at night, it would be possible to mistake him for an older person.'

'If that's the case when his assailant sprung at him with a blunt instrument he would not have been expecting any resistance,' Lewis murmured, rubbing thoughtfully at his chin.

Simon, gave a short, sharp, laugh. 'It must have been a shock when his victim jumped up and fought back. It says here. He was still alive when found.'

'Not for long,' Lewis corrected him.

'But long enough to give a description,' Simon crowed with delight.

Lewis read carefully. 'Age of attacker undetermined, but thought to be young,' he stated, 'well-dressed, medium height. Part of a garment was still clutched in the victim's hand, a quality cloth of high cost.' His eyes travelled the page reading the words again.

'Well,' Simon prompted. 'What do you think?'

Nodding silently Lewis scanned the page yet again. 'I think we should visit this village,' he said in sober tones at last. 'How far away is it?'

Simon studied the map for a minute or two then replied slowly. 'If we start early in the morning we could make it in one day. I feel confident we are back on the trail again,' he concluded with a smile then, holding up a decanter silently asked his companion to join him. 'Let's drink to success,' he added with a sigh of relief.

The small village did not boast a police service of its own, it relied on the nearby township, so the travellers were forced to continue a way further before being able to make more extensive enquiries.

'Well sir,' the officer said politely. 'The victim were a well, liked fellow locally. It was well known he had married above his station.' The man coughed into his clenched fist, clearly uncomfortable saying such things to two obvious gentlemen. 'He was unlucky in business and unfortunate in the choice of a wife, if you see what I mean,' he went on awkwardly. 'He crawled almost a mile looking for help after the attack, dreadful business. Dreadful.' The officer shook his head vigorously. Fussing and clucking like a mother hen he gathered papers from the desk top in front of him.

Simon, and Lewis, looked at each other vaguely amused at the man's agitation they made appropriate noises of commiseration. 'Did you have any suspects?' Simon asked finally.

'Oh yes sir, a few. There were some strangers in the town at the time they were questioned. Then there was some others who had moved on, two to be precise. One was tracked down and questioned, he was eliminated, then a couple of local miscreants were closely questioned, neither completely satisfied us sir, but.' He gave a little shrug.

'So no-one was ever charged?' Lewis queried.

'Not enough evidence, sir,' the officer replied with a crestfallen look.

'It's the strangers in the town that are of most interest,' Simon informed him. 'Would you have any other information for us? Names, descriptions,' he asked hopefully.

'The one we traced lived in the poorer section of town.' The officer scratched at the side of his long, dour, face thoughtfully, his questioning look telling them he did not understand why they were asking. 'But we were satisfied he had nothing to do with the crime,' he replied slowly. 'The other was a wealthy young chap and his sister. Unfortunately we have never been able to establish where they moved on too.'

Lewis sat up straighter his interest peeked. 'Where exactly did these people live in the town?' he asked shooting a knowing glance at Simon.

'On the outskirts,' came the reply. 'The rooms they rented were ransacked before they left. Nice people, well to do,' he added with a sniff. 'That's why my superior thinks they left. People like that don't like to live near trouble.'

Lewis gave him a sharp sideways look from the corner of his eye. 'Wealth is no guarantee of good behaviour,' he snapped.

'You say the rooms were ransacked, by whom?' Simon intervened with his question.

'Thieves,' the officer stated with unconcealed amazement at their stupidity.

'And you have no idea where they have gone?' Simon persisted.

Puzzled at their interest the helpful officer shook his head. 'No sir, we were concentrating on the criminal element around the town,' he said sharply, indignation in his tone. 'We, can't be expected to go round wasting the time of the gentry, now. Can we sir?'

'Fools,' the word exploded from Lewis's lips as they took their leave and returned to their accommodation. 'They let the murderer slip straight through their fingers.

Simon rubbed his eyes tiredly before he murmured. 'The victim must have suffered terribly at my brother's hands, it makes me feel so guilty.'

Lewis clapped his friend on the back. 'You,' he said sternly. 'Must not feel like that. The man showed great stamina it's a pity he wasn't found earlier. But, Edward must have left him for dead. He would not have fled if he thought there was a chance his victim could describe him.'

'So when are we going to visit the address he gave us?' Simon asked, half expecting his companion to want to go immediately, late as the hour was.

'The address he gave us with reluctance,' Lewis reminded him with a twist of his lips and a disbelieving shake of his head. 'He could not comprehend why we would be interested in a gentleman and his sister at all.' He chuckled sardonically. 'Get some rest my boy. We'll breakfast before we go.'

So it was that mid morning saw them entering the premises of Madame Mildred.

The tall, upright woman pressed a spotless, lace edged, handkerchief to her mouth, her spectacles perched pre-cariously on the end of her nose she answered their enquiry tearfully. 'After all the kindness I showed the girl. She had no thought of goodbye.'

'Madame, you must not feel slighted,' Lewis admonished gently. 'Rosie would not have been able to change the events that happened to her. She no doubt felt as badly about it at the time as you do.' Lewis extended a hand towards the owner of the ladies dress emporium and guided her to a chair. 'If you would sit a while I will tell you a little about the girl, it may help you to feel better about her.'

As they talked, Lewis again drank in every detail of the workplace where his Rosie had worked. As he told the tale of the unfortunate girl, he could almost see her perched on a stool, her needle threading in an out of the cloth she would be working.

'Oh dear, I had no idea,' Madame Mildred gasped, her eyeglasses finally dropping from her face and resting against her breast. 'If I had known I would have helped her more,' she moaned in a delicate voice.

'We had hoped we might view the rooms where she had lived whilst we were here,' Simon spoke up at last. 'You do own them, don't you?'

'I have an agreement on the whole building,' she replied with and slight incline of her head. 'Unfortunately, the present tenants are away. Therefore, I am not able to help you,' Madame Mildred said a little sadly. 'But wait, I know someone who could perhaps give you more information on your young lady, Tildy,' she cried, 'Tildy will know.'

Simon and Lewis gazed at one another then, spoke in unison. 'Who's Tildy?'

'They were good friends,' Madame beamed. 'Tildy has married since. I was sorry to lose her services one of my best girls. 'Madame Mildred looked and sounded genuinely sorry. 'I will give you directions.'

Leaving the overpowering premises both men were elated. 'Someone with personal knowledge of her,' Simon whooped. 'Maybe they are still in touch.'

'Let's wait and see,' his companion cautioned wisely directing their carriage towards Canny's Hill, his legal mind refusing to allow his heart to rule his head.

They sat on the over stuffed sofa, rigid as lead soldier's in the strained atmosphere of the *'best room'*, at Tildy's home: The seat too hard to be comfortable, the brightly polished furniture too neat and squarely positioned to give the room a lived in feel.

'For such a large family I'm surprised they keep a room for special occasions,' Simon whispered as he and Lewis gazed about them.

'Not exactly your class my boy, but it's a status. Shows that you're better situated than your neighbour.' He smiled indulgently when he spoke. He knew Simon was not pretentious, he would not intentionally patronise those less fortunate than himself. His words merely emphasised the wide rifts between the social levels.

The door opened with a flurry allowing a tall young woman, with blonde hair, and features that made Lewis think of a doll in a toyshop window, to enter. An equally fair skinned baby perched on her hip.

'I'm sorry,' she said, running her free hand through her hair, embarrassment clouding her pretty face. 'You must think me a sight I was making the most of this brisk wind.' She paused a pink flush touching her cheeks. 'There's always a lot of washing to be done in this house.'

She turned, a noise from the doorway directing her attention to her mother, arms out to relieve her of the baby. Smiling thankfully she handed the child to the elderly woman and closed the door softly on them.

'What exactly can I do for you?' she asked puzzlement filling her wide blue eyes. 'Is there something wrong?'

'Not at all, my dear,' Lewis had risen at her entry. 'Won't you sit down, we would like to ask you about a friend.' He smiled his tone helping to relax her tension.

'You knew her as Rosemary,' Simon stated, shifting his position in his seat so that he could look at her more directly.

Tildy gasped, her hand flying to her mouth. 'Rosemary,' she murmured. 'You have news of her?' Her face told them she expected to hear bad news.

Lewis, his heart sinking his hope of finding Rosie close by disappearing, leaned forward and patted her hand. 'We were hoping there would be news you could give us,' he said with resignation. 'We are searching for her, to take her home. Please tell us whatever you can about the time your knew her?'

93

'How did you find out that we were friends?' Tildy asked, a note of caution entering her sing-song tones.

'Madame Mildred,' Simon told her bluntly.

'Why do you want to know about her? Are you the authorities?' Tildy asked guardedly, then questioned more sharply. 'Are you friends of Robert?'

Simon cast his eyes to the floor and muttered reluctantly, 'not friends. I am ashamed to say I am his brother and his name is not Robert, but Edward.'

Tildy stared in disbelief. 'But, you don't look...you don't behave.' She allowed the words to fade away.

'I think we had better tell you our story first,' Lewis said quietly, preparing to once again recite Rosie's history.

'We didn't mean to upset you so,' Simon added hastily watching when Tildy wiped at the corner of her eye. 'Please tell us all you can about Robert and Rosemary.'

'I'm sorry that he is related to you,' Tildy said softly. 'I didn't trust him or like him, not one bit. It is so strange to hear you referring to Rosemary as Rosie. I don't think I will ever get used to that.'

The conversation stopped and Tildy's mother, Martha, entered with a heavily laden tray of refreshments. 'I expect you'll all be thirsty by now,' she cried, busily setting cups and saucers out before them.

'The police came to the workshop.' Tildy continued with her news when they finished drinking. 'Madame sent them away with a sharp word. She said she would never have entertained anyone in her rooms that had not supplied her with impeccable references. They asked to look at the rooms but Madame wouldn't allow them.'

Lewis's brow creased, 'why not?' he asked.

'She said the rent was paid and therefore they would be trespassing.' Tildy replied with a lift of her shoulders. 'She was sure they had only gone for a short while. Later, after they didn't come back, she took me with her to view the place.'

'And the police were satisfied to be shooed away like that?' Lewis asked again, puzzled this did not seem to fit with what they had been told earlier.

Tildy nodded. 'The rooms were a terrible mess,' she confided. 'I told Madame I thought she should bring the police back, but she said it would make her look a fool,' Tildy cast her eyes to the floor, the room in silence about her.

'The police told us the rooms had been ransacked,' Lewis informed her gently. 'How would they have known?'

'Later, Madame told them she believed her tenants had been robbed that was the excuse she gave for their leaving. She's a very private person, Madame,' Tildy informed them seriously her eyes studied the floor pensively.

'Wait,' she squealed, her head snapping upright. 'Please wait a moment.' With that she jumped up and rushed from the room.

'Here.' She murmured, when she returned, placing a neatly wrapped box on Lewis's lap. 'These are some of her personal items. Madame said I could keep them.'

Lewis heaved himself from his seat the box clutched under his arm. Turning a face distorted with emotion on the occupants of the room he hurried outside.

'Thank you, Tildy,' Simon said gently. 'Although we have told you about Rosie's past, we haven't said much about our intentions, yet you have trusted us with things that must be as precious to you, as they will be to Lewis.'

'You told me you are trying to find her that's enough for me,' Tildy replied. 'Please take her to her real family. People who will care for her properly.' He eyes filled again with unshed tears.

'You realise I intend to make Edward pay for his brutal crimes. You may be called upon in the future,' Simon reminded her.

'Apart from what little you have told me today, I know nothing of his crimes, 'Tildy stated, holding up a hand when Simon's mouth opened, no doubt to tell her more. 'Please

95

don't tell me any more. I will only worry about my friend. When you find her then you can tell me the rest. I will help in any way I can.'

Nodding, Simon thanked her. 'Perhaps we should go and find Lewis,' he said, rising and holding out his hand to help her.

Lewis was sat in the small garden at the front of the house. The unwrapped box on his knee, his head bowed, deep in contemplation of the delicate pieces of porcelain it had revealed. He jumped involuntarily as Simon and Tildy came up beside him. Handling each piece gently he rewrapped Rosie's treasures, slowly with great care, replacing each item back in the box before looking up at them.

'I beg you sir, 'Tildy whispered, 'take care. I dearly want to see Rosemary again.' She leaned down and kissed Lewis on the cheek. Turning she extended her hand to Simon, who surprised her by holding it to his lips before they took an emotional farewell.

'I pray this won't be another dead end,' Lewis said sadly climbing back inside their carriage. 'She's a remarkable young lady. She must have been a tower of strength to Rosie. I wish we could do something in return.'

'We can' Simon replied smartly. 'We can find Rosie and return her to both her old friends, and her new ones.' He gripped Lewis's arm. He was aware that each time they came a little nearer to the girl and each time they found out more about Edwards manipulations, it took a greater toll on the old man. Each new story aged Lewis a little more, bending him under his burden, leaving him sadder and more withdrawn.

'Where do we look now?' Lewis asked in a hollow voice.

'We start by putting ourselves in Edwards shoes, then take it from there,' Simon replied with determination.

Sinking lower in his seat the precious box clasped to his chest, Lewis muttered, 'We know nothing.'

'We know plenty,' Simon corrected him. 'We know this time he made a mistake and was almost caught.'

A perplexed look on his face Lewis stared at his companion silently.

'For the first time we know he was afraid.' Simon recited enthusiastically. 'He must have been or he would not have left in such a hurry, nor left a trail of disruption in his wake. I also think we know he will not return to the coast.'

'Why?'

'When Edward was young and afraid, he hid in closets, in dark isolated places that were hard to find, somewhere not populated. I think,' he said thoughtfully. 'He will be a fair distance from his last deed. Somewhere he can find solitude.' Simon spoke with quiet confidence. 'We will be wasting our time to continue looking around here.' He concluded with satisfaction.

'You sound very positive,' Lewis concurred 'It must be that brotherly bond again.'

'Battersea will be glad to hear of our news,' the younger man sighed, his thoughts suddenly with Molly and Jake. 'At least we know that thus far Rosie had not become one of his victims, so there is no reason to suppose she ever will.'

'What makes you so optimistic?' Lewis questioned, giving his companion a sharp, interrogating look.

Simon chuckled knowingly. 'Because of what we know,' he crowed ticking things off on his fingers to give greater force to his theory. 'We have the benefit of hindsight,' he reminded his companion. 'We know he was about to run out of money may have already been finding his finances tricky. We also know he has used her to earn him money, so she will remain useful to him. He will need her earning power more and more. No old friend, he may work her unmercifully. But, he will keep her alive, and God willing, in good health.'

The carriage, reigned in as Simon finished his speech, his note of optimism just the tonic that had been needed, suddenly they were both ready for a long evening map studying.

THIRTEEN

For a while the two men stayed in Exeter simply studying the surrounding area, searching for somewhere that would fit with Simon's expectations of his brother's behaviour.

They had continued with their usual enquiries, hoping that again by some quirk of fate, they would fall on a piece of news that would put them on the trail again.

Lewis, using his legal standing, made contact with as many of the area's eminent legal men as he could. Worried when he realised what a commotion their enquiries had stirred up.

'There are case files on Edward that would make straight hair curl, ' he told his young friend on his return from his latest visit. 'The police all over the West Country are laying every unsolved crime on their records at his feet.'

'You look really concerned,' Simon remarked, puzzled at his friend's anxious state. 'What are you trying to tell me?'

'Well,' Lewis paused, collecting his thoughts more coherently. 'I hadn't realised that making the enquiries we have, would cause such uproar in the legal world. We have had an exceptional lot of help from the authorities, maybe, now I know why.'

'Tell me,' his companion asked with a frown. 'I'm not at all sure I understand what you are saying.'

'Our enquiries have stirred up a hornets nest that can no longer be denied. If and when Edward is captured, nothing less than a public hanging will satisfy.' Lewis paced about in agitation. 'The general public are becoming too aware of

Edward as a villain. As I say, any and every crime is now being blamed on him.'

'I see, well I think I do,' Simon replied slowly, hands thrust deep in his pockets he paced the room behind his comrade. 'So whatever crimes my brother is guilty of can no longer be dealt with quietly,' he acknowledged. 'Does that really matter?'

'No, yes,' Lewis sighed. 'It will be a big public affair that could lead who knows where,' he said with resignation. 'I have no idea how this will affect your standing in society, my boy,' he added quietly, slumping in a chair.

They sat in silence for long moments before Simon finally spoke up. 'Well this way he won't be able to wriggle out of paying for his actions,' he stated with resignation.

The long and close association between the two unlikely companions had brought them closer than could ever have been expected. In terms of ground covered they had not moved very far along the coast, but they now thought as one. They were developing a sixth sense that helped them sift through the piles of information placed at their disposal.

'What are you doing,' Simon asked, leaning over his friend's shoulder and watching him draw neat circles on the map.

'There are so many area's in this part of the country where a man could hide himself,' he replied. 'I am circling forest and moor, which would you go for in his place. Huh?'

Simon rubbed his chin his hand rasped across stubble and surprised him. Dropping his hand to his side he answered quickly. 'Brotherly link again. Well, wherever I went I would expect to be able to stay for a while, six months a year maybe. He was lucky with the Gimlets, Rosie was young, he could get away with the brother, sister story.' He rubbed again at the short bristles on his face and paced the room.

'Yesss...' prompted Lewis, not sure he was following this train of thought.

'He just about got away with the same tale with Madame Mildred, but he must have known they considered his actions somewhat more than odd,' Simon mused, almost to himself. 'He would certainly not find it easy to continue in that vein. By all accounts Rosie is growing into a remarkable looking young lady. Therefore as she grows and blossoms she will look more like a wife, than a sister.' He tapped at the map before continuing. 'If I were him I would rent a property somewhere that I could be self sufficient for a time.'

Lewis again heard the words in his head, said by Tildy and Madame Mildred, referring to Rosemary as an attractive and extremely pretty girl. 'So,' he said thoughtfully, 'we should be questioning land agents?'

'Yes, I think so.' His young companion replied with conviction. 'Don't forget Edward would probably still have access to money at that time. If he did, he would have no way of knowing it was about to run out. Even then he would not be aware it was going to dry up completely. You do realise,' he added enthusiastically. 'Once he has trapped himself in this position he could very well still be there.'

'It's a long time ago, maybe too long for a land agent to remember,' Lewis remarked, his finger tracing absent circles about the map.

'I don't agree,' Simon replied, looking serious. 'If he is still occupying a property, however remote and unsuitable for normal letting, and,' he added with authority, 'not paying his debts, he will not be forgotten easily.'

Lewis grinned. 'I agree,' he said with a chuckle. 'I have put up every obstacle I could think of and you have successfully squashed each one. I say there is nothing left than to start contacting land agents.'

Simon coughed self-consciously. 'This chase has been a long one,' he said quietly. 'Far longer than either of us expected, so to make an effort to reduce what time is left, I would like to finance the use of messengers.' He turned a questioning face to his friend. 'It could take us forever to

100

criss-cross this and the outlaying areas.' He tapped the map pointedly.

The old man sat heavily in a nearby chair. 'Have you been reading my mind, my boy,' he said tiredly. 'How long has it been now, month after month. I must say I don't relish the thought of going on indefinitely.' He sighed. 'I do so want to see this through to the end, I can't tell you what a worry it has been that time would run out on me first.'

Simon contemplated the aging man aware of the added wrinkles, the widening expanse of hairless head, the droop of his shoulders, whilst he did a few mental sums. 'It has been almost two years since we left Battersea,' he stated with some surprise. 'I too desperately want to see an end to our travels,' he added with feeling. 'And I feel we are very close now.'

'Two years,' Lewis said softly. 'I have lost all track of time I didn't think it was anywhere near that long. I will leave it to you to organise the messengers. Thank you.'

Simon undertook his chosen task with vigilance, refusing to be down hearted when his men turned out to be less than thorough. He had employed all the available men in the district sending them in every direction until his persistence was rewarded.

'I think we've found them,' he shouted excitedly, racing through the Inn to find Lewis, a paper waving in his fist. 'Look, look at this.' He shoved the details into his companion's hand.

With barely concealed excitement the two men hurried to the address of the land agent, waiting with impatience until he was available to talk to them.

'I have been in business many years,' the agent said in a smooth culture voice. 'I wouldn't normally remember. You see, most people don't know what they are looking for. Most can be swayed into what you have to offer without much trouble.'

Lewis liked this homely chap whom, he imagined to be a feet up before the fire person, rather than a hard hitting, business, man. 'So why do you remember this one?' he questioned.

'His rudeness mainly,' the fellow replied. 'He said he was newly married, but wouldn't allow the young lady to enter my premises, that alone was strange. In this day, the women have more and more say in where they want to live.' The agent smiled knowingly and brushed a tiny piece of fluff from his sleeve.

'So you couldn't describe the young lady?' Lewis queried.

The agent shook his head.

'But what makes this man stick in your memory?' Simon persisted, trying to bring the conversation back to the point.

'Newly married young men, in my opinion,' the agent began. 'Are incredibly stupid, they simper over their brides, deferring to them at every move. It changes later,' he added with a depth of feeling. 'But in those early days they simper.'

Simon shuffled his feet and sighed his look stating clearly, this man liked to hear the sound of his own voice.

'The other thing was, he stated his requirements exactly, wasn't interested in anything else that I could offer,' the agent went on hurriedly, his young visitors sigh not being lost on him. 'His main request was isolation. I thought it all very strange indeed.'

'You don't seem fond of the institution of marriage,' Lewis remarked shortly, thinking back on his own all too brief time of wedlock, remembering with surprise how he had simpered. 'I take it you were unable to help this young man. Have you any idea where he would have headed off to?'

'I can't say where they ended up. I sent them to an associate up country. We often help each other out,' he explained unnecessarily. A look of distaste crossed the agent's face. 'I have to say this agent is not the most reputable of persons.' His lips drawn to a thin line he said no more.

Leaving the office, Lewis rubbed his hands together in glee. 'Your hunch has proved correct my boy, this time they are acting as Mr and Mrs.'

'Hmm,' Simon responded tentatively. 'I just hope it didn't spell more trouble for Rosie.'

Realising the concealed meaning behind the younger mans words, Lewis visibly deflated, his mood evaporating like the mist. 'We will have to wait and see, ' he grunted.

It was instant dislike on sight, when they met the oily man called Mr Henry Garth, sitting smugly behind his desk in the untidy office.

'Yes, I believe I know the people you are asking for, Mr Saunders and his wife.' Mr Garth informed them without hesitation, 'her, now't more than a child,' he clicked his tongue and shook his head at them. 'Good looking child though.' His eyes lit in an unholy manner, the unsavoury thoughts in his head visible on his features.

Both men made involuntary movements as they watched Henry Garth flick dirt from beneath his fingernails with a splinter of wood.

'Can you direct us to their abode,' Lewis asked fiercely, his instinct to hit the insolent fellow on his aquiline nose.

'I don't know about that,' Henry whined, scratching the side of his head in mock concern. 'They owe me more than eighteen months rental, they are due to be evicted.'

'When?' Simon thundered his fist thumping on the desk-top, pure hatred crossing his face, he looked prepared to vault the table and take the man by the throat.

Henry Garth clicked his fingers, they all waited whilst a clerk produced several sheets of paper. 'These are the eviction papers,' Henry muttered with more servility, the cold hard stares from his visitors unnerving him.

Lewis grabbed the paperwork, 'so if it hasn't taken place yet, we can pay the debt and arrange to have the premises vacated immediately?' The tone of his voice brooked no argument.

'You her father then?' Henry asked smugly, a touch of awe in his tone. 'I knew as someone would come to get her in the end.'

Simon's threatening gesture wiped the leer from Henry Garth's face, voice raised he yelled. 'The address is all we need.'

'Well,' Henry shouted back in his own defence. 'Who ever you are and whatever you wants with Saunders, you'd better watch yourselves. He's a bad lot,' his tone falling to a normal level he continued. 'A mighty bad lot! Gambles anything in sight, even the girl.' He shot them a cocky smirk as he watched them visibly blanch at his words. 'Treats her like a slave, he does. If you're going out on them moors, I'd go prepared. Off his head he is now, or so I believe.'

His words sunk like pellets of lead into Lewis's heart, were they finally going to find Rosie destroyed, mentally and physically? Would Edward kill her at the last moment rather than allow her to be taken from him?

Lewis paid the debt due, and Simon took meticulous, direction details to what the clerk whispered was the most derelict property they kept.

'What do you think?' Simon asked Lewis as they left the offices and got back into their carriage.

'I think we had better do as he suggests. We had better go well prepared,' he replied vehemently.

The Meeting

FOURTEEN

Standing before the window she had just finished scrubbing, aware of the grime she could not reach, clinging obstinately to the outside of the pane, Rosemary stared past it, at the dark outline of the ruin. It was an outline that dominated the view from the back of the house.

It must have been there when they arrived, she knew. She must have been able to see it when the carriage stopped on the rise, so why had she missed it? Had she been so mesmerised with the building that was to become her new home, she wondered. Had she been so scared she had not been able to see anything else? Now it seemed to dominate her life completely.

The broken walls reached skyward, darkly ominous against the lowering sky, heavy with yet more storm clouds. In the time they had lived there, how long she was not sure. She had found herself wondering if those clouds ever lifted from ground level. The sun steadfastly refused to shine down on them for any length of time.

Below her, Robert was leading the horse into the outbuilding that served as a stable. The carriage already gone, she could not remember when, or to whom, or why. Robert said it was months ago, she thought they had only been living there weeks. If they had lived there so long, why had she never cleaned up before? She wondered. Why had she allowed the place to get so filthy?

'You're stupid,' Robert constantly shouted at her. 'Always forgetting things, you make my life so difficult. I have to do the work for both of us.'

She did not think that to be correct, in her opinion he did almost nothing inside the home. He did look after the horse, she conceded. They needed that horse; there was no other means of travelling the moor.

She dropped into one of the hard, lumpy chairs her mind back on that first day, when Mr Garth had shown them over the premises.

'Why did you tell him we were married?' She sobbed bitter tears at how her brother had betrayed her.

'It's of no importance,' he had shrugged carelessly.

She had run to him, beating her fists against his chest. 'I'm not your wife, I'm your sister.' She did not understand what was happening to her, to them. 'Why have we come here? Why can't we go home?' she wailed, knowing she was driving a barrier between them, but unable to stop herself.

Robert gripped both her flaying hands in one of his own. Holding her away from him at arms length he had roared at her. 'What I do, and why, is my business. You will not question it, ever.'

The look of pure hatred had burned its imprint on her mind, shocking her into immediate silence.

'As my child bride,' he continued more silkily. 'This is your home. This is where you are expected to live. You have already caused me enough trouble, so don't argue with me.' His final words came to her as a threatening hiss.

Fearful, but still determined to know, she questioned. 'Why?'

Turning his back on her and poking about in the corners of the room he had kept her waiting for what seemed an interminable time.

'Mr Garth thinks we are married. So will the rest of the town when word gets around. That is the way I want it,' he replied eventually.

Reluctant to take his word foolishly she persisted. 'I don't understand, why can't we go home,' the tears beginning to flow again.

With a short, sharp laugh of derision, he countered, 'this is home.'

'No, no,' she had wailed thinking he had not understood her. 'I mean home, to London.'

Robert leaned his head close to her face and spoke through clenched teeth. 'Thanks to you, we can never return to London. We have no home other than this one.' He had pushed her roughly aside and strode to the back of the building.

Bemused, her tears dried like magic, she accepted the blame heaped on her shoulders, but still questioned why thanks to her? He could only mean one thing, her mind. So she was mad. Too mad for him to dare to take her back to their friends and associates, and she had made a prisoner of him. In his love for her he had chosen to stay and care for her. Now he could not go home either. No wonder he was so angry with her. She owed him so much.

Slowly rising from her seat, Rosemary made her way outside to Robert. She watched as he roved around the neglected yard, surrounded by the low, functional buildings that, though neglected in appearance, where structurally sound. She thought absently of what a pretty garden the area could make.

Wild ducks rose squawking from a water hole that may once have been a pleasant pond. Cats peered at her from a roof to her left one hissed arching its back she stared back at it. A chicken clucked about her feet the place reminded her of somewhere else.

Somewhere similar, just as neglected, a place that had been turned into a sanctuary with the help of her own hands. She almost saw herself planting young, newly growing bushes, laughing and playing as she did so. She heard someone telling her the bushes had been chosen for the colour of their blooms. The cracked up concrete, and the neglected earth had changed little by little. A voice rang in her ears telling her it would be a haven for them all to enjoy in years to come. She shook head to clear her thoughts.

The memory flitted tantalisingly at the back of her mind, refusing to come forward and be recognised. She shrugged maybe as a child she had been given her own, plot of land. Robert told her the gardens of their home had been extensive.

'Is that hurting it?' she queried looking at an aged sheep, grazing on what stubs of grass it could find, its fleece matted and lumpy, filthy brown tendrils of wool hanging from beneath its belly.

'How would I know,' Robert growled in reply. 'It's too old to be good for anything, even the pot,' he concluded, kicking out at a rabbit that scampered across his path.

Rosemary nodded. She like seeing the animals, it made her feel less alone. But she had known from the beginning that Robert would not tolerate them for long. They would all end up the same way, well cooked on a plate before him.

Scrubbing and beating, dusting and polishing, the chores filled Rosemary's days. Little by little she removed the layers of grime built up over the ages. She could do nothing about the neglected walls and paint work, Her scrubbing had removed much of the peeling surfaces, leaving a leprous look that was almost as offensive as the dirt had been.

'Could we get that Mr Garth to arrange for some repair work to be done?' she asked Robert when he was in one of his rare even, tempered moods. 'The steps in the corner are quite dangerous,' she concluded.

He had not flown into a rage, merely shrugged, smiled half-heartedly and left her. She was very careful these days not to mention home, or London, mentally closing her eyes to the short, comings of their living accommodation.

'If Robert can put up with it for my sake,' she told herself forcibly several times a day. 'Then so can I.'

If only he had been more honest with her, she thought regularly. She would not have run away from him that morning, however long ago it was. They could have left their friends with good feelings, not the ill will they must now feel. If he had trusted her they may have been able to stay in those apartment rooms above Madame Mildred's She had been a kind woman she may even have been prepared to help them.

Staring with unseeing eyes at the abbey ruin, which even in the summer sunshine poked out of the ground like a broken, blackened molar, Rosemary listened to the light, heckling, voices that rose up the stairway to reach her ears. Robert was entertaining, playing cards. He liked her to keep out of the way at times like these.

'We're still waiting,' Robert cried, laughter in his tone.

'I'm thinking,' a male voice replied.

'You think too much, that's your problem.'

She recognised the tones of Henry Garth. She still did not like him but he had supplied her with two buckets of wash for the walls.

'Your request will be dealt with at once,' he had smiled, making her flesh creep when he raised her small hand to his wide mouth.

'You had no right to ask favours of him,' Robert had raged when Henry Garth had left. 'He was my guest here. In future you will remain out of sight whenever I entertain.'

Rosemary smiled, she was quite happy not to be part of the entertainment she disliked Henry Garth and cringed at the thought of his friendship with her brother. Not that he had ever been openly offensive to her, always overly polite in fact. It was the look in his eye and the leer on his lips, which gave her the shivers.

Time had slipped by as she meditated in solitude, the sound of Robert calling her shook her from her thoughts.

110

'Dearest, our guests are leaving,' Robert's voice floated up to her. The day had turned to night outside and she had not noticed.

Making her dutiful way down the steps, Rosemary smiled and stood by Robert's side whilst he said his goodbyes, they waved then, turned back inside.

'I will be away for a few nights from tomorrow,' Robert told her as she busied herself putting the room straight.

'Again?' the word slipped from her lips before she could stop it.

'Are you objecting?' he questioned, his voice rising dangerously. 'I have business to attend to.'

Rosemary stayed silent she doubted the business was more than playing cards with Henry Garth and his dubious associates. But it was happening more often, and Robert's temper on his return was not always a good one.

'I get lonely without you,' she replied at last, realising he was waiting for an answer. 'I miss you,' she added with a sweet smile.

'Why, when have I ever been away before?' Robert queried, his tone full of curiosity.

'You were away last week, or was it the week before,' Rosemary screwed up her forehead in thought, the days and weeks all rolled into one since they had come to the moor to live.

Robert laughed. 'You are mistaken my dear, I have never left you. It's all in your imagination,' he said walking to her side and placing an arm about her. 'I would never leave you unless it were of utmost importance, as it is now.'

'But…' she persisted. You have been away on several occasions. I know you have.'

Concern clouded Roberts face as he looked at her. 'I hope you are not getting ill again,' he said softly, staring at her intently. 'Your mind is playing tricks on you. I suggest you go up and rest.' He pushed her towards the steps. 'We will talk about this again when I get back.'

Rosemary did as she were told and prepared herself for sleep. She was sure, no positive. Her brother had been away on several trips, which he called business. She was beginning to wonder, unkindly maybe, if it was Robert who's mind was in question. After all it had been him, not her who had suffered the nightmares when they first came here. Him that had cursed his father and called for a non-existent brother, when she had cradled him against her breast, soothing his fears and mopping his perspiring brow until he calmed his emotions.

He had railed and raged at her when she asked him about these bad dreams that had bedevilled his nights for a while.

'Last night,' she told him once. 'You cried because your mother had died, leaving you to the mercy of another woman. Did we have different mothers?' she asked. It would explain why they were so unalike, why her colouring was so much fairer than his.

'How dare you question me,' he had yelled, flying into a rage. 'Someone who doesn't even know what day it is, pushing your bad dreams onto me, making out that I suffer instead of you.'

She had known they were not her dreams, but refrained from asking about them any more. She never knew whether he remembered his nightly, raving's. The dreams had slowly ceased and she put them all to the back of her mind until they surfaced at times like this, when Robert caused her to question herself again.

Alone, Rosemary wandered aimlessly on the moor, eventually arriving to her usual spot inside the abbey wall. It had taken a long time to venture inside this place, but once achieved she had found a strange, peaceful feeling, that was otherwise alien to her.

Whatever the weather of the day the wind and rain never reached her here. The wind blocked by the thick, jagged walls, the rain held off by the sections of crumbling roof still

112

hanging precariously in place. On sunny days, the rays shone brightly on the open section of ground at one end, it was always hotter and brighter than outside. It glistened and reflected on the granite stonework of the floor. Inside the Abbey time seemed to stand still.

She sat on a small, slightly humped platform of stone that rested in the covered corner of the ruin. When it rained, the water seeped under the walls and ran down where the floor inclined and puddled under her seat. She thought of it as a bridge, a place of safety. She came here when she had tedious work like sewing to do. With a cushion beneath her she could sit for hours darning and repairing to keep their home, and clothing in order.

Returning, thinking about the evening meal and whether Robert would be coming home for it, she was greeted by the presence of the travelling merchant.

'Hello there,' the old man and his son greeted her in unison.

Rosemary hurried to the side of the large, flat backed, cart they trundled their goods in. 'Oh it is nice to see you, Mr Shepherd,' she cried. 'And you too, Will,' she smiled, putting a hand up to touch the bent old man, sitting in the drivers seat.

'And it's always a pleasure to see your smiling face, my dear,' the old man said kindly. 'What can we leave you today?'

In the early days Robert had made the purchases from the Shepherd's travelling shop. Until he realised how much of the provisions they ran out of before the next visit was due. Reluctantly he had handed the chore over to his sister, though not the finances.

'Robert's away,' she said sadly, 'He has left me no money.'

'That's al'right,' Will volunteered, 'he paid a sum of money in advance. He said if we ever came when he was away he would settle up the difference next time. So?'

Rosemary was amazed, so Robert had expected to be away a lot. Pushing her disappointment to one side she busied herself with choosing supplies, the ever helpful Will dancing attendance and carrying the heavier goods to the house for her.

Take care of yourself,' Rosemary said to the old man, when her shopping was completed. She liked Mr Shepherd, she felt sorry for him, his joints were visibly swollen and painful but he always had a smile for her.

'See he gets some rest,' she whispered to Will, before he took his leave.

'Oi'll do me best,' the lad whispered back with a cheeky grin, then ran round and sprang up beside his father, waving farewell until they were out of sight.

Rosemary watched them bump away over the rough moor. She wished they came more often she liked the company. Turning aside she returned to her duties, prepared to wait on her brother, and any of his friends, if he chose to return that evening.

CHAPTER FIFTEEN

The day was humid, hot and sticky, the exhausting temperature held promise of a storm to come. Pulling and pushing the bag of animal feed, Rosemary was quickly wet through from her exertion. And the bag is only half full, she thought, marvelling at how light Robert made them seem when he handled them. On days such as this she appreciated how much more energy her brother put into the homestead that she failed to credit him for.

When, like now, Robert stayed away for weeks at a time, it fell to her to clean out the animal bedding and top up their feed. She ached from the physical effort involved. Besides, she was more than a little scared of the animals. In particular she felt intimidated by the horse. She always knew when her brother had gone with Henry Garth because he left the horse behind. With lack of exercise the animal grew steadily more skittish, picking up the smell of the girl's fear. She truly wished that Robert would not leave her to look after it.

Wiping her perspiring forehead on her upper arm, her hands being far too grime encrusted to place near her, she felt the first heavy drops of rain. The sky had darkened ominously above her, night was still several hours away, but the sky it seemed could not tell the time.

Leaning her head against the wood of the barn door she let the cool drops plop on her face and neck, slow at first then driving to a sudden frenzy they soaked her, sending her scuttling inside. She watched from the window as the dry, parched moor soaked up the blessed rain the sky lifting again little by little freshness invading the air.

Just as suddenly thunder crashed and lightning cracked. The deluge hammered on the roof of the lonely homestead. Water seeped through every nook and cranny, making her want to weep when it ruined the hours of work she had done that day, sweeping and cleaning her home. Feeling scared and alone she listened to the cries of the animals, the thud of hooves as the horse reared against his confinement.

Watching through the window Rosemary was horrified to see water streaming into the yard, flowing from under the buildings at a rapid pace. Fearful of finding the house floating away beneath her she ran up the rickety steps and hid beneath the covers of her own, small bed.

She stirred the room dark around her, her eyes heavy with sleep. She did not remember the storm abating, nor could she remember undressing and getting into bed. Now something had woken her. The bedroom door squeaked on its hinges, she peered blearily at the doorway until she made out the figure of Robert. The rancid smell of him washed over the tiny room.

'Robert,' she cried in trepidation, 'where have you been, for so long?' Her head turned in agitation there was something badly wrong, why would Robert be here in her room? A room so small there was no escaping from it.

She received no answer and she struggled to sit up, pushing herself backwards into the corner of the bed against the wall, pulling the covers along with her. 'Are you alone?' Her voice came out in a harsh croak, fear of his friends crowding in behind him robbing her of her speech.

In three strides Robert was beside her, she heard his feet against the floor and a snigger from his lips then, felt his fist as he grabbed the meagre covers from her hand and yanked, stripping them from the bed completely.

Mewling like a frightened animal, the cool night air and her sudden terror made her shiver and her teeth chatter. She pressed closer to the wall. 'Robert, Robert,' she sobbed. Holding out a thin arm she endeavoured to keep him at bay,

116

whilst wailing. 'What is the matter, Robert? Please go away. Go to your room and leave me alone,' she begged.

Instead he sat on the edge of the bed effectively trapping her in the corner of her choice. A foolish move she realised too late. She shuddered pushing futilely at his chest, his ale sodden breath making her want to heave.

His hand flew out and grabbed her ankle in a vice like grip. In one movement she was pulled bodily back into the centre of the bed, her night attire twisting about the top of her legs, his free hand beginning to knead painfully at her small breasts.

Rosemary felt a wave of pain as he pulled her down, her head smashed against the wall briefly robbing her of her senses, the room revolved and nausea threatened.

Releasing her ankle he placed his hand heavily on her middle, leaning down on his elbow knocking what little breath she had from her body. His free hand continued to stroke and caress her breasts, crooning all the while like a father soothing a small child, his foul breath washing over her face in waves.

Sobbing uncontrollably, unable to understand why he was acting in this way, or move from under his weight, Rosemary begged and pleaded for him to stop. His hand left her breast and trailed its slow way down her side, pinching and stroking it prepared to explore other parts of her body.

'Oh, please, please no,' she moaned, her mind in turmoil at his actions, instinctively crossing her legs tightly against his invasion. 'Robert,' she screamed his hand forcing her thighs apart, his fingers digging cruelly into her flesh, his nails tearing at her skin when he invaded her private area with a cruel force.

'Shut up,' he muttered, his sour breath sickening her, his lips found her mouth and smothered her with evil, wet kisses. 'You're my wife, I can do this when ever I want.'

She struggled, her powerless arms pushing at his chest. 'No, Robert, no,' she pleaded, thrashing her head from side to side to avoid his mouth. 'I'm your sister, not your wife,' she pleaded in vain. 'Listen to me.' Huge racking sobs caught in her throat. 'Listen Robert, you are my brother,' she screamed uselessly, he was oblivious to her futile efforts, which seemed to inflame his passion more than diminish it.

His hand left her middle, rising and smashing against the side of her face, rattling her teeth and knocking her almost senseless. A black void opened in her brain and she lost the use of her limbs. She lay inert, at his mercy.

He stood swaying, murmuring at her, 'but I love you, I need you,' he told her, his words slurred tottering in his efforts to strip off his lower garments.

Numb with horror and pain her thoughts refusing to show her a way out of her predicament she lay still. Knowing she was unable to resist his evil intentions, endeavouring to close her mind to his actions, she only vaguely heard, and felt, the ripping of her night shift the buttons as they popped to the floor when he wrestled with his own shirt. She turned her face away from the silhouetted outline of his naked body, refusing to acknowledge him, or what he was about to do.

Straddling her he forced himself inside, ignoring the cry of pain that filled the room. He covered her face with slimy, evil, wet kisses. Wrestling her legs apart with his knees he raised himself upright, saliva dripped from his open mouth onto her chest as he lifted her buttocks in his hands. His fingers dug cruelly into her flesh, his body pumped against hers, crying aloud with elation when he finally reached the climax of his activities.

Seconds later he climbed from her inert body, bent to the floor and scooped up his clothing, tottered mildly as he straightened up again, then turned and left the room.

Rosemary lay she had no idea for how long. Her body racked with physical pain, her mind tormented by her own thoughts. Why, how had she let this happen? Was she so afraid of his violence her brain had been paralysed with fear? A sharp sliver of light peeped through the flimsy covering to the window, dawn was breaking. A voice screamed in her head. This had been a nightmare. Robert would not do such a thing. She moved, pain telling her otherwise. She would rather die than allow him to violate her in such a manner. Curling painfully into a tight ball she wept until there were no more tears left.

Lifting herself tentatively from the bed, disgusted by the sticky mess that covered the lower part of her body, she went to the chipped, china bowl she always kept filled with water and scrubbed at herself. The cool temperature soothed her chaffed, sore, flesh. She could wash away the evidence from her skin but how could she ever wash the reality from her mind?

The long rays of bright sunshine danced at her, mocking the bruised and aching limbs. She dressed with care and made her hesitant way down the steps to the kitchen.

Robert sat at the table, ignorant of the mud covered floor, still awash in places with water from the last night's storm. He was washed shaved and smartly dressed. He beamed at her. 'Good morning,' he cried brightly. Then looking more closely asked with concern. 'Are you ill?'

Rosemary stared unable to speak.

'I've been waiting for ages,' he went on, his voice sickly smooth and silky. 'You're so late, it's unlike you, oh dear me, did I wake you when I came in. I was very late.'

Tears flowed unheeded down her face and she stared at him. This was not the Robert of last night. She had not been able to see him clearly, but she had felt his straggly hair, his unshaven face, her own cheeks and chin were rubbed raw because of it. She had smelt his horrific breath and the sweat and grime she knew would be on his body.

'I did look in on you, but you were sound asleep,' he assured her with a serine smile.

She sat gingerly at the table, sobs and the smell of wet, rotting wood, choking her. 'That's not true, Robert. You know it isn't,' she cried accusingly. 'You know what you did...' She plunged her head in her hands unable to look at him.

He rose and came round the table laying a gentle hand on the small of her back. 'Have you been having those bad dreams again,' he asked in a conciliatory tone.

She cringed instinctively from his touch her body moving without her command, instantly triggering his temper.

'What evil are you trying to level at me now?' he yelled, spitting the words across her face, spraying her again with minute droplets of saliva.

'I'm not saying anything,' she whispered. 'You were drunk, you didn't know what you were doing.' Too late she realised, for her own safety she should have played along with his game.

'You're nothing,' he screamed, flouncing away from her, picking up and smashing a plate on the already littered floor. 'Nothing but trash from the gutter.' He rushed back at her putting his hand under her chin and snapping her head up to look at him. 'No man will ever want you,' he hissed. 'You're a tramp, a vagabond, the burden of my life. Someone I will have to carry until the day I die.' He took his hand from beneath her chin, her head falling on her chest, her eyes focused on the floor, not seeing the raised hand that landed open palm, on the side of her face knocking her sideways. With a look of pure contempt he stormed off into the rain sodden yard.

Rosemary laid her head on the rough surface of the table, her face stung, her body ached and her heart was heavy and sore. What on earth was happening now? she questioned her bemused brain. Was she mad? Or was Robert? If he was not mad, he was sick. How would she ever know? There was nobody to ask.

Standing stiffly, leaning her hands heavily on the table she surveyed the state of the home she did her best to make habitable. Today was going to be another hot and humid one, yesterdays storm had only cleared the air for a short while.

No doubt Henry Garth would arrive before the day was out, with several other unsavoury guests in tow, and heaven only knew what the evening and night would bring for her.

She shuddered straightening her back telling herself sternly she was not to think that far ahead. After last night, it was unthinkable.

In the meantime there was plenty of work to be done.

CHAPTER SIXTEEN

Henry Garth did not come to the house that day, or any other day after.

'Are your friends not coming to play cards?' she asked tentatively several days later, she sat opposite her brother's sullen figure.

'I have no friends,' he snapped. 'Friends are as fickle as my family,' he raged. 'They take everything you can give, then turn on you when least expected.'

Rosemary said nothing. She was being extremely careful about choosing her words. Robert had made no further reference to the night he had returned, and she had deemed it wiser to do the same.

'I thought you were looking bored,' she said softly, giving her reason for raising the subject.

'I am,' he replied, with no hint of animosity in his tone. 'I think I will ride out tomorrow, thank you dear sister for your thoughtfulness.'

Now when Robert stayed away he thankfully would take the dreaded horse with him, she half smiled to herself at the thought, the pleasure dissipating when she recalled his last return.

As time rolled by and Robert made no repeat of his unsavoury action she had relaxed her vigilance. Her body had healed leaving no scars and she had successfully pushed the incident to the back of her mind, other more important issue's taking its place.

'Mr Shepherd called today,' she informed him.

'Good, maybe I can have a decent meal then,' Robert snarled.

Rosemary stood before him her hands twisting at her middle. 'He called to say he could not allow us any more credit. He gave me a bill to pass on to you. It's quite considerable,' She reached in her skirt pocket and handed it to him.

He accepted the paper she had given him, carelessly screwing it in his palm and tossing the crumpled ball onto the floor. 'This is nothing to do with me,' he warned in a low tone. 'If the old fool is so besotted with you he gives you goods you can't pay for, that's his affair, not mine. I gave him a sum of money he should have stopped when it run out.'

'But that was month's ago,' Rosemary cried. 'We would have starved if he had stopped then.'

'Starved!' he shouted spinning on his heel and glaring at her. 'What have we got animals in the yard for? We won't starve.'

Her own temper rising at his injustice, she snapped back at him. 'If you had been in the yard recently you would know that you have already eaten half of the animals we had. I need some money to buy provisions, the cupboards are empty.'

'God help me,' he yelled, raising his arm heavenward, 'save me from the grabbing hands of this trollop.'

Her mouth opening and closing, she watched him stomp from the room and out of the house. She was used to his name-calling, but calling on God for help was something she had never heard him do before. How he expected her to continue to feed them both was beyond her comprehension. She had already slaughtered and cooked the small animals. There was no way she could stomach having to do the same with the larger ones.

Several hours later, the sound of heavy knocking on the door at the front of the house roused her from the washing she was dunking in a bucket in the yard. Wiping her hands on her skirt Rosemary made her way through the kitchen to stand in the dim hallway. Something about the knocking told her this was not good news. Shouts and curses began to accompany the banging, which was growing ever more energetic as she listened.

Rushing up the steps to an upper window, her eyes searched the yard and surrounding moor with anxious haste. Robert could not be far away the horse was still in the stable.

The sound of splintering wood brought her feet racing back to the hall again. Her hand clasped over her mouth she crept to the nearest front window. A short, thick set, man in a heavy tweed, coat was walking slowly away from the building. She ducked down instinctively when he turned and gazed back, his hand on his hips, his stance defiant. Her heart pounding she peeped out fearfully. Looking past him she was thankful to see her brother striding towards them across the moor.

To her surprise Roberts face was wreathed in smiles, he was clearly glad to greet the visitor.

She watched him raise a hand and hail the fellow who in turn waved his fist under her brother's nose. An animated conversation pursued. Finally, turning his visitor about and placing a friendly arm across his shoulder, Robert led the man back towards the house. She heard his tongue click in agitation when he saw the splintered woodwork of the door.

'That was really unnecessary,' he said smoothly leading the fellow inside.

'Never mind the bloody door. I'll flay the hide off you, you jumped up jackanapes,' the man yelled, stopping short when they came face to face with Rosemary.

'Sorry,' he stammered, his already blotchy face turning a darker red. 'I didn't know you had company.'

'She lives here,' Robert informed him smiling and waving the man to a seat, ignoring his visitor's anger completely much to Rosemary's concern

'Nobody answered my knocking,' the fellow mumbled a frown on his thickset forehead. He glared from one to the other.

'You frightened me,' she replied in a shaky voice, studying his bull neck and wide shoulders with apprehension.

'Huh, maybe so,' he grunted, his appearance as rough as the tweed coat he was wearing. Extracting a dark coloured bottle from his pocket he motioned for Robert to follow him into the kitchen. 'Let's sort this out like gentlemen,' he said. Robert complied.

On several occasions since his loss of Henry Garth's friendship her brother had brought home other unsavoury characters. She had learned to run and hide if she was fortunate enough to see them coming. This one had taken her unaware.

She sat, listening to the rise and fall of voices, although dangerously high from time to time there was no more thumping or cursing.

'May we join you,' Robert queried, they both made their unsteady way to her side.

Groaning inwardly she realised the dark bottle had been full of strong liquor, both men seemed mellow in spirit but unsteady on their feet.

Collecting up the sewing she had been busy with she prepared to leave the room, stopped by Robert's hand when it shot out and grabbed her shoulder forcing her back into her seat.

'A little female company is just what we need,' he said slyly.

She shivered from cold, and fear. The nights were drawing in and the mist had begun to hang over the moor, the heat all but leeched out of the autumn sun. She resumed her sewing, watching from beneath her lids whilst the two men talked of things she knew nothing about.

Taking her by surprise Robert's hand snaked out and lifted the hem of her skirt. 'Have you ever seen such a well turned ankle?' he asked his companion, she struggled to pull her skirt from his hand.

She tugged so violently that Robert toppled from his seat, falling in an ungainly heap on the floor. Looking up, she was just in time to see the rough fellow putting his tongue back inside his slack mouth, licking at his lips in a very suggestive manner.

'Come, come now,' Robert giggled, crawling on his knees in front of her. 'Stand up and show our friend your wonderful figure.' Despite the giggle, Rosemary knew how close he was to losing his temper.

Pulling her to her feet, sewing still clutched in her hand, he placed himself behind her, running his greedy hands from her hips to her armpits, extending his reach and cupping her breasts, squeezing them gently. His elbows dug into her waist warning her silently what would happen if she moved. She stared mutely at the ground embarrassment flooding her body with heat.

'See how ready she is for you,' Robert laughed, playing with the upright nipples he had teased from hiding. Cursing her body for duplicity against her a tear slipped from the corner of her eye.

Her brother was in debt to this heathen and she was how he intended to pay it off. Rosemary froze the knowledge hitting her with force.

Leering and drooling openly the rough man rose to his feet, unsteadily he lurched towards her, then miraculously tripped, she could not be sure on what, possibly his own feet. He fell flat on his face making no attempt to save himself. The force of the fall caused foul liquid to ooze from his mouth and form a puddle where he lay.

'Well,' Robert chuckled heartily. 'It must be a lucky day for you.' He released her pushing her back in the chair. 'The fellow could never hold his drink,' he cried, falling backwards into his own chair laughing hysterically.

Galvanised into action Rosemary threw aside her sewing, picked up the hem of her skirt and raced to her room, attempting to bar the door when Robert pushed through it.

'We're not going to waste this fine chance, are we?' he said with menace. A fat, half smoked cigar was clutched between his fingers he put it to his mouth and puffed on it, the end glowing red, the choking smell filling the small room. Blowing slow circles of smoke he advanced and Rosemary retreated, forcing her to stop when she backed up against the far wall.

Stuffing the cigar between his lips he grabbed her shoulders, with one swift flick of his foot he knocked her legs from beneath her and propelled her down on the bed, totally at his mercy.

'No, Robert, no not again,' she cried, knowing her protests would be of no avail.

Leaning down his curled fingers grabbed the front of her bodice, tearing it from her he let hot ash fall on her exposed skin leaving ugly red speckles when he brushed it away. The sight fascinated him and he tapped the cigar again allowing more ash to fall on her, watching as more small red, painful spots appeared. He giggled like a child with a favoured toy.

'It hurts,' she writhed and squealed involuntarily, knowing immediately it had been the wrong thing to do.

'Hurts does it?' he laughed, taking another long pull at the cigar in his mouth, then sprinkled hot ash liberally over her exposed breasts.

Clamping her teeth together she flinched refusing to make another sound.

Laughing, Robert stroked the hot end of the cigar in a line down the cleft between her breasts whispering. 'You don't know what pain is. Nobody does, except me.'

Rosemary writhed silently, unable to shake him off but desperate to stop his actions. His fist slammed into her jaw. 'You deserve that,' he hissed. 'My friend has travelled backwards and forwards to London for you. Not for anyone

127

else, only you. He deserved to be rewarded and what did you do. You cried. 'His voice became a squeak, reminding her befuddled brain of a child in a tantrum

She went limp, closing her eyes, an action, which terrified her because he was clearly capable of inflicting terrible damage to her body, but hoping it would convince him he had hurt her enough.

Throwing her skirt over her head muttering that no one was going to tell him what he could and could not do, he stubbed out his cigar on her groin. The excruciating pain lifting her knees in an involuntary movement, the smell of burning hair and flesh filling her nostrils with its acrid perfume. Dragging her legs down in vice like fists, Robert mounted her. The few futile attempts she made to stop him only heightening his desire then, he cried and yelled in exultation, calling loudly on the name of his god to bless his actions whilst he took his satisfaction.

His exertion completed he grunted his way out of the room, leaving Rosemary to stare in horror at her bleeding body. She was living a nightmare. She heard him slip and curse as he descended the steps.

'Who broke my bloody cigar?' he shouted drunkenly.

She knew he had again sunk into his own private world. Even if faced with his deeds he would be unable to believe himself capable of such actions. He would no doubt ask her stupid, solicitous questions about her bruises, never making any referral to what had happened.

Limping down the steps, she was just in time to see Robert pushing their visitor through the broken doorway, askance she heard him detail explicit sexual exploits that he was supposed to have taken with herself.

'I did?' the fellow questioned foolishly 'Are you sure, I don't recall.'

'That'll teach you to hold your liquor in future,' Robert laughed slapping him heavily on the back. 'Safe journey,' he cried.

Muddled and puzzled the chap kept turning back as he climbed the rise in the growing twilight. 'I did, you're sure?'

Feeling sick to her stomach Rosemary turned away, the fellow would never know whether he had done those things or not. Eventually he would believe that he had. But Robert had proved the winner. The man would never again come to their door to collect his debt, much or little.

'Maybe I should accompany him to town,' Robert mused, he stood inside the closed door. 'What do you think?' he turned and asked her sweetly.

Rosemary shrugged but did not reply, uncaring for either of them.

'Yes, you're right you always are, it would be the hospitable thing to do,' he cried excitedly. Gathering up his outdoor attire he made for the back yard, and his horse.

Whether he was going to accompany his friend to town or not, did not matter to Rosemary. All she knew for sure was, she would thankfully not see Robert again for some considerable time.

SEVENTEEN

Robert's actions took on a regular routine, following the same cycle week after week. He stayed away for indefinite periods usually two or three days, allowing Rosemary time to recoup some sanity and heal her body. On his return he would use her as a wife, an uncared for wife.

During his time at home he made no attempt to supply the food cupboard, yet, clearly expected to be fed in a normal manner. He neither offered, nor asked about money.

Rosemary had learned two hard lessons, firstly to submit to his physical demands without resistance. Secondly, driven by desperation she had learned to pick his pockets when he was deep in a drunken stupor. In the beginning this action had cost her great mental stress. The knowledge that Robert always had a goodly amount of coins about his person, and fear of a beating if she could not supply his meals helped her to come to terms with her behaviour.

This all gave way to another secret. To supply the table it was necessary for her to make furtive treks across the moor to the nearest farm, which also placed great strain on her under nourished body. She had no idea how far she travelled in miles to do her shopping only knowing how many hours the walk took her.

The moment Robert rode off on one of mysterious trips she threw a shawl about her shoulders and hurried away across the moor.

'Why won't you let me drop these provisions at your door?' the farmer asked, giving her a rare lift home.

'No, I couldn't think of bringing you all this way out just to deliver such small amounts,' she protested fearfully.

'But I go to town once every week, that's where I'm going now,' he grinned as he spoke, turning his head to look at her. 'If you ever want to have a trip into town, tell me and I'll stop off and pick you up,' he offered kindly. 'It would do you good, my wife was only saying last time you came how tired and pale you look.'

'Thank you, I'll remember that if I ever need to go,' she promised waiting for him to draw the horse and buggy to a halt on the rise.

'Mind how you go,' he called, helping her to climb from her seat beside him and gather her purchases in her arms. He waved to her retreating figure.

It made her sad when people were kind to her, she would like to be more friendly but fear of Robert finding out, and what he would do, stopped her.

Not that she had long to consider her feelings, dumping her goods unceremoniously in the kitchen she was again overcome with nausea, rushing outside to the yard the sickness overtook her. The farmer's wife was right, she thought, leaning against the wall panting from her sudden exertion. She did feel under the weather and she blamed her brother. What else could she expect on the amount she allowed herself to eat? Robert's coins did not provide over flowing cupboards, therefore she had to ensure his plate was always full, often leaving her own far too empty.

Several days ago she had been carrying a bundle of newly dried clothing from the yard into the house. She had woken up on the kitchen floor the clothes beneath her, her arms still clutched about them. It worried her. She needed to rest more, she told herself making her way back inside the house.

Settling into what she considered her own armchair, she tucked her feet up beside her and closed her eyes. She would just sit quietly for a minute or two, she thought. Waking with a start sometime later, realising she had fallen asleep and suddenly fearful that Robert would come home unexpectedly and find no chores done, she sat up in haste. Putting her feet to the floor she began to stand then, doubled over when her stomach lurched inside her, knocking her sick and breathless. Sitting gingerly back in her seat she waited for the strange feeling to subside.

Gaping down at her body open-mouthed she pressed gently with her hands around her stomach region her fingers probing lightly about her skin. The area was tender and bloated and movement fluttered beneath her palm.

'How could I be so stupid,' she cried in awe and disbelief. 'I'm with child!'

She should have known, she knew how children were conceived. How often had she watched the animals in the yard get pregnant and give birth. How could she not have realised it would one day happen to her? With it came a flood of emotion chasing across her brain. Excitement and happiness, followed by wonder and amazement, then came apprehension and fear.

She leaned her head back and closed her eyes her hands still caressing her swollen middle. Childbirth, it stirred a memory that danced tantalizingly out of reach. She allowed her mind to drift, it was a regular game, faces, and places often visited her on these occasions, not that she could put names to any of it. Yet she found them strangely comforting despite her lack of knowledge, she often thanked them silently for keeping her sane. Slowly her mood changed and she thought of her brother.

'What am I going to tell him?' she wailed loudly. 'How will I ever make him believe the truth?'

Somehow she had to make him accountable for his actions. She had to force him to take her back to civilisation. It was not just their survival now, but the life of their child, also. Terrified of his reactions she knew she would have no rest now until he returned. She was not to know at that moment Robert would stay away, this time, longer than ever before.

He had been home all morning and she still had not found the courage to speak to him. Finally, knowing the deed had to be done sooner, rather than later, she squared her shoulders and stood before him.

'Robert,' she began in a small, hesitant voice. 'I have something to tell you well, discuss with you,' she corrected, seating herself back in her chair she picked up her sewing. If she did not keep her hands busy he would see how much she was shaking with fear of him.

He failed to look up, merely mumbled, 'hmm...'

She swallowed hard. 'Robert I am expecting a child,' she said softly, her eyes fixed on her work, unable to raise her head to look at him.

'What makes you say that,' his words were a harsh whisper that brought her head up to face him. His neck and cheeks were already ablaze, red hot with anger.

'The signs,' she stammered, flustered, her practiced speech forgotten. 'The changes in my body.'

'When?' He shot the word like an arrow straight at her.

'About five or six month's as near as I can judge,' she whispered, fear claiming her heart, she had considered him in a mellow mood she had been wrong.

Standing he covered the two steps required to hunch over her. He glared down watching as she twisted the needle and thread in her nervous fingers. Words tumbled from her lips in an effort to explain and placate him at the same time.

'You have to understand,' she pleaded. She wanted to shout that it was his actions that had put her in this position, but knew better than to refer to it. 'Why do you look so shocked?' she cried in amazement. She knew he was capable of acting as though he had blotted everything from his mind, but inside she believed he knew exactly what he did.

'Who is it?' he yelled, spraying her with spittle. 'Tell me his name?'

'But Robert you know very well,' she sobbed, unwanted tears filling her eyes. 'Why are you asking such a question? You know exactly what has been happening.'

'Henry Garth,' he said, his voice so low she strained to hear his words. 'I know it is him. Tell me, tell me it's him, isn't it?' He swung on his heel turning a full circle, flaying his arm uselessly about him before he leaned down and grabbed her wrist, his grip like a vice he twisted her arm. Yelling at her now, his anger making him almost incoherent, he went on more to himself than her.

'I knew he would do this,' he rasped, his eyes bulging, his lips dragged back from his teeth. 'He thought he had won you at cards when I lost all my money. I knew he would go back on his word.' His hand twisted on her wrist, burning her flesh.

'Robert,' she wept. 'You know who it was. Not Henry Garth I have not seen him. You're hurting me,' she wailed.

Ignoring her he leaned closer. 'How often does he come here?' he hissed. 'Does he watch to see when I leave, have you got some sort of signal?'

Rosemary stared mesmerized at the tiny red veins flecking his goggling eyes and the angry tick that was playing under the skin of his temples. He was mad. Completely mad she could not believe what she was hearing. How could he put the blame for his own actions on an innocent man, however distasteful she thought the person to be?

His fingers left her arm and he turned, still muttering to himself and stamped from one end of the room to the other, he ranted and raged as he paced. Opening his arms and raising them high in the air he called upon God to deliver him from his cursed sister. He screamed about the retribution he would take on his old friend, Henry. She cringed in her chair watching him.

Rushing back at her he clutched at her hand, squeezing it in his fist, he cursed her. 'You slut, you are the whore from

134

hell,' he raved, throwing one profanity after another into her face.

Rosemary screamed in pain the sewing needle she had been holding drove deep into her palm, twisting and breaking, Robert crushed her hand more tightly in his. Blood dripped between his fingers and dropped on her lap, he was totally unaware of it.

'I should throw you out, send you to your lover,' he yelled, releasing her hand and spitting squarely in her face. 'You disgust me. You turn my stomach, I never want to look at you again.' He fled, charging up the steps and retreating to his own room, his oaths trailing after him.

Wiping her face with the edge of her skirt, she nursed her injured limb. Opening her hand with difficulty and steeling herself against more pain, she carefully removed the embedded metal from her flesh hurriedly wrapping the article she had been sewing around her injury to soak up the blood. The pain of her actions momentarily robbed her of sight and her head reeled. She was not sure which hurt the most, her injury, or Robert's behaviour.

Rosemary's mind chased in circles day and night, she worried about the developing child inside her. If it survived the birth what would he, or she be like, what did life hold for it anyway? Could any infant survive their rigorous life?

'Robert please calm down,' she begged constantly when he raged about their home, destroying everything in his path.

'You're a witch,' he yelled, 'an evil, twisted witch. You should be burned for your sins,' he ranted at her.

'I am not the one guilty of sin,' she replied calmly, beyond tears, or fear now.

He would hold up his fist to her and she never flinched.

'There is nothing more you can do to me, Robert,' she told him quietly on one of these occasions. 'Except kill me, and that would be blessed relief.'

He roared at her like an injured, trapped animal and fled to his room sobbing.

Eventually his temper subsided and he began to act even more strangely. Shying away from her nervously, refusing to look at her growing shape. He began to pray, to chant his prayers out loud as he walked from room to room.

'Robert, please will you gather your senses and behave in a normal manner?' she requested one morning. She was tired of this continual childish treatment and it had to stop.

'One of us has to beg for your sin to be forgiven,' he replied defiantly, his eyes fixed firmly on the table. 'God, can't just do it like that, you have to earn it.' He informed her earnestly. 'You won't make any effort to do so therefore, I must.'

More frightened than she had ever been of his violence, Rosemary shrank inside at his words. How could he have convinced himself in this manner, she was not the one in need of forgiveness, was she? She watched in amazement when her brother sank to his knees, putting his palms together before his face, his eyes turned upwards and began to pray loudly his eulogy covering years of misdeeds on her part.

'God,' he cried finally. 'She is only young. She has no parents to guide her, release her from this burden she carries. Make your saints help her. Let her be as she used to be.' Then lifting his voice higher he continued. 'Don't punish my sister, please stop punishing her she didn't know what she was doing.'

He stopped shouting heavenwards and doubled over, tears flowing endlessly down his cheeks. Rosemary stretched out a hand and watched it hover falteringly above his bent head then, snatched it back a new fear gripping her. Was this more of his play-acting? Was he going to do something awful to her, to the baby inside her? Then would he blame his actions on God, telling her it was the way his God had answered his prayer.

Something about him, she decided, reminded her of that eerie, flat, calm that comes before the worst thunderstorms. Suddenly she was terrified, would he act before or after the

136

birth? He no longer made nocturnal visits to her room. After many sleepless nights, waiting and listening for a noise from him, she had relaxed enough to sleep again. Maybe this was his way of lulling her to a secure mind. She shivered.

'I'm going to town for provisions,' he informed her without looking in her direction. 'We have empty cupboards again, I will never know what you do with all that I buy.'

She bit back the retort she would like to make. He had never asked how she managed all those months he was more away than home. Thankfully she watched him leave. She could no longer have trekked across the moor anyway, though she missed the minimal contact with the outside world. Robert, she knew, would be gone most of the day, which would give her time to rest.

Her nightly vigils would have to start again, she decided. With her brother, it would be better to anticipate the worst, and be prepared.

EIGHTEEN

The Refuge was quieter than usual. The weather was inclement for the time of year. Molly sat impatiently waiting for her husband to finish reading the latest news from the West Country.

Jake paced backwards and forwards as he read. 'Where are the children?' he asked absently looking up briefly.

'Dora has them, outside,' she replied, almost jiggling in her seat with anxiety. 'What does it say?' she begged.

'Here,' he said thrusting the paper at her his face unreadable. 'You had better see for yourself.'

Molly scanned the news, then began again and digested it more slowly. 'What does it mean?' she asked, her pale face turned up to her husband waiting for him to explain.

Jake stood watching her he was so still it frightened her. 'They have been very honest,' he said. 'They have been at pains not to give us too much hope.'

'But there say they are sure they have found her,' she said, a mixture of joy and fear in her tone.

'True,' Jake replied, 'but they also list all they have learned about Edward so far. Although it doesn't say so in so many words,' he went on. 'I don't think they expect to find Rosie... Alive!'

'Oh, I've prayed so hard that it would all end happily,' Molly said softly, a tear shimmering on her long lashes. 'It's been so long since they left and so much has happened.'

Jake nodded, thinking his own thoughts about Ninny and the rest of the family. 'I had half expected that Lewis would return when he heard about Ninny,' he admitted.

'No,' Molly replied forcefully. 'He's far too committed to finding Rosie. I do hope they find her alive, and well.'

'I'm going,' Jake cried. 'It's time I'm going to meet them, see what's happening for myself.'

'But they say here, they will send to tell us the minute it is over,' Molly answered, jumping up flustered at the thought of her husband leaving as well.

'However they find her, I should be there,' Jake told her, his eyes beseeching her for understanding.

Molly turned and walked away she left the building and stood, contemplating as she watched her children play tag around the garden. She smiled at Dora, dozing on her seat. Rosie meant as much to her and Jake, as Sammy and Emily did. She had longed for the girl to be returned to them. Now she was scared, terrified of what Lewis, and Simon were about to find. She felt the warmth of him as Jake came to stand behind her, his arms going protectively about her middle, his head resting on the back of her shoulder.

'When will you leave?' she asked softly.

'In the morning,' he answered, kissing her tenderly on the cheek.

NINETEEN

Simon continued to rage at the top of his voice about Henry Garth as they bumped and swayed, racing the carriage at break neck speed across the moor.

'He's the most odious man I have ever met. All I wanted to do was hit him,' he ranted, punching a clenched fist into his open palm to demonstrate his wishes.

Lewis sat silently beside his companion, concentrating on controlling the horse, endeavouring to avoid the worst of the ruts and ridges without loosing pace. 'We have her know,' he shouted against the wind to his young friend, 'save your energy for when we get there. It may be needed,' he added in a tone of warning.

'If Edward is as mad as that Garth fellow says,' Simon yelled back, the horror on his face telling Lewis exactly what he meant.

'Have you given any thought to how we should deal with him?' Lewis questioned. Instinct was commanding their actions at this moment they had made no plan of campaign.

'What do you think he meant about gambling her away?' Simon asked, the wind whipping at his words. 'You do think she will still be there, when we get to the house.'

Lewis shrugged. 'He could have given her away to someone else, you mean?' He said flatly. 'I don't want to think of that as a possibility.'

Simon fell silent. He knew it would kill his companion if that were the case. At his age Lewis could not continue receiving these body blows, each disappointment took its toll on his health and well being.

140

'Should we have waited for the police?' Lewis questioned with uncertainty.

'No time,' Simon confirmed. 'Confronted, Edward will wriggle out of this situation somehow. Guile is what will trap him. If he saw uniforms he would run, and the chase would begin again.'

'Whoa, steady, steady,' Lewis cried, as the horse missed his footing the carriage juddering.

'Why did you pay the rent?' Simon queried, turning to look at the older man. 'It seemed a strange thing to do if we are going to take her away with us.'

'We have no idea what we will find.' Lewis turned his head. 'There is an outside chance Rosie will be completely on her own. She may not need our help. She could have grown into the life she is leading,' he shouted back.

'I think you are being far too liberal with your thinking,' his companion replied. 'I'm sure she won't want to stay.'

'I hope with all my heart you're right,' he boomed. 'But, he, Edward, may have damaged her mind more than we can understand. She may see us as enemies.'

'What will you do if that's the case?' Simon questioned.

'Go back to the odious Garth and secure the house for as long as possible. Then settle in the area and try to help her,' Lewis answered flatly.

Simon fell silent he believed what he was hearing. Lewis would live the rest of his days as close at hand as he could.

The trip across the moor was taking forever, more because neither of them knew exactly where they were going. It had looked much closer on the sketchy map drawn by the clerk.

'We are going in the right direction?' Simon asked at last, his eyes scanning the blank horizon.

'Yes, yes, look,' Lewis cried, drawing the horse to a slower pace as they crested the ridge.

Simon shuddered, 'What a peculiar place to build a home,' he breathed, staring at the gloomy building in the hollow.

'There is no doubt this is the right place,' Lewis responded. 'It gives me the creeps.'

'What's that?' Simon pointed past the homestead at the black, jagged stonework sticking up out of the ground.

'A ruin of some sort,' Lewis replied thoughtfully. 'The clerk mention an old Abbey, that's probably it.'

'Let's get on with it,' the younger man murmured, his hand on his companion's arm

Lewis visibly squared his shoulders before he set the horse down the incline. 'Surely we will find the place empty,' he muttered his eyes searching the building for signs of life.

The carriage nosed through the broken gateway and up to the front door the air of neglect demoralising, they dismounted looking with heavy hearts at the grimy windows, the splintered door.

'She's in there, I know it,' Lewis whispered, his voice trembling. With hesitant steps he went up to the door and knocked on it loudly.

Long minutes passed with no answer. Rapping again, he called through the woodwork, 'Rosie, Rosemary.'

'Should I go round the back?' Simon asked in a low tone. 'She may flee in fright.'

'Wait, let's see if she will open the door. If not, then we'll both go to the back,' Lewis responded, rapping and calling again.

'Rosie, Rosie it's Lewis. You won't remember me but I've known you for many years. I've come all the way from London to find you. Molly and Jake are waiting for you. Won't you open the door and talk to me.'

Simon, who had his ear against the woodwork, touched his friend's arm. ' Listen, there's a shuffle inside,' he whispered

'Rosie darling, open the door I am your friend. Simon here with me, he is also a friend. You have no need to fear us,' he continued to call in calm tones. 'Rosie,' he implored. 'I knew you when you were a little girl, when you lived by the riverside with Molly and Jake, and Lenny and Dora, and Dirty Sam.' His voice tailed off a sob choking his words, his eyes flickering from door to windows in hopes of seeing some sign of life.

They both heard the rustle from within. 'We are friends,' Lewis renewed his efforts. 'We have come to take you away from Robert. To take you home to safety,' he cried.

Gently pushing Lewis to one side Simon put his mouth to the door. 'Rosemary,' he called softly. 'We are friends, we've come to take you back to your home, and your family.' He turned to his companion and whispered. 'She knows herself as Rosemary, not Rosie.'

Silence fell inside, and out.

'She won't know the name Rosie, it might frighten her,' Simon went on, 'Let her digest what we have told her.'

'What if it's Edward and not Rosie inside?' Lewis whispered back, his fears visible on his features.

Suddenly the door creaked and opened the tiniest crack. An eye and a sliver of face could be seen in the dimness.

'You won't remember me, I know all that has happened to you,' Lewis whispered not wanting to frighten her. 'I have even talked to your friend Tildy,' he told her patiently. He smiled as widely as he could. 'The last time we saw each other you were about eleven years old,' he went on in a sing song voice, trying to calm both her fears, and his own.

'Is Robert in there?' Simon asked gently his ever, searching eyes telling how he expected his brother to jump out on him at any moment.

The door cracked an inch or so wider and they saw her shake her head as she stared at them, the door was heavy in her hands, it scraped against the floor. Smiling tenderly Lewis extended his arm slowly and gripped the edge of the door

143

pushing gently he opened it wide enough to enter. His breath taken by the shock of the skeletal figure he saw standing in the hallway. 'Oh my God,' he hissed, as he allowed Simon to pass him.

'Shall we go inside,' Simon asked gently, not waiting for Lewis to complete closing the door before he ushered the pathetically thin, shabby female further into the house.

Leading her to the window, where the best of the late afternoon light was still penetrating, Simon stared into the face of the unknown girl he had spent so long searching for. The pallor of her skin and the darkly circled eyes, pulled at his emotions. 'He will never hurt you again,' he vowed almost tearfully.

'Do you remember me, Rosie?' Lewis asked hopefully, stepping up beside them his eyes drinking in her features, his heart pounding painfully in his chest.

'My name is Rosemary, sir,' is all she answered, yet her eyes roved about his face as though searching for something that eluded her.

'Quite right,' Lewis replied with a cough. 'Rosie was my personal pet name for you.' His hands had gone to her arms, his urge to draw her to his chest and cuddle her almost readable on his face. A loud wail rent the air and Rosie a tender smile cracking her features excused herself.

They watched as she climbed a set of broken steps, returning moments later with a bundle secured under each arm.

'You are sure this is, Rosie?' Simon questioned. 'She's nothing like we had expected,' he added as Lewis nodded vigorously.

Stepping forward Lewis reached for the squirming bundle that looked in danger of slipping through her arm, looking down his stare was returned by a pair of coal, black eyes, young as the baby was, they assessed him in return. Looking from the silent scrutiny of the child in his arms, he stared at the crying bundle which Rosie was unwrapping where she sat in a battered armchair. Ignoring her visitors, she got on with the business of feeding her baby. The yells stifled instantly as the infant began to suckle. Crooning softly, she rocked gently and gazed lovingly at her child.

Lewis sat heavily on the edge of a seat. Looking up helplessly at his companion he asked the unspoken question, what do we do now.

Feeling somewhat stupid Simon spoke first. 'Are you married, Rosemary?' he asked, his face telling of his shock.

'No sir,' she replied. Unable to lie to these people whom for some reason she trusted instinctively. 'He tells everyone that we are, but he's my brother really.'

Lewis was shaken at her blunt tone. 'Who exactly tells people you are married?' he queried softly. 'Who is your brother?'

'Robert, of course,' she replied as though he were foolish.

A trick of the light glistened on the girl's hair giving the impression of a halo about her head. Both men stared at her. 'These are Edwards children?' Simon asked in amazement.

Lewis nodded not taking his eyes from Rosie, who looked up, puzzlement clouding her face.

'Phew, what a turn up for the family tree,' he murmured, slumping heavily in an armchair with a broken arm.

A tiny fist snaked from the cover cradled in Lewis's arms, a small thumb diving deep into the rosebud mouth sounds of the child's vigorous sucking filled the room.

'How old are the babies?' Lewis asked his curiosity peeked.

'About three months sir,' Rosie answered proudly. A broad smile lighting up her face. Mother love etched on her features.

'Boy's, or girl's?' Lewis queried, looking from mother to each child in turn, his mind digesting the sudden change in circumstances.

'You are holding Nancy, she's the good, quiet one,' she replied still smiling. 'This one is Daniel, he needs lots of attention.' She dropped a kiss on the spiky black hair, sprouting from the tiny head still nuzzling at her breast.

'How did you chose the names?' Lewis asked, curious to hear her answer.

Looking directly at him she replied unabashed. 'That I don't know sir, they just seemed to come to me, and I liked them.'

'If I told you,' Lewis began quietly. 'That a young woman called Nancy had been almost a mother to you when you were very small, and later, that you made a friend of a young man called Daniel, and felt very sorry for him when he was taken into custody. Would that stir any memories for you?'

She shook a sad head, 'I don't remember being young,' she replied with honesty, covering her breast as she moved the child from her. Smiling she allowed Lewis to stand up and hand her Nancy, at the same time, Simon stepped forward and relieved her of Daniel now snuggled contentedly. With the awkwardness of a single man, he sat gingerly back in his seat, the child cuddled stiffly in his arms.

Walking away on the pretext of his legs being cramped, Lewis made his way into the kitchen. There he stared out of the window at a couple of ducks pecking absently as wisps of straw in the yard. He lifted a finger and brushed at his cheek knowing it was wet. 'Dear God,' he muttered as he looked around him. 'How has she survived?' he moaned peering into empty cupboards and searching for facilities he knew he would not find.

Going back to Rosie's side he hunched down with difficulty, bringing his face level with hers. 'Are you sure you don't remember me, Rosie?' he asked softly, watching as she shook her head. 'You have accepted me, and Simon here,' he jerked a thumb at his companion. 'You have no fear of us, why is that?'

She shook her head softly. 'Robert,' she said. 'He, has always told me I lived in a mansion, in London when I was a little girl, he said we were rich. I used to believe him.' A blush

146

covered her face and she looked steadily into the old man's eyes. 'Then I began not to believe him. I don't know who I am or where I come from. Neither, do I know you, sir,' she replied timidly, 'I wish I did, but something inside tells me to trust you. It's as though I have always known you would come.' She smiled past Lewis at Simon, still holding the sleeping baby, embracing him in her statement.

'So,' 'he said softly not wanting to frighten her at this stage. 'You will understand when I say we have come from London to take you, and your children home with us. Will you come? Will you trust us enough to leave with us, now?' The painful position was hurting his legs but he resisted the urge to stand up. He had so hoped the sight of him, of his talk of the family left behind, would jog her mind and open the locked door for her.

Cocking her head to one side she replied sweetly. 'When Robert comes.'

'When do you expect Robert home?' Simon asked, wanting to help his face telling how awkward he was feeling.

'It could be days. Sir,' she answered smiling serenely

'Why don't we take you and the babies to the Tavern in town,' Lewis suggested, hating the way she insisted on calling him sir all the time. 'Once you are settled comfortably, we can come back for Robert,' he coaxed. 'He can join us later.' He lifted an enquiring eyebrow and plastered a smile on his lips. It clearly asked, would she trust that much?

Rosie stared from one to the other, confusion on her face, a mental tussle taking place in her mind. What would Robert do if he returned and found her gone, she wondered, still fearful of his tantrums? Then again, would he be pleased she was no longer there? He hated her and the twins, prayed daylong for his deliverance from them. She had feared he would damage them instead he had retreated into himself, acting as though she no longer existed.

'Will you be taking Robert home to London as well?' she asked, that was his dearest wish she knew that.

147

'We hope so,' Lewis and Simon both answered at once.

'Then if you think I should, sir,' she replied softly.

Breathing a huge sigh of relief, Lewis stood, stamping lightly with his feet to ease his pain. He cast about him surveying the furnishings, everything was clean and tidy if old and often broken, he could think of nothing she would want to take, but he asked the question anyway.

'Is there anything you want to take with you, my dear?'

'I have very little,' she said honestly. 'The babies clothing, such as it is.'

Anxious now to be out of this place Simon almost shouted. 'Don't worry about any of that, we will get new once we are in town. Just let's hurry.' He stood, clutching the child to his chest, already making for the door.

Laughing with relief, happier than he had been in a long time, Lewis found a shawl and wrapped it protectively about Rosie's shoulders, his urge to enfold her in his arms palpable in the air about them. Then he led her outside to their carriage.

'Goodness,' she said, a laugh in her voice. 'I hardly remember the last time I travelled like this.' She gazed around, whether looking for her brother or saying a mental farewell, they would never know.

Simon appointed himself driver, handing over his bundle, then, jumping up to the high seat, leaving Lewis to settle the family in comfort.

The journey back was taken at a more sedate pace, the light fading around them. Elation at the success of their mission making him call to them every few minutes, ensuring their comfort and safety as he picked his careful way across the moor.

'He doesn't mean to be a nuisance,' Lewis informed his young companion with a smile. 'We've been searching for you for two, long years. He's almost as happy as I am that we have found you at last.'

She turned to him, the features of her face unclear in the darkness, but he had heard her gasp. 'Two years, sir?' she asked. 'Have I been away from home for that long.'

'Much longer than that my dear,' Lewis told her tenderly. 'You were eleven years old when you were stolen from your family. Now you must be seventeen, or eighteen. It's been a very long time indeed.'

'Stolen, by whom?' she queried, awe reducing her voice to a whisper.

'It is a very long story, which I will gladly tell you later,' he promised. 'For now, both you and the babies should rest.'

TWENTY

The rhythmic rocking of the journey's steady progress, lulled Rosie and the babies to sleep, leaving Lewis to study the person he had dreamed about finding for so long.

Simon had been right to question her authenticity; she was greatly changed from how he remembered her. Yet, he had known her instantly.

The thought of all she had suffered made him sick to his stomach, his desire to see Edward hang from the gallows growing stronger with ever hour. As he swayed gently from side to side with the motion of the carriage, he mentally composed the letter he would gladly send to Molly and Jake in London. He knew when they had arrived at their selected residence, by the noise that Simon was making.

'Landlord, landlord,' he yelled. 'Bring help out here, at once.'

Lewis gently shook Rosie awake and helped her to alight, she stood blinking as the landlord, his wife and two maids, hurried to their assistance. Each maid accepting, and cooing over a child, the two men helped Rosie, now overcome with the warmth of the interior, and the rich smell of food cooking, to her room.

'Hot water,' Lewis requested, looking at the maids, 'and,' he added a little ruefully, 'could one of you young ladies spare a decent night shift, for our friend?'

'My uncle owns the village shop,' one of the girls offered. 'If you make a list of your requirements, I will go and attempt to get them for you.'

150

Thankfully Simon hurried to supply her with all she would need, and she scurried away. 'The village will know our business before morning,' he informed Lewis with a worried frown.

'It matters not,' Lewis assured him. 'I have already told mine host that Rosie is my grand daughter run away from home. I have taken the liberty of asking his wife to scout the village for a wet nurse. In her state she cannot be expected to continue to feed both babies on her own.'

Within an hour of their arrival, not one, but two nurses had been employed, one for the twins, one for Rosie. The local trader had hurried to the Inn his arms full of the requirements Simon had requested. A doctor had been sent for and a messenger dispatched to Battersea. Lewis was busy instructing the two remaining messengers who were about to be sent post haste, to the Gimlets, and to Tildy.

To Tildy he sent a request that she join them as quickly as possible. He liked the strong-minded, young woman, and had high hopes that she would help him to crack the block that was covering Rosie's memory. He prayed that meeting someone from the past she could recall would help her.

In all, the evening was the busiest they had spent in a long time, everyone was more than glad when they were able to take some rest.

'I'm off to the authorities,' Simon, informed his companion briskly as he left the breakfast table. 'I think I have all the paperwork needed.'

'I was under the impression the local police force only numbered two,' Lewis said, his eyes opening wide with concern.

'I didn't want to worry you with details,' Simon told him a thoughtful frown on his face. 'I've arranged to go further up the coast where there is more help available,' he confirmed with a half smile. 'You see to Rosie and the twins, I'll deal with this.'

151

It was mid afternoon when a small army of militia, gathered on horseback outside the Inn the leader dismounting and entering in search of Simon.

'We are ready to be off,' he informed him officially. 'You will be joining us sir.' He clicked his heels and bowed his head in salute.

'Me?' Simon questioned stupefied, looking from Lewis to the uniformed person clearly waiting for him. 'I didn't expect to have to join you.'

'Well, sir,' the policeman went on steadfastly. 'You being his brother we need you to identify him, and you may be able to talk him into coming with us quietly.'

'He's never listened to me before,' Simon exploded. 'So why should he be expected to now?' He looked at his companion for moral support.

'I think one of us should go,' Lewis said firmly, rising as though to take his young friend's place.

Staying him with a hand on his shoulder, Simon nodded, 'Very well,' he muttered reluctantly. 'I'll go.'

The babble of voices, snorting and stamping of horses, filled the Inn as they waited impatiently for the off, Simon prevaricated, he really did not want to do this and was making his preparations last as long as possible.

'A messenger sir,' the landlord popped his head around the door waving the official looking document first at Lewis, then at his other well to-do guest.

Accepting the rolled paper thrust into his hand, Simon reached into his pocket and rewarded the man with a few coins, before turning aside to read the missive.

'It is from the local constabulary,' he informed everyone. 'It seems my brother has been under our noses all the time,' he told his adversary who had stepped up beside him. 'He has been drinking himself stupid in several local watering holes. And was finally turned out bodily for his inability to pay, only this morning.' He smiled. 'I would assume that means he is on his way back to the hovel on the moor.'

The officer perused the paper handed to him as they walked out into the fresh air. 'In that case,' he said confidently. 'I think he will be home barely anytime at all before we get there.' He waved a hand to bring his men to order.

Simon stared at him puzzled. 'It said he was turned out this morning,' he stated limply.

'Aye sir, but I know that particular publican. He will have taken anything of value before he turned your brother out,' he nodded wisely. ' He will be on foot, without doubt.'

With mounting dismay Simon accepted his fate and went to collect his horse, falling in line behind the group leaving the Inn yard. Eventually he found himself once again on that rise looking down on the unpleasant homestead he had hoped never to see again.

Beckoning, the officer indicated that Simon should accompany him to the door. They dismounted and could hear the sound of breaking furniture, together with loud cursing. Animal like roars alternated with the thumping and splintering of wood, liberally sprinkled with foul oaths, told them clearly Edward was already aware that Rosie and his children had gone.

'We'll go round the back. I think,' the officer muttered, heading off in that direction.

Simon followed dutifully, not sure why, to the flimsy kitchen doorway. Pushing it quietly inwards both men entered coming instantly face to face with a raging demon.

'Who the hell are you?' Edward cried, a spindly wooden stool held above his head menacingly. 'Who said you could enter my home?' he yelled, heaving the stool, which crashed against the wall and fell apart.

Simon stared foolishly, mouth agape. This man held no resemblance to the brother he recalled. His brother was a dandified man this one looked more like an ape. His hair was long and unruly, his beard unkempt, his appearance that of the lowest of the low. A torn cloak still clung to his shoulders,

153

whether tattered on the long journey home or from his raging temper since being in the house, Simon would never know. What amazed him was how it failed completely to impede his actions in any way.

Edward gazed back, recognition and disbelief in his eyes, head angling for a second he squinted, joy and fear chasing across his features like the flicker of a candle flame.

Men crowded in the narrow doorway behind them, the officer took a step towards Edward. With a deep roar of rage Edward leaped straight at Simon, his hands held like claws.

Involuntarily Simon stepped back, his retreat hampered by the cracked sink and water pump. In a mid air leap his brother completely changed direction; with the dexterity of an acrobat he lunged through the broken framework of what had been the kitchen window. While Simon cringed from the expected assault, Edward gripped the edges of his cloak, and rolled his body through the opening and out into the yard, liberally littered with broken items.

Stumbling at first he picked himself up and ran, weaving his way across the ground, sure footed in the grime and sludge, deftly avoiding the men who slipped and slid in their efforts to apprehend him. Gaining vital seconds Edward picked up speed and ran across the moor in the direction of the Abbey.

'Get after him. Get after him,' the officer roared, stabbing a finger in the air after Edward. 'Come on man. To the horses,' he instructed Simon then turned back to the front of the house. 'We've got to catch him.'

Bemused, Simon again followed without question. Other men joined them all scrambling to collect their horses, some ran on foot in chase of their villain. Pandemonium reigned.

Simon could see his brother, his cloak billowing behind him, charging across the moor in the fading light. Digging his heels sharply in his horse he urged the animal to speed and flew after him not waiting for the horse to stop before leaping from its back when the ground got progressively more boulder strewn and precarious.

'Edward, stop, Edward,' he yelled at the top of his voice, he slipped and slid from one pile of rubble to another, his breath coming in harsh, rasping pants that hurt his chest and seared his throat.

A manic laugh reached his ears Edward paused only momentarily to look back at him.

Using every ounce of strength and determination Simon pushed his efforts harder and closed the gap between them. Leaning forward to extend his arm he gripped the cloth of his brother's cloak and yanked with all his might, hoping to bring the fleeing figure to a stand still.

Edward deftly shrugged his shoulders, the cloak falling away from him, leaving Simon faltering on a boulder, the loose cloth dangling from his hand.

'Nice try,' the officer in charge said with admiration as he drew level. 'Look,' he cried, turning back to Edward and pointing. 'What's the fool going to do now?'

Edward was slowly scaling the blackened, Abbey wall, the broken stonework forming giant steps that aided his accent. Simon turned to watch, heaving and shuddering he fought to control his breathing and stared upwards. His brother had chosen the tallest part of the crumbling walls. It looked solid enough, but Simon found himself holding his breath, expecting the stonework to disintegrate under Edward's weight at any moment.

The climbing figure stopped and gazed down, Simon was sure he was looking directly at him. A light glinting from the row of white teeth his wide grin exposed. Peal after peal of maddening laughter reached them and bounced from the ruined walls, ringing about them.

'Edward, come back,' he roared. 'We need to talk,' he shouted, knowing his pleas were wasted, he watched his brother climbing higher, and higher.

One by one, men clambered over the stonework that surrounded the Abbey, the noise of their stumbling over the loose boulders filling the air. Nudging and jostling one another they gaped at the spectacle.

'Look, look,' the gasp went round the group crowded inside the ruin all faces turned skyward. Edward reached the highest point of the wall his silhouette dark and foreboding against the eerie twilight.

'Edward, come down, there is nowhere else to go,' Simon shouted, unsure whether his words would carry that far upwards uncertain why he was even trying to talk to his brother, a cauldron of mixed emotions stirring inside him.

If they had, Edward ignored them. He stood, feet apart, arms raised heavenward, under some spell of his own making oblivious to his perilous position or the people beneath. He was yelling but no words came to them, his face turned skywards, his voice blown away by any breeze there may have been at that height.

'What's he doing praying?' one man whispered to his neighbour, the sibilant sound of the question echoing in the unnatural quiet.

'Making his peace with God,' another replied, his low words sounding just as harsh.

'More like a pact with the devil,' yet another growled.

Ignoring them, Simon watched in silent horror. The men around him also watching the puppet like actions of the person, poised high above them.

Slowly, slowly, Edward lowered his arms from the heavens and stretched them out to his sides. For long minutes he stood perfectly still, the only movement the clouds behind him, the only sound the occasional scrape of a boot against a stone as someone shuffled his feet. Then in the manner of a graceful bird he launched himself into mid air, a laugh following his body to the ground where it crashed at the foot of the wall with a sickening thud of pulverising bones.

As one, every man had fallen backwards, shuffling away from the falling form. Now, with the exception of Simon, they surged forward to examine the broken body.

'I'm, very sorry,' the officer said quietly, after he had directed his men to remove the body and again joined Simon. 'I don't imagine he felt much,' he added. 'Must have died instantly. Mad as a hatter,' he muttered.

Simon nodded silently. He had hated his brother, wanted more than anything to see him hang, until this moment. Now he felt empty, failed, he should have tried harder to talk him down from the wall. If those fools had not crowded into that silly kitchen he could have talked to Edward, he was sure about that. Got some answers maybe to all the questions they had been asking for so long.

As though reading his mind the officer said softly. 'Don't feel bad. We would never have captured him. He had no intention of being taken alive.'

'I know,' Simon replied. 'I was just thinking how he had suffered in his life,' he looked directly at the disbelieving official. 'I know what you must be thinking,' he gave a small smile. 'I wanted to see justice done as well. But I have the misfortune of knowing what a loveless childhood my brother had to contend with. His own mother died, and my mother, loving soul that she was to me, hated Edward, our father was incapable of showing any love to either of us.'

The officer clapped a sympathetic hand on Simon's back. 'Don't try putting the blame on people, not yourself or anyone else,' he said with an air of authority. 'Evil is born, not created, and that man was evil. Nothing in his life, easy or hard, would have changed the ending.' With that he turned and walked stiffly back to his horse.

'No one will ever know that for sure,' Simon murmured into the darkness before turning and joining them.

The stop for official purposes was a short one. Simon made a brief statement that the body strapped across the back of the horse he accompanied, was indeed that of his brother

157

Edward Saunderman, then he was allowed to return to the Inn.

'So Edward has won, once again,' Lewis commented, his face telling how heartily sorry he felt for his young friend.

'How do you mean?' Simon queried, too tired to think for him self.

'He chose his end,' Lewis said softly. 'He won't have to face judgement. Nor, the hangman's rope,' he added gently.

TWENTY ONE

Lewis looked questioningly at the doctor. 'Why does she sleep so much?' he asked with concern, his glance flickering back to Rosie, in the bed.

'Exhaustion,' the doctor replied, he stood back and surveyed his patient, 'her unconscious mind revelling in the relief of being safe at last, maybe. She was on the point of fatal collapse when you called me,' he pointed out kindly. 'I think her body has just shut down temporarily, she had suffered greatly, and it needs time to heal itself.'

Lewis cringed visibly at the thought of her suffering then, smiled he had been scrupulously honest with this man whom, he judged to be about the same age as himself. There had been no other way; they had all witnessed the many scars on Rosie, which told them as much as she could about her suffering.

'Do you mind if I ask you a question?' he asked quietly, a little unsure of his ground on the point he wished to raise.

The doctor looked at him, 'not at all,' he murmured, a twitch catching the corner of his mouth. 'But let me guess what it is you want to know. Will the children be of sound mind, bearing in mind who their father was?'

Lewis nodded, thankful for the doctors understanding.

'Well, the answer is, only time will tell,' he replied evenly. 'But you have to remember they have the sweetness of your grand daughter along with the cruelty of their father. You have to watch for signs as they grow up, and,' he added with a note of caution. 'If you should feel uneasy about them take action early. Traits of this kind can often be alleviated if dealt with at a young age.' He nodded his head sagely, lifting a finger and wagging it in the air.

Lewis inclined his head again, feeling a little foolish but thankful at the same time. 'And Rosie?'

'Her mind you mean,' the doctor, rubbed at his chin and picked his words. 'There my friend,' he said bluntly. 'I am out of my depth. Her body I can heal, her mind, if you can't jog it open, will have to be dealt with by people more experienced than I am.'

'Thank you for your honesty,' Lewis replied, shaking the man's hand.

'She could live quite contentedly,' the doctor said thoughtfully, ' without ever knowing her past. She will accept what you tell her, learn to love and trust her family all over again and that will be the end of it,' he smiled. 'That's how I would treat it if I were in your place,' he confided.

'If I were in her position, ' Lewis replied, looking lovingly at Rosie. 'I don't think I could accept life on those conditions. It would eat me alive always trying to recall the past. Knowing this child as I do, I feel that is how she will react as well.'

The doctor shrugged. 'My immediate problem is more basic, I'm afraid,' he went on. 'She had a difficult time at the birth of the twins. A lesser person would not have survived, maybe her years of depravation helped her through that period,' he looked sadly at his companion. 'I fear she may never be able to have more children.'

'Nature is a wonderful thing,' Lewis commented, almost brushing aside the doctor's concerns. 'That is something else only time will tell. At this moment it is neither here, nor there. Getting her well is our priority.' He tempered his words with a smile, not wishing to upset the man who had so far shown such consideration.

'Take heart dear fellow,' the doctor said, before turning and issuing last minute instructions to the nurse. 'She is with you now, and love can do so much more than science.' With those words of comfort, he took his leave, allowing Lewis to stand and ponder the problem.

Watching the sleeping form in the bed, emotion welled inside him. His mind flying back to the many times he had stood by another woman's bedside. A more primitive bedside in the austere confines of a prison, all those years ago, when Molly had been fighting for her life, so much had happened since then, so much, he told himself, that Rosie might never, ever, remember.

'Rosie,' he murmured in a whisper to himself. 'Rosemary remember.' Then added, 'please.'

The Rosie he had spent such long months searching for was dead and gone, he realised that. In her place was a girl who had been forced into womanhood, without the benefit of love or care. That he could love this Rosie every bit as much was not in question. He could love her equally, if not more, and he would spend the rest of his life proving it to her.

His reverie was interrupted by a quiet rapping of knuckles at the door turning, he was amazed and delighted to see the magical appearance of Jake's head.

'But I only despatched a messenger a couple of days ago,' he cried, being hushed by the nurse and lowering his tone immediately.

'I couldn't wait,' Jake whispered back, coming to his old friend and throwing his arms about him in a smothering hug. 'When you sent to say you were on her trail, I had to come.'

'How did you find us?' Lewis questioned, his brain refusing to accept the sight before him.

'It wasn't hard,' Jake grinned telling his tale,' the whole country seems to know all about you, and where you are.'

Reaching up and placing a hand on his young prodigy's shoulder, Lewis led him to the bedside. 'There she is,' he whispered, 'There's our Rosie.'

'Oh, my God,' Jake moaned his hand flying to his mouth, as he surveyed the pale, thin, sleeping female in the bed. 'Tell me all,' he demanded.

'Later,' Lewis promised softly his mind slipping instantly back to his reverie. 'I was just standing here thinking about Molly,' he said tenderly, looking from Rosie to Jake. 'Remembering the day you two married in that prison ward.'

Jake smiled back. 'We didn't tell Molly for month's that Rosie was gone,' he admitted. 'She used to ask about her every day,' Jake turned haunted eyes on his friend. 'We used to leave it to Ninny to make up stories about her, remember. So that she wouldn't worry,' he recalled quietly. 'It all seems so long ago, another lifetime away.'

'It was just before Sammy was born,' Lewis went on. 'After that her name was cleared and they released her,' He smiled before continuing, 'Molly was so happy that day she was waiting for us, sitting in that chair, the baby cradled in her arms, her face alight with joy. We had to ruin it for her,' he recalled painfully. 'We had to tell her the truth. I didn't think she would ever forgive us all for lying to her.'

'That's Molly,' Jake replied. 'You have to remember she had already lost Rosie once before when Nancy escaped with her, it was heartbreak for a second time,' Jake replied with emotion. 'But she did,' he added on a brighter note, 'and now she can't wait to have everyone back home again.'

'Yes,' Lewis agreed, 'Ninny always said the lives of Molly and this child were too closely linked for them never to see each other again.' He closed his lips in a tight line. 'It does no good dwelling on thoughts of the past,' he said hastily, 'we have to plan for the future.'

As they watched, Rosie's eyes flickered open. 'Hello child,' Lewis said with a wide grin, stepping round to the side of the bed. 'How are you feeling?' There was no light of recognition on Rosie face, which saddened his old heart, but he went on regardless. 'Are you well enough for a visitor?' He beckoned to his companion bringing him to his side. 'Rosie, this is Jake,' he told her. 'You used to think of him as your father.'

162

Jake pulled a chair beside the bed, taking one of Rosie's hands in his own he said nothing, his emotions choking his voice he blinked back tears. Rosie looked at him with compassion then said softly, 'hello, Jake.'

Holding out thin arms she silently asked for, and returned a loving embrace. 'I have looked forward to meeting you,' she said gently with a sweet smile. 'I hope Molly is well.'

Jake's head jerked and he peered closely into Rosie's face. 'Molly, you asked about Molly.' He said a little foolishly.

Rosie smiled at Lewis bobbing her head towards him. 'I have been told a great deal about all my friends,' she confided a musical chuckle in her words.

'I'll leave you two to get acquainted,' Lewis said tenderly, turning to leave the room. 'Tell her all about the riverbank, and the people she used to know,' he instructed Jake softly, adding in a whisper. 'Then I have something to show you. Don't forget to tell her about Daniel,' he added brightly seeing Rosie turn her head to look at him. With a finger to his lips he winked at her. 'I'll tell him all about it later,' he promised her, receiving a mischievous grin in return.

Walking back into the bar of the Inn, Lewis was in time to greet Simon on his return. 'Have you made the arrangements for Edwards burial?' he asked solicitously, noting the dark circles under his companion's eyes and the tired look on his face.

Shaking his head the young man said nothing, accepting the drink that was placed before him he took a deep swallow from the glass before speaking. 'I'm expecting them to hang his body from the gibbet for public viewing,' he muttered darkly, wiping the back of his hand across his mouth. 'We haven't heard the last of this. The questions they are asking make me suspect they will be satisfied with nothing less than a live scapegoat,' he thumped his glass on the bar, his torso visibly sagging, he related his harrowoing experience with the authorities.

163

'The police?' Lewis interrupted, and questioned with surprise. 'You, do you mean, they want to pin these crimes on you?'

'Well they have no intention of letting me bury my brother,' Simon responded heatedly. 'They said, not until they have satisfied themselves there is no other person responsible for any or all of his misdemeanours.' he spat the words across the bar at him.

'Oh,' Lewis said flatly. 'I had been half afraid of this. I fear much of it has been my fault.' He looked away, studying his feet, rather than his companion.

'In what way?' Simon questioned sharply.

'In hindsight, I realise. If I had carried out our enquiries with a little more thought, and a little less bravado,' he muttered, embarrassment turning his cheeks pink. 'The country would not be so stirred up. So what are they asking of you?'

Simon stretched his limbs before answering. His look telling his companion he thought his last statement to be a lot of nonsense. 'I don't think it's me they want,' he said quietly. 'I don't really know who, maybe they think Edward had an accomplice. But they assure me they still have a lot of enquiries to make.'

'Well it is a day of news, ' Lewis informed him, in a lighter tone. 'Jake is here, he's sitting with Rosie.'

As he spoke a maid appeared with a bulky folded paper, bearing a plain seal. 'Please, sir,' she said bobbing a curtsy. 'This has just come for you.' She handed it to Lewis.

'It's from the good Mrs Gimlet,' he cried, tearing off the seal. 'She says she is delighted we have found Rosie. Sorry to hear she has had such a bad time of things. She goes on at length about her feelings for the girl,' he added, looking up from the writing with a wry smile. 'Unfortunately her husband's poor health stops her from joining us, but she is sure we will look after the child well.' Lewis grinned as he read. 'She also states she hopes Robert will be caught and punished for his crimes.'

'Funny,' Simon said, taking the missive and reading it for himself, 'how everyone thinks of Rosie as a child. I will send and tell her how Edward has taken his own life. Did you not tell her about the twins?' he queried, accepting Lewis's shake of the head as an answer. 'Then I'll tell her when I write. That will no doubt give her plenty to dream about.'

'I'll go and tell Rosie about this,' he tapped the papers that Simon handed back to him. 'You rest a while. I'll send Jake in to talk to you. He doesn't know about the twins either,' he added with a grin. 'I'll leave that to you, I think.'

Jake had been both elated, and upset at Simon's news about the babies. He had stared, bemused at the tiny bundles, held in the nurse's arms.

'This is Nancy,' Simon said, putting an affectionate finger under the little girls chin. 'And this little demon is, Daniel,' he grinned as he introduced his niece and nephew to Jake.

'I don't know what to think,' Jake admitted quietly shaking his head in disbelief, after the babies had been sent back to their mother. 'Nothing is as I expected it to be. Somehow I never envisioned what has come to pass.'

'It was a fair shock to Lewis and myself,' Simon chuckled, sitting back and running his fingers through his hair. 'You get used to it after a while and it all seems quite natural,' he said with compassion.

'I will never be able to thank you enough,' Jake began, a catch in his throat, opening his hands in a helpless gesture. 'Neither you, nor Lewis, would have been blamed if you had given up the chase and returned home without her.' He looked squarely at the young man to whom he owed so much. 'Lewis knows my finances well, I am by no means rich, but I have enough. It has cost you two a king's ransom to get this far. Molly and I have discussed it all,' humiliation made his words falter. 'I, we, would like to make some contribution to the cost. It's the least we can do.'

Simon clapped his companion on the back. 'Think nothing of it. I was intending to do this on my own, anyway. Even if Lewis had not joined me, I would still have spent the money,' he smiled as he spoke. 'I can afford it. Lewis you must talk to for yourself, but I am sure that, like me, he will refuse.' He rose, the clatter from the next room telling them the evening meal was being served.

'Your turn will come, my friend,' he assured Jake as they prepared to join their associate for dinner. 'There are years ahead when Rosie and those children will need your help and protection.'

TWENTY TWO

Simon smiled warmly. 'It's so good to see you here, Tildy,' he told her. 'The nurse has promised to tell us the moment Rosie wakes. Please sit down and take tea with me.' He extended his arm to a table under the window, already set with tea things. 'Bring another cup, please,' he instructed the maid who had only that minute finished laying the table.

Removing her small hat, and laying it carefully to one side, Tildy asked seriously. 'Please tell me honestly, how is she?'

Smiling to himself at the latest fashion for ladies to wear these tiny, headpieces Simon poured the tea before replying. Then leaving out nothing he regaled her with all that had happened.

Shuddering, as she heard of Edwards ending, she said, 'how gruesome. To deliberately throw yourself from a wall, are you sure he didn't just miss his footing? Robert never struck me as someone that would end his own life, whatever trouble he was facing.'

'I can agree, and disagree with you,' Simon replied. 'Generally I would have said my brother's self esteem was far too large for such an action. But I believe the balance of his mind was tilted. One half of him knew exactly what crimes he had committed and what his punishment would be if caught. The other believed himself to be a persecuted man.' Reaching across the table he removed Tildy's empty cup, placing it with his own, out of the way, then leaned his arms on the tabletop.

167

'Rosemary, Rosie, does she know that Robert is dead?' Tildy asked, dabbing delicately at her mouth with a small handkerchief.

'Yes,' Simon said nodding, 'thankfully Lewis and Jake, undertook that task.'

'How did she take it?' Tildy questioned, her clear blue, eyes surveying his face. 'However badly Robert treated her, she continued to adore and defend him when I knew her,' she added.

'In that case I have to say surprisingly well.' he told her, his lips turning down at the corners in a mockery of a smile. 'She said she had more or less expected it. She also said, he would be pleased to be with his God at last.'

Her hand flying to her throat, Tildy expressed complete surprise. 'But I never knew him to be of a religious inclination.'

'From what we can gather,' Simon informed her quietly. 'He had turned to his own form of religion since he found out Rosie was pregnant. Refused to acknowledge it had anything to do with him, blamed all his troubles on her and did little else but ask God for his deliverance. He became a bit of a hell fire and damnation type apparently.'

Tildy sat quietly digesting all she had heard, her brow creased with worry lines. 'Has she remembered anyone from her past Lewis, Jake?' she enquired.

'Sadly no,' he replied, just as the nurse popped her head round the door.

'Mistress Rosie is awake,' she informed them.

Standing up and visibly squaring her shoulders, Tildy smoothed her skirt before she allowed herself to be led to her friend's bedside.

'Such a pity, Tildy can only stay for a few days,' Lewis cried as he bustled in to sit in the seat the woman had just vacated. 'It will be so good for Rosie to have someone near her own age to talk too.'

'Ah,' Simon replied, smiling. 'I hadn't realised I was so ancient.'

'My dear boy, no, I didn't mean,' Lewis stuttered with embarrassment. Then laughed when he realised Simon was only teasing. 'It does my heart good to see everyone happy.'

'You're much better than I expected you to be,' Tildy cried rushing to Rosie's side and hugging her affectionately. Pulling back and holding her at arms length she examined what she saw. 'You're very thin, and you look tired,' she admitted, reaching out and lifting a lock of her friend's neglected hair. 'Otherwise quite perky,' she stated with a laugh. 'We'll soon have you once again looking like that smart young seamstress that worked for Madame Mildred,' she assured. Reaching for the silver backed hairbrush on the bedside table she began gently to brush the pale brown waves.

'It's so lovely to see you,' Rosie responded with delight. 'You seem so different, grown up,' she added her wide eyes looking up at Tildy, awe in her tone.

'How about you, with twins,' Tildy responded replacing the brush. She peered lovingly into the crib beside the bed. 'One day they must come to Canny's Hill and play with my daughter.' Turning her attention back to Rosie she asked thoughtfully. 'How do you feel about your rescue?' Leaning over she took her friends hand and held it tightly, at the same time seating herself comfortably on the edge of the bed. 'How are you getting on with Lewis, and Jake, and Simon?' she went on not waiting for answers to her rapid questions.

'They're wonderful,' Rosie replied with sincerity. 'It's as though I have always known them, yet I don't know them at all,' she giggled shyly. 'They have told me such strange stories about the things that I am supposed to have done. I can't believe any of it happened really,' she added in disbelief. 'I will always be grateful to them for coming to find me. I don't think I could have gone on the way things were,

169

not much longer,' she admitted, her voice low and full of emotion.

'I'm sorry about Robert,' Tildy said softly. 'I know how you felt about him, but if what they tell me is true, the things he did, and all that,' she blushed as she tried to be diplomatic in her approach. 'Maybe it is for the best,' she admitted, shrugging.

'My feelings for Robert changed a long time ago,' Rosie said flatly.

Rising Tildy reached into the crib and picked up a baby the tone in her friends voice when she spoke of her brother had shocked her. Robert, or whatever his real name was, must have been very cruel to have turned love to hate in such a fashion.

'That's Daniel you're holding,' Rosie spoke softly. 'He's the hungry one. He also gave me the most trouble when he was born.'

Tildy placed a finger on the baby's lip, it was immediately sucked into his greedy little mouth, the noise he made, making both girls laugh out loud. 'So I can see,' Tildy replied. 'You had a doctor for the birth?' she asked, looking directly at Rosie who shook her head in reply. 'Then how did you cope?' she cried, thinking back on the birth of her own dear little Bethany.

'Robert was away,' Rosie said in a low whisper, 'he was often away for days on end. I had pains that got worse as the day wore on. I knew it was time,' she nodded more to herself than her visitor. 'Nancy came quite easily. I didn't know what to do at first it was just instinct. I've watched the animals you see,' she told her. 'I thought it was all over when I had dealt with Nancy. I wrapped her in a cloth and laid her on the seat. I was going to clean myself up when it started again.'

Tildy listened in silence, Simon had told her about the hovel. 'I'm trying to imagine it,' she murmured, waiting for Rosie to continue.

'Daniel was twisted he didn't come head first like Nancy,' Rosie's voice took on a far away tone she was lost, back in that dreadful room reliving the experience. 'It hurt,' she turned pain filled eyes to her friend. 'So much, and there was so much blood. Then he was crying, yelling at the top of his lungs,' her face twisted into a brief grimace clearing and becoming wreathed in smiles. 'I think that's why he's always hungry,' she laughed.

'Their faces are those of strangers, yet I trust Lewis and the others,' Rosie said changing the subject, turning her gaze away from the baby her face serious. 'Do you think that is wrong of me?'

Tildy leaned forward and kissed the side of her friend's face. 'No dear, I think they all love you dearly. The only thing I find strange, wrong,' she corrected. 'Is trying to remember to call you Rosie, and think of Robert as Edward,' laughing she handed Daniel to his wet nurse who had arrived to take him for his feed.

'I think you're very brave,' she added seriously. 'In your place I'm sure I would be doubting, and questioning everyone and everything.'

'It could all have been worse,' Rosie chuckled, a twinkle filling her eye.

'How?' Tildy queried puzzlement creasing her brow.

'They could have changed my name completely.'

Tildy spluttered, laughter welling up inside her as she voiced a few weird and wonderful names. Like children the girls played up to each other, endeavouring to find all the worst names they could think of, the time flying by and their conversation skipping from one subject to another.

The babies were returned to the crib, Nancy's little face staring intently at the visitor, Daniel fast asleep.

'They are lovely,' Tildy murmured, 'it still seems so strange that you are unable to remember anything before you came to our town, and met me.'

171

'Oh I have images,' Rosie admitted. 'Fleeting glimpses of things that play on the edges of my mind, that's why I was convinced I was mad, as Robert told me I was. Now I hope,' she said with a bright smile, ' those same glimpses will help me to recognise people when I finally meet them.'

'I can't wait for you to meet my own daughter, Bethany,' Tildy spoke softly, her hand patting lightly on Nancy's back in an effort to sooth her to sleep. 'She's a poppet, and she'll love you all as much as I do.'

'I will look forward to it,' Rosie replied. 'Now that I know Robert, oh dear, Edward, was not my brother, I feel better about taking the children out into the world,' she admitted quietly.

'You must never be ashamed,' Tildy begged, her arms going protectively about her friend. 'Believe me you were not responsible for the things that happened to you.'

TWENTY THREE

The smartly tailored man stood firm, the policeman by his side giving him all the courage he required to demand that his orders be carried out.

'You can't do this,' Lewis cried, red in the face and angry as a raging bull.

'I repeat,' the man stated in official tones. 'Is anyone here a blood relative to this young woman?'

He stared from face to face belligerently, intimidation in every fibre of his being.

'No,' Simon replied for the.n all. He was worried about the condition of his old friend. Lewis was building up to explosion point, it would do his heart no good. 'Look,' he said defensively. 'You know my brother was responsible for all these crimes, why can't you just accept it. He's dead now, the cases should be closed. Why are you looking for a scapegoat?'

The official ignored him, standing erect and pulling at his cuffs he directed his question at Lewis. 'Are you this woman's real grandfather?'

'No,' Lewis moaned, tears of desperation in his voice. 'She is an orphan,' he explained. 'I was her lawyer before I retired, I think of myself as her chosen grandfather.' He let his words tail off, they would count for nothing in legal terms, and he knew it.

The man smirked as he cast his eyes about the room again. 'Are, either of you two gentlemen related to her?' he asked Jake and Simon.

Shaking his head with sorrow, Simon replied. 'No, I am the uncle of her children, this man here,' he extended his arm to point at Jake. 'Is the person that took her in as a child, he brought her up until the day of her abduction.'

The 'huh,' that dropped from the officials lips, clanged around the otherwise, silent room ominously. He had been questioning Rosie all morning, and just announced that he intended to take her into custody.

'You can't possibly take her into custody,' Lewis yelled, 'Look at her man, she's in no fit state of health to stand up to it for a start,' he paced about the room, gesturing to Rosie who stood quietly in a corner. 'She's barely more than a child herself, you can't possible think she could be responsible for any of Edwards crimes.'

'Somebody gave him the ideas, and harboured him, co-operated with him,' the man informed them with a satisfied smack of his lips. 'That is almost as big a crime as actually committing the deeds. If you were a lawyer, as you say. You will know that for a fact,' his sarcasm was directed at Lewis.

Now,' he added with a smirk. 'The only person who can challenge my orders would be a blood relative. As there is no such person in this room will you please step aside and allow me to do my duty.'

'Where will you be taking her?' Jake spoke up at last. 'Will we be able to visit her?'

With exaggerated calm the official sighed, 'she is not going to a police cell. We are not that unfeeling. She will be going to hospital, where her present state of health will be taken into consideration.'

'Will she be treated for her memory loss?' Jake cross-questioned. A shrug was his only reply.

His patience finally running out the official stepped up to Lewis waving papers under his nose. 'You, should know, until we are satisfied with the answers that only she can give. We will do as we see fit.'

Rosie, who up to that moment had remained silent, burst into tears, crying, 'my babies, what about my babies?'

Three men turned instinctively towards her, each taking a step in her direction, stopping instantly when the command 'leave her,' rang from the official's lips.

Signalling for his men to do their duty, he ignored her tears, and her cry, encouraging them to march her outside, leaving Lewis and Jake both calling after her.

'The children will be cared for, I will see to it personally,' Lewis cried, beside himself with anger.

'I'll take them to Molly,' Jake yelled, watching them push her roughly into the waiting carriage, a policeman on either side of her. All three men chased outside to watch the carriage slide away, picking up speed and disappearing along the road.

'History is repeating itself,' Lewis wailed in desperation.

'I should have taken her back to London the moment I arrived,' Jake growled. 'They couldn't have taken her then.'

'Don't be fool man,' Simon snapped. 'They would have come after you, then both of you would be in custody now.'

'Jake I'm so sorry,' Lewis moaned. 'But Simon is right, we considered departing for London despite her state of health. But within hours of our being here it was clear the authorities were not satisfied with Edward's death. They would never have willingly allowed her to leave.'

Jake glared defiantly at his friends, 'we kept Molly hidden for years.' He grunted.

'Yes,' Lewis replied quietly, 'and look what happened when they finally caught up with her.' His temper subsiding, he was endeavouring to find some reasoning behind the latest development. 'Anyway, Jake,' he warned. 'The less they have to look into that area of your past, and Molly's, the better. It would not help Rosie at all if it came to light at this moment.'

'But the list of crimes,' Jake groaned, his face pained. 'She would have been about eight years old when some of them were committed. How can they lay them at her door?'

'Simon was right,' Lewis admitted reluctantly. 'They have made her the excuse for closing many open cases. I have never witnessed such a thing before, but I have heard colleges speak about it.'

'They can't mean it,' Simon said hopefully following his friends back into the Inn. 'They really can't. They will let her go in a day or so, you see.'

Lewis sank into a chair, leaning forward his elbows digging into his knees he dropped his head into his hands. 'I wish I could believe that my boy,' he mumbled brokenly.

'He suggested I was using my families money to cover up her duplicity,' Simon added heavily, referring to the official, his stare fixed on the window where he watched an aimless leaf detached itself from a tree, and drift on the breeze to the ground.

'He was certainly not impressed with the fact that one of Rosie's children is the new Earl, or that you are his regent,' Jake snorted disgustedly. 'Did you see his look of distain?'

Simon turned his attention back to his friends. 'But I am not Daniels regent,' he reminded them. 'His next of kin is his regent, that's Rosie. She is a very rich young lady now. I hope when this trouble is satisfactorily settled, she will allow me to help her with the task of running the estate.'

Stunned silence filled the room and both men considered what they had heard. Jake fixed a sceptical gaze on his companion and let out a low whistle, Lewis jumped up from his seat and wiped a hand across his eyes in confusion.

'Of course, you're right my boy,' he said, staggering a little. 'Why had I not realised that for myself.' He looked strained and tired suddenly, reacting to the news as if it were a fresh blow to him personally.

'Well whether the authorities realise it or not, it didn't make any difference to his attitude,' Jake muttered his own attitude sullen and resentful.

'Her doctor's testimony counted for nothing,' Lewis repeated unnecessarily. 'It is hard to look back across the years,' he wandered wearily back and forth talking in quiet tones. 'If you look at Edwards catalogue of crimes, and believe he had no help whatsoever.'

'But to suggest she harboured him, helped him,' Simon replied in awe.

'Strictly speaking that is exactly what she did,' Lewis reminded them firmly ceasing his pacing and taking his legal stance. 'Unknowingly she cared for him. Washed his blood stained clothes, or threw them away if they were badly damaged. Believed him to have been in drunken brawls, endured his temper tantrums, and his cruelty to her person. Instead she blamed it all on herself, for in her words, *'being the mad one'*. Never once did it occur to her to go to the authorities, not even when he was committing incest. None of this will be in her favour.'

'But she couldn't, she didn't know any better, she was in his power she didn't understand any of this,' Jake yelled, colour flooding his face as he listened to the words.

'I doubt they will take that into consideration,' Lewis concluded.

'Who's side are you taking,' Jake roared, his hands fisting by his side, his torso tense and leaning forward ready to spring at anyone who was against him.

'Calm down,' Simon cried, placing a hand on Jake's shoulder to defuse the situation. 'Lewis is only telling it from the viewpoint of a stranger, in particular a stranger who wants to believe this person guilty more than anything else. Think about it Jake,' he urged.

Jake opened his mouth to comment, then closed it again, and nodded unhappily.

'She told me she had seen my face many times in her dreams,' he said quietly changing the subject completely. 'I asked her if she knew me.' He looked helplessly at Lewis when he spoke. 'I thought it meant she remembered me, for a second I was so happy.' Unshed tears shimmered in his eyes. 'She must remember something, perhaps it will all come back to her now,' he added hope turning his words to a plea.

'It's hard the first time you see her,' Lewis agreed. 'We were searching for a child the picture in our minds was that of a child. And here she is a young woman.'

Simon understood the melancholy that had descended on the room but could not allow it to grip their souls instead he tapped the official papers left for them. 'It says here,' he told them. 'She will be taken to a local clinic, no doubt owned by that slippery little man they referred to as the police doctor.'

'Well, I didn't trust him,' Jake thundered. 'Did you hear what he told that smarmy official. Self induced, he said, I heard him.'

Simon nodded, he also had heard the whispered words, and felt exactly like Jake in his mistrust of the man who had claimed he would have Rosie's memory restored within days. By what method, he asked himself.

'I think we need to look a little closer at this clinic,' Simon suggested looking purposefully at Lewis, who inclined his head in agreement.

'What good will that do,' Jake groaned.

'Much as you would like to we cannot charge in and physically remove Rosie from the hands of the authorities,' Simon said with a patient sigh. 'We have to be practical and follow any line that is open to us in hope, hope that we can make nonsense of their claims legally.'

'Well, there is one thing I can do,' Jake replied with determination. 'I can get those twins into Molly's care before they decide to arrest them as well.' He spun round to look at Simon. 'Oh, that is if it's all right with you? You being their uncle,' he added self- consciously.

'Fine by me,' Simon smiled his permission. 'I'll travel with you. It's essential to see that Daniel's title is passed to him properly that all the necessary papers are signed im- mediately. Being the mother of an Earl may be of help to Rosie in the future. Will you manage whilst we are away?' he asked of his old friend.

Lewis waved a hand and nodded agreement. 'I'll move my headquarters nearer to this clinic,' he said quietly, studying the papers.

The start of their journey to London was irritatingly delayed, neither of the nurses employed by Lewis and Simon were prepared to leave their hometown.

'I have a friend, her daughter might be able to help you,' one of the women offered timidly.

'What experience has she had?' Jake questioned.

The woman smirked. 'Apart from umpteen brothers and sisters you mean, sir,' she quipped 'She's the eldest in the family, been looking after babes since she were no more than a babe herself,' the woman added proudly.

'Fetch her, please,' Simon requested with a smile of thanks.

The woman had returned before the children's packing had been completed, with a tall, freckle, faced girl, whose frizzy red hair stood about her face like a tipsy halo.

'This is Harriett, I have explained what you need of her, sir,' she said bobbing her knee, and leaving the girl with her new employers.

'Do you think you can cope with two babies who will no longer have their wet nurse?' Jake asked with a sceptical look from under his brows.

Harriett nodded, 'I'm sure, sir,' she said her voice bright and musical to the ear.

'You will be away from home for a considerable time,' Simon told her kindly. 'Will that worry you?'

'Our house is very overcrowded,' she said in a matter of fact manner. 'My parents will welcome one less, they won't mind, neither will I.'

'What's your full name,' Jake asked, his tone sharp, his face dubious.

'Just Harriett, sir,' she replied.

Shrugging, Jake sent her to get her things and add them the packing already being taken care of.

'What do you think?' he asked Simon, 'she seems very young to me.'

'But very capable,' Simon replied with a warm smile. 'I'm sure between us we will cope excellently well. I'm more worried about leaving Lewis, than how we will fare on the journey.'

Jakes head snapped up to stare at the man standing next to him. 'You think this is all too much for him.' he barked.

'He is not as agile as he was,' Simon admitted grudgingly. 'But it's more his state of mind that concerns me. He is more worried about Rosie than we think. He feels frustrated because there is nothing he can do. It will be weeks, months before they are satisfied about the girl's memory, that much we all know. If she never recovers it she has no defence against the charges. If on the other hand she does recover it and starts talking about being a vagrant, living under bridges in London. Her case could be lost before it even starts.'

'Whew,' Jake whistled. 'Put like that, I see what you mean. Perhaps I shouldn't go,' he queried, uncertainty replacing his previous determination.

'No. London is the best place for the children,' Simon assured him. 'Molly will mother them until Rosie can do it herself. I will return post haste and remain by our good friends side through thick and thin,' he promised.

TWENTY FOUR

Days ran into one another as the slow journey progressed to London. Harriett had experienced far more trouble than anticipated with the twins,

'I was told they were already accepting more solid food than they seem to be,' she apologised to Simon on the first evenings stop. 'Daniel in particular seems set against anything other than mother's milk.' Fear lingered in her eyes when she spoke. 'I will try harder,' she promised in a small voice.

Simon patted her arm. 'My ears are still ringing with my nephews lusty yells,' he replied laughing. 'Fear not, your position as their nurse is safe. Daniel has always been a demanding baby, run along and get something to eat yourself and try to get some rest,' he called after her.

Daniel had yelled less on the second day but both babies had proved sickly, necessitating a constantly open carriage window despite the stiff, cool breeze.

'If only that wet nurse had come along,' Jake growled, watching Harriett clean up her charges, yet again.

'Be reasonable man,' Simon retorted shortly. 'The woman had a young family of her own that needed her.' In truth he was as impatient as Jake to get home, but they owed it to Rosie to keep her children healthy.

Jake thumped a fist into the palm of his hand. 'I'm sorry,' he replied breathing deeply to calm his nerves. 'It's just this constant stopping and starting. I know it's not the girl's fault that the children are sick.'

'How are you enjoying the journey?' Simon asked in a rare moment of quiet, both babies, and Jake, were asleep. Cradled snugly one either side of Harriett the children look angelic.

She flashed him a wide smile. 'I've never been out of our town before,' she admitted. Her eyes feasted on the rolling fields and the distant hills either side of the road. 'It's beautiful,' she whispered in awe.

'I'm afraid you won't find London as beautiful,' Simon responded with a half smile. He had quite taken to this soft-spoken girl who was valiantly struggling to keep the peace between her charges and her employer.

'I've heard tales about London,' she replied shyly. 'I'm sure it can't be as bad as they say. Anyway I'll manage,' she added defiantly.

'I'm sure you will,' Simon reassured her. 'We will be there tomorrow, so you can see things for yourself soon enough.'

The sound of the carriage rolling onto the dock brought Molly racing to the Refuge door. About to throw herself inside to the occupants she stopped short at the sight of the small face, with its wiry red, hair framed in the window staring at her. She stood puzzled, gazing from the girl to the babies and back again.

Jake sprang to her side. 'No my love, this is not Rosie,' he told her softly. 'This is Harriett, and these are Rosie twins. Harriett is their nurse.' He placed a protective arm about his quivering wife. 'There is such a lot to tell you later,' he said dropping a kiss on the tip of her nose before going to help Simon and their trusty driver with all their belongings.

Harriett stepped forward and handed the sleeping Nancy into Molly's arms. 'This is Nancy she's been rather sickly since we left,' the girl told her with a touch of authority. Then reaching back inside the carriage she lifted the other bundle into her own arms, saying with a smile. 'This one is Daniel, he's the noisy one.'

Placing his arms around the waist of each woman Jake led them inside his home where he was greeted with squeals of delight from his own children. Samuel and Emily threw themselves at him.

Lifting each child, hugging and kissing them he twirled them in the air before placing them back on the floor, finally lifting Emily again so that she could peer at each baby in turn.' These are Rosie's twins,' he announced to the crowd of faces gathering to see what was going on.

'Dora,' Molly called, gently lifting Daniel from Harriett. 'Take out guest to Rosie's old room and see she is made comfortable please.'

Showing her widest, toothless grin, Dora hurried the girl away. 'This was Rosie's room,' she confirmed, pushing at a door on the upper floor.' Then course it were Ninny's afore she died,' she chattered on. 'But we always thinks of it as Rosie's.' She dropped her plump body on the edge of the bed and bounced, chuckling gleefully, her straw like hair fluttering up and down at the sides of her head with her jerky movements.

'Did you see our little girl?' Dora asked, her own face childlike in its curiosity.

'No,' Harriett admitted, she sat beside the old woman. 'But I know a lot about her, she's not a little girl anymore. Those babies downstairs are hers,' she explained patiently.

'Where's she gone to then?' Dora questioned, looking as though she were about to cry.

Taking the old hand in her own, Harriet endeavoured to explain in simple language all that Simon had told her during the long hours of their journey. Repeating much of what she had to say until she was sure the old woman had retained the gist of the story.

The next few hours flew by. Simon took his leave to hurry off and attend to his own business. Molly and Harriett dealt with the children, all of them. Dora and Lizzie, the cook, threw their energies into a family meal.

'I know I brought them home without asking, but will you be able to cope with two extra children?' Jake questioned his wife as they shared a tender moment together, at last.

'Harriett has already agreed to stay on permanently,' she told him smiling. 'She was ready to leave home anyway, so she is not anxious to return to the West Country for a while. She's a very capable girl I will enjoy having her to help,' she assured him. 'Will you go back to Lewis and Rosie, when Simon does?'

'I don't know,' he admitted honestly. 'Simon has suggested he needs someone here to oversee the estate. He left it in the hands of managers thinking he would be away a few months not years. I have a feeling he was asking me to undertake the job,' he shrugged. 'I felt useless there,' he told her as she nestled against his chest. 'Lewis and Simon had everything under control, all I could do was get angry and upset everyone.' He rested his cheek on his wife's head, 'I missed you all so much,' he whispered tenderly.

'But will you want to go back and keep Lewis company?' she persisted. 'I don't want you to feel trapped here with us.'

'I would probably drive the old man mad,' he confided. 'He's perfectly capable of getting the job done without me.'

'I can't take it all in,' she murmured against his neck. 'Our baby with babies of her own, we've missed all that growing up. The last time I saw her she was so excited about our wedding, do you remember? She couldn't stop trying on that new dress she was going to wear for the ceremony. We were choosing flowers,' Molly's words trailed off as the recalled the still painful memory of her own arrest.

Jake bent and kissed her, long and passionately. 'That's all in the past now,' he told her firmly. 'We must think ahead, look forward to all being together again.' His words held less conviction than he would have liked.

Turning and walking to the window Molly leaned her head against the cold pane, and gazed at what little she could see of the darkening garden. 'Tell me everything?' she

184

begged, emotion strangling her voice. 'However bad it is, please don't miss it out. I need to know everything that has happened to our girl.'

Standing behind her his arms about her waist, Jake told her all he could, their tears mingling as the darkened window reflected their faces back at them. The tale finally completed, Molly turned and sobbed against his chest.

TWENTY FIVE

Tildy leaned close, placing her mouth to Lewis's ear she asked, 'why don't they clear the court?'

Barely able to hear what she was saying above the babble of noise about them, Lewis was at a loss for words. 'I have never seen such an unruly crowd in all my life,' he yelled back at her.

'What does Bernard think of it,' Tildy again pressed her mouth close to Lewis, who shrugged helplessly.

Following Simon's instructions they had employed, with difficulty, a young local lawyer. The whole of the West Country was alight with '*hang Rosie the murderess*' fever and finding any sort of legal help had been a thankless task. Bernard Foster was doing it because he desperately needed the money on offer, not because he believed in his clients, innocence.

Tildy gazed around the packed room, the tall blank walls with their pealing paint glared back at her. Windows set high above them let little light in through the barred surfaces, the pale rays that did penetrate dancing on the swirls of smoky air far above her head. 'Why did they wait so long to notify us of this hearing?' she questioned, trying hard to make some sense of what was happening.

Again Lewis shrugged. 'Because they did not want us to have time to put up any defence,' he stated bluntly. 'I sent for you the minute I heard, I apologise for the short notice,' he almost shouted his words into her face, ducking as a missile sailed across the room and over his head, thudding against a

186

far wall. 'Bernard and I have spent two full days putting the facts in some sort of order.'

'Do you think Bernard can carry this off,' Tildy asked dubiously, viewing the young lawyer from the corner of her eye.

'He will never make a memorable figurehead,' Lewis admitted, 'though his knowledge of the law is quite extensive.' He looked tiredly at the young woman by his side. 'I've been to the clinic everyday,' he told her.

Tildy nodded, 'I know,' she said sympathetically her pain for the old man's suffering written on her features. 'And they won't let you see her. It's a disgrace, after they promised you limited visiting rights.' She twisted her gloved hands together nervously. 'What do you expect to happen here today?'

'It's a legal proceeding,' he yelled, 'necessary for them to be able to continue to hold her in custody. Effectively this will give them the right to hold Rosie indefinitely.'

The noise stopped, an eerie silence falling on the crowd as a door opened and Rosie was led in shackled between two burly officers. Tildy's gasp of dismay drowned by the sigh of satisfaction that rippled about the room.

Standing behind a big, well, chipped and scarred table, Rosie was a tiny lost figure, thin and pale, her eyes cast to the ground her face slack and emotionless.

'What's wrong with her?' Tildy whispered harshly. 'She isn't even looking our way. I so wanted her to know we were here for her.'

Lewis turned a worried face to his companion. 'Drugs,' he mumbled. 'I've seen opium sodden men look in exactly that way.' Despite his low tone anger could be heard close to the surface.

A chair was placed behind Rosie and the men either side of her pushed her backwards into it, there she sat, in her shapeless white shift, her mind in a world of its own, oblivious to the proceeding concerning her. Her hair had grown and hung matted and lifeless about her shoulders. Her skin, Tildy noted, had a greenish tinge.

'Her skin looks green to me,' she murmured, squinting to be sure it was not simply her imagination. 'Isn't it arsenic, that does that?'

'So much for the care and attention they promised,' Lewis hissed. 'They are killing her with medication.' He searched for and gripped his companion's hand. 'I'm so glad you're here with me,' he choked.

Tildy fell silent for a long moment, then having made up her mind, informed him in no uncertain terms of her decision. 'You must come home with me today,' she said firmly. 'This cannot go on any longer. We will fight this together. I will not take no for an answer,' she stated flatly.

The gavel banged on the table and the robed judge took his place. The noise in the room had gradually increased again, making it necessary for the gavel to thud on the table several times more.

Twenty minutes of shouting took place. Bernard tried earnestly to state his case, his voice being drowned by the jeers of the crowd no effort being made to quieten them. Then it was over and Rosie was being led away again.

Choking back her tears, Tildy cried. 'She looked like a frightened bird caught in a trap.'

Straightening his old bones Lewis led the way outside, the fresh air making them light headed after the leaden fog of the stuffy room they had been sitting in.

'Did you hear the names they called her?' Tildy whispered, her brave front slipping, her words vehement. 'How can people pre-judge a situation like that, they know nothing about it, or Rosie.'

Bernard joined them on the steps fronting the elegant building. 'It looks bleak,' he admitted reluctantly. 'They wouldn't even listen to me.'

Lewis patted his shoulder half-heartedly. 'I know, she has already been tried and found guilty,' he said sadly.

188

'Your best bet would be to get her to another part of the country,' Bernard said with little enthusiasm. ' Somewhere she would get an honest hearing, though how you do that is beyond me.'

'I agree with you,' Lewis responded. 'Yet, I don't think it likely to happen.'

A bright fire greeted them in the house on Canny's Hill, Martha hurried to despatch Tildy's husband, and her son, to prepare the best room for their visitor. 'Consider it yours for as long as you need,' she told him with a welcoming smile.

Savouring the tea he was sharing with Tildy, tired from the days activities and grateful for being allowed to share a home after years of impersonal Inn rooms, Lewis stretched his feet to the blaze and stared into the flickering flames.

'It's time,' he cried, jumping up without warning and rummaging in his possessions for paper, pen and ink, plonking them all on a side table, which he carried carefully to place in front of his chair.

Bemused, Tildy watched him. 'What are you doing?' she half laughed eying Lewis who made great show of settling himself to the task in hand.

'Over the years,' he said quietly, pen poised motionless in mid air. 'I have done many favours in my business, successful favours that have led to high rewards for the people involved,' his head bobbed in confirmation as he spoke. 'I have at times, with effort far above what would normally be expected, managed to get some of these folk out of very compromising situations.'

Tildy nodded silently watching him. 'I'm still not sure I understand, 'she said at length.

'My dear, it's time to remind these people. In short I need a few favours in return. My old friend Ninny would say, it is time to eat a little humble pie. Whatever it takes to get Rosie home again,' he added as he bestowed a gentle look on her.

189

Two weeks passed from the day that Lewis despatched his letters to his old acquaintances, until the day that Tildy entered his room with news that a messenger waited for him outside.

'Thank goodness,' he replied, heaving his wide frame from the chair and heading for the door.

'I hope it's good news,' she said, kissing his cheek when he passed her.

The day wore on with a succession of packages and letters arriving, the old man was dancing with joy, digesting everything that came to him.

'Not one of them has turned me down,' he crowed when asked for the latest news. 'They have all given more than I could ever have expected,' he cried, his face beaming, hope oozing from his pores.

'You are a well respected man,' she told him softly.

'First we dismiss Bernard Foster, ' he told her happily. 'Then we wait for Simon, because all of these people are now in direct contact with him. Unfortunately our nearly Earl, will himself owe a few favours after this. I will apologise for that fact when he arrives.' He smiled at her puzzled face. 'I know you don't understand at this moment but you will. Rosie will be returned to us, you wait and see.' With that he threw his arms about her and hugged her with a strength neither had suspected he possessed.

In the week they waited for Simon to return, Lewis fretted and fussed, willing the time to pass faster than it could. Tildy gave up questioning him and resigned herself to waiting patiently by his side.

'Simon, and friend,' Martha announced importantly ushering them into Lewis's room.

Tildy surveyed the short, beefy fellow that she estimated to be about thirty years of age, whilst Simon and Lewis greeted each other.

'Why the need of a bodyguard?' Lewis questioned almost fearfully, 'is there trouble?'

'Bide your time old friend,' Simon said, wagging a finger in Lewis's face, then greeting Tildy with much warmth before introducing them both to his companion. 'Meet Albert, everyone,' he pulled his companion to the centre of the room where he formally introduced the family.

'Did you do everything I requested?' the old man asked in agitation.

'I did, gladly,' he replied, a cheeky grin on his face.

'I apologise for placing such a strain on you,' Lewis continued to fuss, his brow creased with worry lines.

'There is nothing I wouldn't do for Rosie,' Simon responded, something in his tone bringing Tildy's head round to look at him. 'Don't worry about it any more.'

'How did your journey go, with the babies?' she asked, slipping her arm through his and walking him outside for a few moments of private chat.

'I must confess I haven't seen a great deal of them,' he admitted with a shamed face. 'Harriett the young nurse, coped wonderfully well. She has stayed on with Molly and Jake,' he informed her thankfully. 'The twins will be all right whatever happens.' He patted the hand resting in the crook of his arm in reassurance.

'And you?' Tildy questioned, giving him a sideways glance. 'Did you get all your business affairs completed?'

He nodded pressing his lips together. 'And a great deal more, I hope,' he added.

'Rosie?' she looked directly into his eyes noting the small blush that tinged his cheek and smiled. 'I'm glad,' she said softly, accepting his grateful grin as acknowledgement of her unasked question.

Early the following morning Simon returned, his beefy companion Albert sitting in the driving seat of a large, and handsome carriage.

Greeting him by the roadside Lewis questioned anxiously. 'Everything ready?' The two men shook hands warmly, clapping each other on the back and wishing each other the best of luck.'

Tildy watched her curiosity growing by the minute.

'You know what to do?' Simon called as he hefted himself back up to his vacant seat.

'I do. We will be waiting,' Lewis replied with great seriousness.

Tildy stood beside him for a long while and they watched the carriage disappear from sight, their hands casually linked in joint reassurance.

'Whatever it is you are up to,' she whispered. 'I pray that it works.' She bobbed her head from side to side as though searching for anyone eavesdropping on their conversation. The light wind teased at the hem of her skirt, lifting it to flap about her ankles as she stared along the road.

'I pray I have left nothing to chance,' the old man replied. 'That neither Simon, nor I have overlooked any vital detail.' His hand tightened about her fingers and he raised them to his lips. 'I'm so glad I lived long enough to meet you young lady,' he told her softly, kissing her knuckles. 'I couldn't have done this without you. You have been my strength.'

TWENTY SIX

A poker-faced nurse pursed her lips at them and repeated in her nasal tones again. 'She is much too ill for visitors. You have been told.'

Simon stared, equally straight faced back at her. 'I am aware of what you say,' he told her in a steely manner. 'But I repeat my request to be told this by the clinic director.'

Crossing her arms across her ample bosom, the nurse refused to be intimidated and replied just as firmly. 'And I have told you he is too busy to be disturbed.'

She made a noise of distaste in her throat walking away across the plush waiting area. Simon smiled at his companion saying, 'if she is hoping to put us off with her unpleasant attitude. It won't work.' They seated themselves, prepared to wait as long as necessary.

'How long before they arrive?' Albert questioned.

'Within two hours,' Simon replied, settling himself more comfortably in his chair.

'Oh lord,' Albert moaned. 'You mean we have to look at miss sour face over there for that long.' He covered his eyes with his hands in mock horror then, dropping them turned a serious face to his superior. 'What will you do if he changes his mind and decides to see you?'

Laughing Simon ignored the play-acting. 'Tell him the truth. Explain exactly what is about to happen, and why,' he said simply. He had purposely chosen the chairs they sat in. Exactly opposite the desk the harridan of a nurse sat behind. He intended to pass the time with idle chit chat if it annoyed her, so much the better.

During the next hour or so a steady procession of people made their way to the opulent waiting area, each making their own individual effort to persuade Simon that he was wasting both his own time, and theirs.

'I have plenty of time to waste,' he informed them with an arrogant smile at the acid faced nurse, watching her increasing discomfort with a measure of pleasure.

'Can you hear that, sir,' Albert nudged his superior as he gleefully imparted the news. 'Listen.'

Grinning, Simon got to his feet, the noise from outside growing by the minute. 'By heaven they've arrived,' he cried, letting out an audible sigh of relief. He had been more worried than he would allow his companion to realise 'They have made good time,' he cried gratefully.

The clatter of many horse hooves ringing on the cobbles outside filled the air, loud shouted, official sounding orders echoed deep inside the clinic walls. Office and consulting room doors opened and enquiring heads popped out in all directions.

Simon fixed his eyes on the nurse, smiling with glee when the outer door opened and she espied the scarlet uniforms. Two erect military figures marched smartly up to him clicking their heels and saluting noisily.

'Pleased to see you,' he greeted them, his face split by the widest grin he accepted the offered credentials.

'Captain Fisher and company at your command,' the officer replied sharply.

From the corner of his eye Simon noted the hurried departure of the nurse, her seat overturning in her haste to find the doctor in charge. A peal of laughter that he was unable to contain any longer left his lips as he watched her scuttle away.

The Captain smoothed at his neatly trimmed moustache and cast enquiring grey eyes over the civilians amused features.

Simon's body shook with suppressed laughter, much of it the release valve for his pent up nerves. With a visible effort he brought himself to attention and stood silently with his three associates. They made no move, expecting the nurse to return, which she did within minutes.

'The director will see you now,' she stammered, almost bobbing a curtsy to the man she had berated with her knife edged tongue only hours before.

Indicating that Albert and one soldier should wait within hearing distance of the directors, office door, Simon beckoned Captain Fisher to join him.

'Wait outside here one moment,' he whispered before following the nurse into the office alone, remaining at the door whilst she left and carefully leaving it a few inches open before turning into the opulent room.

Face to face with the evil little man who had helped to forcibly remove Rosie, all those weeks ago, he was delighted to note the beads of perspiration on his adversaries, forehead and upper lip. This time he had the upper hand, and they both knew it.

Striding across the lush carpeting, Simon stood before the small, balding man sitting behind the protection of a large desk. 'I have come to see Madame Saunderman,' he stated, brusquely.

'My nurse had already told you, she is too ill for visitors,' the doctor whined, shrinking where he sat.

'If she is so ill she cannot receive visitors. I take it her trial will be postponed until her recovery,' he queried, his voice loud yet sickly sweet.

'Postponed, never. Why should it be,' the doctor blustered, his face reddening rapidly in his agitation, his body jerking spasmodically up and down on his chair.

'I see,' Simon mused. 'So you are telling me she is well enough to stand up in court but not well enough for visitors. I do beg your pardon.' His tone had taken on a deadly calm.

195

The director licked his lips feverishly. 'Not at all,' he stammered. 'I didn't say.' He mopped his brow with a white handkerchief pulled from his coat pocket. 'Where the trial is concerned I have no say.'

'Let me understand you,' Simon purred, gazing around the expensively furnished office. 'You have no say at all in when this woman is taken to trial. You do not get asked for your opinion on the condition of her health? Hmm.' He waited as the man first nodded, then shook his head, then nodded again, abject fear blazing from his eyes.

'So, you are prepared to put on trial someone who is so ill,' he went on a little less softly. 'She cannot speak to others, cannot answer for herself.' He paused casting his eye deliberately about him watching the fellows discomfort grow rapidly. 'Someone too ill to answer the questions that will be asked of her,' his voice as he spoke belied his churning gut, his calm outward appearance covering a rising temper.

The director wiped drips of perspiration from his temple on the sleeve of his coat. 'She will have representation. It has nothing to do with me,' he groaned.

'Can she in fact answer questions?' Simon asked in silky tones.

'You have been told. No,' the doctor shouted, jumping up.

Striding back to the door, Simon pulled it open wide to admit the waiting soldier. Standing to one side he allowed Captain Fisher to pass.

'Captain Fisher, this good doctor is the director of this clinic. A private clinic of means I would say, not the place you would expect to house a prisoner,' he added, more to himself than his audience. 'He is also the official Police doctor responsible for Rosie. I will ask him to repeat the answers to the questions I have already put to him.' He turned back to the man.

Holding up a restraining hand Captain Fisher spoke. 'The clinic may be expensive, but the walls are thin. I heard every word clearly.' Reaching into his pocket, he pulled forth a

196

bulky package bearing a large, official seal. The package bore the name of the clinic director.

'It is my duty to hand you this,' he said, his voice boomed around the room. 'I must insist you read it in my presence,' he intoned.

With a shaky hand the director received the missive breaking the seal and reading it slowly, blanching as he turned the pages. White faced he looked up at the Captain. Fear turned the whites of his eyes a sickly yellow.

'Before you take us to your patient. You will complete this statement and sign these documents,' Simon commanded, leaning across the desktop almost nose to nose with the despicable little man. His knuckles gleamed whitely where they rested on the desk he was having great trouble resisting the urge to thrust them into the doctor's throat.

Walking back out into the hallway, leaving the director in the capable hands of the Captain he commandeered a passing nurse. Gesturing to Albert and the waiting soldier, he called through the director's doorway. 'Join me as soon as he has done what is required.' Captain Fisher clicked his heels in acknowledgement and Simon urged the nurse to take them to Rosie.

Outside the door of Rosie's room, Captain Fisher and the reluctant doctor caught up with them. The captain held up a parchment.

'A freely given statement that the patient known as Rosie Saunderman is too ill to stand trial,' he intoned without emotion. 'It is here, recommended that for the sake of her health she be removed to London where it has been arranged for eminent doctors to continue her treatment. It concludes that the good doctor here, feels it will be some considerable months before this woman's health will permit her to stand trial.' A smile twitched at his lips when he looked at Simon. 'Soldier,' he commanded, rolling the parchment, pulling sealing wax and a match from his pocket.

Simon watched a melted blob of wax seal the roll. Captain Fisher pressed his ring into the soft surface of the wax and handed the roll to his subordinate. 'This document is to be taken directly to the Dartmouth Court House,' he instructed. 'There, you are to personally oversee it's reading. Ensure that its contents are noted officially and return to me. Take two men with you in case of trouble,' he warned.

Nodding, the soldier took the papers asking, 'where will I find you, sir?'

'On the road to London, I imagine you will have no difficulty. I don't expect to make very good time, not with a dangerously ill patient.' He glared at the doctor who visibly cringed under the onslaught of words.

With a smart click of his boots the soldier left.

The doctor looked smaller and less eminent with every move made about him. His slumped figure shivered uncontrollably. Simon stopped briefly to wonder why? They were intimidating him, he agreed, but this man was physically scared of something other than them. Presumably, he reasoned to himself some local chief of police feathering his own nest, at the countries expense.

'Now lets go in and see your patient,' Captain Fisher said, pushing the door open and standing to one side.

The smell of the room overpowered them the minute they entered. Both men choked as it hit the back of their throats. Captain Fisher coughed a rasping sound the aroma searing his nostrils.

'Are you sure she's still alive,' Simon roared, the acid smell making his eyes water and filling his lungs.

'Yes, yes she is alive,' the doctor cried as Simon grabbed him forcibly by the coat front. 'She's sedated. We've been carrying out tests,' he hesitated at the look on his assailants face. 'To clear her mind,' he rushed on his voice little more than a squeak.

'Trying to kill her more like,' Albert spoke up, his face twisted with rage and disgust.

The table by the high bedside was covered with jars of noxious looking liquid's, strange colours reflected from them in the weak light that filtered through the lightly covered window.

They stared down at the ashen face of Rosie where she lay in the bed. Her hair straggled out in damp tendrils a few clinging tenaciously to the sides of her sunken cheeks. The sweet cloying smell drifting up from her form made Simon feel nauseous, he stepped closer to the bed.

'Wash her, brush her hair and dress her warmly,' he growled at the cowering nurse by his side. 'And be quick about it,' he commanded then fled the room.

Seconds later the nurse crept from the doorway to find him leaning heavily against the wall, his chest heaving in his efforts to control his emotions. 'Please sir,' she whispered fearfully. 'The lady has no clothing of her own.'

He nodded, disgust and frustration churning his innards, then turned away marching from the building, too angry to respond to the frightened figure. Fate seemed to thwart him at every turn, he had hoped to be able to scoop Rosie into his arms and flee with her instantly. Every hour spent affecting her release gave rise to the fear of interruption. The paperwork could not be questioned, he was sure of that, but there was always that element of the unexpected and it worried him.

A chorus of catcalls greeted him as he stepped outside, surprise at the gathered crowd pulling him to a standstill. Taking a deep breath he plunged on through the throng who made ever attempt to stop his progress along the street.

Ignoring the jeers he went silently about his business, returning to the clinic some thirty minutes later, his arms laden with purchases. Elbowing people aside he entered and returned to Rosie's room tossing the goods on the end of the bed and instructing the nurse to hurry.

'I have commandeered the medications,' Captain Fisher told him quietly. 'We may need them on the journey, anyway

199

her new doctors will need to know what this brute has been administering to her.'

Returning to the doctor's office, Simon walked in without the courtesy of a knock to announce his arrival. The doctor took immediate refuge behind his desk where he cowered, visibly.

'The mother of the Earl of Berwick has been made ready for her departure. When she is well again,' he warned ominously. 'Rest assured I will make it my aim in life to encourage her to see that your so called clinic, is closed down.'

The doctors head pivoted on his neck, his face changing colour as he repeated, 'Earl of Berwick.'

'By the way your jaw has slipped,' Simon said, smirking at the man looking stupid with his mouth gaping open. 'I take it they omitted to tell you exactly who you were tampering with. Well, let this be a lesson to you. Greed is not always rewarded.' For the briefest of moments he felt sorry for the little man who was obviously being used as a pawn in someone else's game.

'This man is Simon Saunderman,' Captain Fisher explained, entering the room he laid a hand on Simon's shoulder having overheard the conversation so far. 'He is the brother to Edward Saunderman, and you know who he was! Not only was he the criminal responsible for the crimes committed but, also an Earl.' He explained slowly and evenly as though to a backward child. 'He was also the father of Rosie's children, and is now dead. The male of the twins born to her some months ago is now the fourth Earl of Berwick. It would have paid you better,' he added with a satisfied smirk. 'To have made your own enquiries about the background of your patient, Edward Saunderman, the man responsible for all of the crimes, was the third Earl of Berwick.'

Simon had taken great delight in watching a rainbow of colours cross the doctor's contorted face, his figure shrivelling as he listened to the details. They turned and left a broken man behind them.

Albert met them at the door the inert figure of Rosie cradled in his arms. Captain Fisher stepped forward and tucked her cloak and blanket more securely about her legs before leading them outside to the waiting carriage.

Anticipating the worst, Simon had arranged for a narrow, make shift bed, to be fitted in the roomy interior, Rosie was placed gently on top of it. Like magic the red coated, soldiers appeared and surrounded the carriage and its occupants, protecting them from the unruly crowd showing a tendency to violence. Captain Fisher mounted his own horse and yelled his orders and they pulled away from the front of the clinic. Rosie once more safely delivered into their hands.

The journey back to Lewis and Tildy was a slow affair. The carriage escorted by townsfolk as well as soldiers, they ran for several miles along the roadside with them. The occasional missile being hurled from a distance, shouting and jeering dying as their breath became laboured from their exertions.

'I fully understand your fears, now,' Captain Fisher called into the window at Simon. 'She would not have stood a chance in a court in this part of the country. If the journey gets too much,' he indicated the prone figure of Rosie. 'Let me know.'

'I'll say,' Simon replied with deep relief poking his head from the window. 'I was glad to have your support,' he grinned. 'Thank you,' he called when the captain moved away to the head of his men. Then looking back at his patient he murmured. ' Fear not, I'll be the last person to put her in any danger now.'

TWENTY SEVEN

Lewis and Tildy stood hand in hand at the roadside, watching the carriage and the troop of soldiers that made their way up the hill and pulled to stop in front of them.

'You know my feelings on this matter,' Captain Fisher informed Simon and Lewis, they all stood to one side allowing Tildy and Martha to oversee Rosie's removal from carriage to house.

Lewis nodded soberly. 'Yes, I fully understand and I thank you for your co-operation. The local doctor is waiting inside to examine her, hopefully in a few days I will feel more at ease about completing the rest of this arduous journey to the capital.' He extended his hand to the captain and pumped the soldiers arm up and down as he spoke.

'It will be necessary for me to leave two men here,' the soldier informed him in official tones. 'I am directly responsible to our government, I cannot neglect my official duty and permit you to keep her unsupervised.'

'She will be quite safe with us,' Simon shouted, his frustrations of the day making his voice sharper than he intended.

'I'm sure,' Captain Fisher replied civilly. 'Officially I should not allow this break at all. The young lady is not only my responsibility, technically she is my prisoner I have to be sure.'

'Of course,' Lewis murmured. 'We have all been so delighted that she is safely back with us we are forgetting that point. Please feel free to leave as many men here as you wish,' he added quietly thinking of the preparation that had already taken place in readiness for this moment.

Tildy had spent her day in hectic activity, turning her home upside down to accommodate the expected party.

'This is putting your family to so much trouble,' Lewis had apologised gazing forlornly at the upheaval he was creating. 'I must admit I hadn't thought the details through properly, only now do I realise how much work is involved.'

'The girl is one of our own,' Martha had snapped at him. 'We would do this much for any member of our family, so what else would we expect to do for her?'

A bedroom had been turned into a simple hospital ward. Lewis had gladly shopped for the necessary furnishings.

'It looks more like an apothecary shop than a bedroom,' Tildy laughed.

'Captain,' Simon called to the assembled gathering still waiting at the roadside, anxious to ensure the initial bustle of settling the patient had been completed. 'Could I ask a favour of you?'

The Captain held the reigns of his impatiently snorting horse, the stamp of hooves on the ground filling their ears. He inclined his head. 'If I can help.'

'Could you house the trusty Albert with your men? I think he would feel more comfortable bedding down with them, than trying to fit in here,' Simon waved an absent arm at the house as he spoke.

'Delighted to have his company,' the soldier replied, nodding his ascent. 'We'll leave now, I will return daily to check on progress,' he kept his voice low his words meant for Simon only. Then barking his orders, his men escorted the carriage away up the hill and out of sight.

'You are causing a stir in our peaceful little town,' the doctor said, addressing Lewis as he puffed his way down the stairs having completed his examination of Rosie.

'How is she?' he enquired in return.

The doctor shook his head he had carefully scanned the paperwork offered to him by the good Captain. 'I have no idea what effects these drugs will have on her, or how long they will take to release their hold on her system,' his words held a touch of embarrassment. 'To be honest,' he admitted. 'I have not even heard of one or two of them.' He ran a finger about the high collar of his shirt in an effort to get more air through his windpipe. 'I am no expert, the things that are listed here frighten me, what the eventual outcome on her health will be.' He shrugged in a helpless gesture, not saying any more.

'Can you tell us when she is likely to wake up?' Tildy asked.

'From all that I hear she is a remarkably resilient young woman,' the doctor told her kindly. 'A bit like yourself,' he patted Tildy on her hand, turning to Lewis he added proudly. 'I helped to bring this young lady into the world, I know what she is capably of.' He beamed at his audience then, returned to the matter in hand. 'Maybe a day or so, get as much liquid into her as possible. If she wakes in pain, send for me at once.' With that he took his leave.

Tildy and Lewis walked outside to watch him depart. 'Maybe now you will tell me how this has all come about?' she asked, tucking her hand in the crook of her old friend's arm. 'All I know is what you told us all the day before yesterday, Rosie would be staying here to recover before going on to London. It's a miracle how did you make it happen?'

Lewis led her to a sheltered bench and wrapped his arm about her shoulder to give her a little protection from the cool air. 'It was Bernard Foster,' he began, 'and a chain of thoughts.'

'If you remember, Bernard said she would only get a fair trial in another part of the country. That evening as we sat before the fire I began thinking. London is where it all started and that's where Edwards crimes should be judged.'

'But,' Tildy interrupted.'

Lewis put a gentle finger on her lips to silence her. 'I know,' he continued. 'It would take an act of Parliament to make it happen. That was exactly what turned my thoughts to an old client who is now a newly elected Member of Parliament.' He paused, settling his rotund figure a little more comfortably. 'In turn I recalled what I had done for him and others, and so, the idea of contacting them and asking for help was born.' He smiled at her. 'It was Simon who had to agree to do most of the work. I could only approach them from afar, he had to follow up with his own personal guarantees, and talk them into bending whatever rules they could. '

'But a whole troop of the Queen's soldier,' Tildy replied in awe, her face telling him she did not underestimate his part in all that had happened, at all.

'That wasn't in my request,' he assured her. 'I simply told everyone what sort of treatment one of the Queen's subjects was receiving in this part of the country. All I wanted was a letter from some government body to effectively gain Rosie's release from the authorities here in the west country, and return her to London, where hopefully she will get a fair hearing. The rest has surpassed all my expectations.' He placed the palm of his hand on his heart to emphasize his honesty.

'This clinic?' Tildy asked with a tremble. 'Did they really think it would help Rosie's mind?'

Lewis shook a sad head. 'I think maybe they were trying to kill her in a manner that would not be questioned. It would merely be stated that she failed to respond to treatment,' he said softly.

'There's more to it than that,' Simon growled, joining them, overhearing the tale end of the conversation. 'You could be right it might just have been to save the cost of a trial. I couldn't work out what that doctor was getting out of it. A large fee for the use of his expensive clinic, yes.' He

205

shook his head in disbelief. 'He wasn't working on his own authority. Of that I'm sure.'

'No doubt what you say is true my boy. It would have added up to a tidy sum being paid by local authorities. If it could have been made to last long enough, it could have meant a healthy retirement for someone. It's inconsequential as too whom.' Lewis pondered his words for a moment then, brightened. 'I wish I could have seen the doctors face when he realised who he had been dealing with,' he chuckled.

'It was almost as satisfactory as punching him between those beady little eyes,' Simon assured them with a grin.

'The drugs that have been administered could cause some dependency,' Lewis warned them both, bringing the subject back to Rosie. 'I have been studying some of them during the wait. In fact I have gathered all I could find on the subject,' he told them quietly. 'It could be harrowing for the family,' he added, looking again at Tildy. 'Would you like me to engage a nurse?'

'With two able bodied women in the house, not at all,' Tildy replied firmly. Standing she pulled herself up to her full height, her hands smoothing her crumpled skirt as she spoke. 'Let's hear no more about it. Now I will go and see to my own sleeping arrangement. I will sleep in the room with her,' she informed them both, her tone brooking no argument. 'Rosie must not be allowed to wake up alone.

'What would we do without her,' Lewis muttered, both men watched her return to the house.

'We mustn't forget her long suffering husband,' Simon reminded him. 'Donald has tolerated a lot, many men would have objected in his place.'

'He will not be forgotten,' Lewis promised with a smile. 'Though I rather feel his love for his wife, and her strong character would quickly overcome any objections he may have wanted to raise. His has the sort of love my old heart would wish for Rosie to find eventually,' he concluded tenderly.

Simon looked a trifle uncomfortable under his old friend's scrutiny a soft, pink blush creeping up his neck. Spots of rain touched his cheek and he looked upwards at the gathering cloud layer before speaking again. 'I feel totally humbled by the amount that people will do for others, sometimes for near strangers,' he replied quietly, awe and amazement on his face.

'Not quite what your cosseted upbringing would have led you to expect,' Lewis responded kindly with a satisfied smile.

TWENTY EIGHT

Jake strode purposefully up the stairs in the Refuge, ignoring the shouted greetings of the regulars, already enjoying their mid-day meal. His mind fixed on reaching the nursery, and imparting his news.

Big, structural alterations had been carried out to the Refuge, since his return with the twins. An extra room had been built on and two existing bedrooms combined to make one large nursery, used by all four children. A bed for Harriett was discreetly secluded in one corner, along with two high, sided cots for the babies. Molly and her children spent most of their days in this room. Less and less of her efforts were put into the day to day running of the Refuge, not that Jake minded in the least, that side of their life was a well oiled cog, thanks to their loyal and supportive friends. So well established was it, he felt sure it would ran smoothly without either of them for an extended length of time.

As he entered the bright and airy room, Jake heard the gasps from Molly and Harriett, who both turned their attention to him immediately.

'Well,' Molly whispered finally, 'Did he say, yes.'

Jake nodded, momentarily robbed of words as he took in the picture of his wife placing protective cushions around the sitting figure of baby Daniel. The children were growing so bonny, under the loving ministrations of these two women. 'Rosie is missing so much,' he croaked emotionally, a tear prickling the back of his eyelid. 'Yes he has agreed to take the case.'

'Congratulations,' Molly cried, jumping up and throwing herself into his arms. 'I knew you would succeed.'

'Father,' Samuel's voice interrupted the moment. 'Could you help me with this problem?' he requested, from where he sat at his desk in the portion of the room used for the children's lessons.

Jake walked to his son's side and peered down at his work, taking only a minute to assess the boy's concern. Then, ruffling his son's hair affectionately he stood back and watched him return to his work with renewed confidence. Samuel was a bright boy, old for his age he thought as he studied him. He no longer wished to be treated as a child. Jake knew that sooner rather than later, he would have to over ride Molly's wish to keep her son near at hand. He understood his wife's fear of letting her children grow away from her. After all, he reasoned, her own childhood had not been a loving one, she knew all about being a lonely, unhappy youngster. But the boy deserved the best in education he had a brain worthy of it. He needed to stretch his wings, to go away to school.

Right now Sammy professed that he wanted to be either a doctor, or a lawyer, when he grew up. Molly laughed, Jake was not quite sure what she expected her son to become he secretly believed she never thought of him as ever being anything other than a dependent child. Jake understood both of his son's choices, he was being heavily influenced by the events around him, which was only to be expected, he thought. Then again Samuel was bright enough to become either.

At the behest of Simon and Lewis, Jake had spent a lot of time lately searching for legal help. His search had taken him to Lincoln's Inn Fields. Today had been his third visit in his quest to find the best legal man he could. He was aware, yet wary, of the plan the pair had concocted to move Rosie to London and prayed that it would work. Simon had been at pains to ensure they knew his every move, before he returned to Lewis. In the meantime it fell to Jake to do his best in return. Lewis had furnished him with a list of names some of which, he knew would have retired, but it had been a starting place.

Jake had contacted each man in turn taking their advice and listening to their recommendations, one name had cropped up over and over again that of Alexander Howell, and that is who he had been to see this morning.

His heart in his mouth Jake had approached the man five days ago.

'What makes you think I could be the right man for this case?' the lawyer had questioned thoughtfully.

'So many people recommended you,' Jake replied honestly, studying the tall, broad shouldered man sitting opposite him. 'One told me how interested you were in the Battersea murders when they were big news, so long ago.'

Alexander chewed on the side of his mouth, his bushy eyebrows coming together across the bridge of his nose when he frowned then, relaxed and gave a half smile. 'I drove my poor wife mad,' he confessed. 'I spent every spare hour searching for clues, loop holes, anything that would give an angle on who was committing these atrocities. Yes I could be interested.' His hand rubbed his chiselled chin absently as he considered the request. 'But I would need a lot more information before I agreed to take it on.

Jake had hurried back the following day, at the lawyer's request. This time he had taken every scrap of paperwork and sat for several hours filling in all the details of Rosie's story that he knew. An appointment had been made for this morning, when the lawyer had promised a decision. It had cost the family a number of sleepless nights now thankfully they could look to the whole case moving on.

'This case will be all consuming for everyone involved,' Alexander Howell had told Jake in no uncertain terms. 'My wife, bless her for her love and understanding, has agreed to

210

live with that fact. Are you prepared to do the same?' He had shot the question at Jake taking him completely by surprise.

'My wife and I have lived with nothing else in our heads for years,' Jake retorted, anger and hurt rising in his voice. 'Our dearest friend, and the uncle of Rosie's children, have spent years searching the West Country for her. Our commitment is above questioning so how can you ask?'

Holding up a conciliatory hand Alexander apologised. 'I have to be sure. It is going to take every ounce of effort, and strain every fibre of our being to win this case. Now let's go over the details once more.'

For two hours Jake had sat and talked. He had not minded. If it gave them success in the end he would talk forever.

Now standing in the nursery, telling the women every detail of the morning's events, Dora puffed in on them.

'There's a messenger down with Lenny,' she informed them shakily.

Jake went to her side he could feel her fearful shivering and understood. Over the years Dora had learned to fear the bad news that most of the messengers had brought them. 'It's all right, Dora,' he soothed. 'This time it should be good news. Stay here and help Harriett with the children,' he suggested, nodding to Molly he gestured for her to join him.

Welcoming the man who had visited them on more than one occasion in the past, Jake took the papers from him and read them. 'They have her safe at Tildy's,' he cried, Molly reached up and endeavoured to peer over his shoulder.

'Did you see her,' Molly addressed her question to the messenger who, had stayed overnight as their guest on several occasions and knew most of their story by now. He shook his head.

'But I heard her, an I was only there but minutes,' he confessed a grimace on his tired face.

'Heard her,' Molly cocked her head and looked at him, 'in what way?' she asked.

'Enough to make your blood run cold,' he said with a chill of horror, 'Fearful screaming and wailing. Mr Lewis, he has given me instruction to hurry back, I only hopes it's not so I can return and tell you the worst,' he added with a mournful certainty.

Molly looked from him to Jake, her mouth opening and closing as she tried to form a question.

'It says here that her health is completely broken.' Jake choked on his words then went on his head going dizzy as he digested what he read. 'They have given her a drug dependency that is stripping her body of any assistance it may have given to aid her recovery,' he moaned. 'Despite all their efforts they are gravely worried. Simon asks us to pray that all our endeavours will not prove to be wasted ones.' A sob broke from him and he handed the paper to his wife.

'It can't happen,' she cried, tears flowing freely down her pretty face. 'Not after so much and when we have at last got her the help she needed. Dear God, no,' she wailed. 'Don't let it happen.'

TWENTY NINE

Joining Lewis by Rosie's bedside, Simon whispered. 'What have you done with our trusty nurses?'

'Sent them for some much needed rest,' he replied huskily. 'They are worn out.' His head turned to allow him to study the room, which, he knew had been a pretty bedroom before, with his help, it had been so transformed. 'I must find a way to compensate the family for the trouble we have put them too,' he muttered, more to himself than his comrade.

Simon let the comment pass they would both see that the family were rewarded. 'Her recovery is taking so long,' he moaned. 'The days were stretching into one another.'

'And been far more harrowing than even I imagined,' Lewis admitted tiredly.

Simon nodded. He was well aware how Rosie's pain was affecting his old friend. It had taken all his-own strength to watch as she thrashed about in an agony they were unable to relieve. Lewis had found a release valve in walking. He spent hours of his time walking through the fields and by the river. Tildy's daughter Bethany, often balanced on the crook of his arm, her small arms linked about his old neck, or walking her wobbly walk by his side, her tiny hand clutching his. Talking their own brand of baby talk they chatted away reviewing the world around them. He, on the other hand, had not been able to turn away.

'He's helping in his own manner,' Tildy assured Simon when he apologised for Lewis's inability to cope with their patient. 'He takes a great worry from my mind just looking after my child,' she smiled reassuringly.

'What did the good Captain have to say?' Lewis queried, he had heard the clatter of the daily visit but chosen not to leave the room.

'He's despatched some of his men back to London, keeping only a few to wait. He understands she cannot be transported in this state of health. I sent Albert back with them,' he nodded at Rosie in the bed. 'Her sleep seems deeper than usual?' he said thoughtfully staring at the dull, grey skin of her face, and the black circles ringing her eyes. 'I wish this area boasted a more eminent medical man though.'

'The man we have is doing his best,' Lewis reminded him a little sharply. 'Is the good Captain upset that he will be in some measure of trouble when he returns to London, after all this was a very unofficial stop.'

'He's sent word with his men that the patient was taken violently ill on the journey, he had no alternative but to stop,' Simon told him. 'I haven't said so, but I intend to write and thank his superior for the excellent service Fisher has given us. That should take the sting from any ill feeling there may be.'

'Well done,' Lewis congratulated quietly. 'Excellent way to repay him for all he has done.'

'Who knows what demons she is suffering,' Simon said softly gently lifting one of Rosie's lifeless hands and stroking it with his own. 'If my brother were still alive, I would willingly kill him myself,' he murmured with feeling.

'Take heart,' Lewis responded with a smile. 'She is not one for giving in. She's fighting all the way. My fear is that her young mind will over dose on all that has been expected of it and close down completely on her.' He hunched forward in his seat gazing closely at the wan face, watching every slight movement of muscle, every involuntary flicker of her eyelids, almost willing her to return to them.

'Should we hire a nurse? It's not right for Tildy and Martha to be put to this much trouble,' Simon questioned, his eyes not leaving Rosie's face either.

'No,' Lewis replied sharply. 'It would be unkind to hurt their feelings in such a way. We, I, must try to help more, in whatever small way I can,' he added a little guiltily.

Simon agreed readily. 'I have no wish to offend them,' he told his friend.

'She blames herself,' Lewis stated bluntly.

Simon's head swivelled, 'who?'

'Tildy,' Lewis replied, putting a cautionary finger to his lips. 'She feels she should have done more to stop Edward taking her from here in the first place. The time when Rosie ran to them for help.'

'Rubbish,' Simon hissed, his body jerking in a gesture of disgust. 'Fisher's army could not have stopped Edward doing what he wanted never mind one young girl and her family.'

A cough brought their eyes back to the bed as Rosie's lips twitched in the tiniest of smiles and her mouth opened to whisper, 'hello.'

Whooping for joy, uncaring of waking others Simon almost smothered her in a hug of delight. Pushing him aside, Lewis held a china bowl to her lips and encouraged her to sip at the soothing water.

'How are you feeling?' he asked tenderly, 'you've been in your own world for a very long time, we've all been worried about you.'

Rosie allowed her eyes to wander past him, then asked, 'where am I?'

'Here darling, with me,' Tildy cried rushing into the room roused by the noise. 'Oh it's so good to see you awake.' A tear splashed on Rosie's skin when she leaned over to kiss the thin face.

A puzzled frown creased Rosie's brow briefly. 'I don't understand,' she whispered, looking at the faces crowding over her.

'Just rest,' Simon told her. 'We will explain everything when you are stronger.'

The next few days saw a remarkable change in the patient, as her appetite increased so did her strength, and her determination to recover from the sudden, unaccountable attacks of panic that over whelmed her from time to time.

'We have a message from Jake,' Lewis told her as they sat together in the family room. 'Do you remember Jake?' he asked kindly.

'Yes, he took my babies to London with him,' she replied, reaching out and stroking the fine, fair hair of the plump baby girl playing happily at her feet.

'Thank goodness,' Lewis sighed with relief. 'We have been so fearful of mentioning the children to you. Indeed we have been fearful that you might not even remember them,' he told her, wondering how they had all come to the unspoken agreement to keep quiet.

'Have you news of them?' she asked, her eyes clouding with fear. 'Nothing bad has happened to them?'

His old heart tore apart at the look of terror on her face and her totally vulnerable state. With difficulty he raised a smile. 'They are well, and growing fast. They sit on their own now, and Daniel eats enough for two,' he assured her. Then told her the news he felt to be most important. 'Jake has secured you a Queen's counsellor, a Mr Alexander Howell of Lincolns Inn Fields no less. Isn't that great news,' he added, a tinge of excitement creeping into his voice.

'Very,' Rosie replied without enthusiasm. 'What else does he say about Daniel and Nancy?'

Lewis rose and reached for a paper from the top of a pile of official documents, stored on a side table. Handing it to Rosie he said gently. 'Read it for yourself.'

'It's from Molly,' she looked up questioningly, before reading on. Tears swam silently down her face and tripped off her chin as she scanned the page.

Doing a mental somersault, Lewis kicked himself. They had all been so busy tiptoeing around her health problem they had overlooked the one thing that had meant most to her and may have helped with her inner struggles. That may have been the one single thing, which would give her a reason to live. They had not talked to her about her children.

'I think it is time you were allowed to see those rascals again for yourself,' Lewis stated with emotion, making up his mind on the spot. 'If you think you can stand the journey we will inform Captain Fisher and start for London as soon as possible.'

The beautific smile he received in return was more thanks than he could ever have expected. Leaving her with her letter he rushed about the house issuing his orders.

'It's good news, Simon my boy,' he called when he found his companion busy writing. 'We are taking her to London, at once, she wants to see her children.' He waited expectantly, would Simon put up an argument against it?

Instead the young man smiled calmly, 'I have been expecting it,' he admitted.

'Captain Fisher was also saying he could not delay the return much longer,' he went on. 'His men will be glad to get going.'

With relief Lewis went on to tell the other occupants of the house.

'Any mother would miss her children.' Tildy responded when she was told. 'I was hoping she would ask for them, a tiny bit of me was scared her mind had blotted them from her memory.'

'I'll go and inform the Captain,' Simon offered, 'We leave tomorrow then.'

Copious tears, many hugs and kisses, and the constant words, 'thank you', accompanied their leaving.

'We will never be able to repay their kindness,' Lewis muttered, wiping a hand across his eyes. 'I have grown so fond of your young friend,' he told Rosie. 'And that little angel of a daughter.' He sniffed loudly before pulling a handkerchief from his pocket and blowing his nose.

217

It was an impressive display of uniforms that accompanied their journey through the town and out into the countryside, less than had been required to bring her to Canny's Hill, but enough to create a lot of interest.

The interior of the carriage proved hot and stuffy, Rosie, rocked by the motion of the wheels dozed fitfully between watching the countryside roll by. Lewis suffered the discomfort of the hard seating in silence. His old bones feeling every jolt, his spine jarred at every bump, his chest tightening in the dusty air. 'I'm grown too old for all this travelling,' he told nobody in particular.

Early in the afternoon Captain Fisher despatched a rider to go ahead and secure rooms at a suitable hostelry, for their night's stop. The Innkeeper to be told he was receiving a family of the highest standing, but no further details to be discussed. His concern for their comfort touching.

A satisfying hot meal awaited their arrival at the chosen tavern, their host and his wife, waiting on them in a royal manner. After quenching her thirst and nibbling on a little white meat Rosie retired to her room, allowing the landlords wife and a maid to help her to bed.

'The young lady is sleeping like a baby,' the wife informed Lewis on her return to the dining area. 'Poor wee lass, she looks as though she has been very ill.' She clucked her tongue in genuine concern as she busied herself clearing away the dishes.

'If you don't mind, my boy, I think I will retire as well,' Lewis informed Simon wearily. 'The journey has proved more tiring for me than our patient,' he quipped as he left the room.

The following days travel proved little different from the last, except for the sun. Today the clouds hung low and rain sprinkled the countryside at regular intervals. The interior of the carriage was no less humid and dust laden.

Rosie spent her waking time fanning her face with a small, ornate ivory fan that Simon had been thoughtful enough to provide for her: Occasionally leaning across to waft the pretty object in the air around Lewis's head.

Hating to waste his time, Lewis tried with as much patience as he could muster, to write up his notes and a few personal messages in preparation to their return home. Though Rosie was much brighter and more chatty today, Lewis found the travelling hours long and tedious, his bones ached, his body felt leaden and sluggish, not his usual self at all.

'You are much taken with your writing,' Rosie ventured. 'I hope the contents are not as serious as the look on your face.' Her lips turned in a small, but expressive smile that made her look healthier than he had seen her since her rescue. The effort plucked at Lewis's heartstrings. Suddenly he wanted to be home, in his own Town house where he had first met this child and taken a liking to her pert ways. He wanted desperately to turn time back, but knew it could never happen. Instead he wished whole-heartedly for her to remember those days of her childhood.

'Just a few personal notes, my dear,' he said with a sigh, patting her hand as he spoke. 'You know the sort of little items that get forgotten but are a useful way to pass the journey.' He smiled tenderly at her, his face telling her of the love he felt for her.

'I'm sorry,' she mumbled quietly. 'I don't wish to be a bad travelling companion, I will leave you to your work.' She closed her eyes allowing herself to be lulled to sleep once more.

Tucking the light cover gently about her knees, Lewis leaned over and kissed her softly on the cheek. 'Sleep now,' he whispered. 'It will do you far more good than my useless chatter.'

THIRTY

Simon stretched down an arm to shake Lewis by the shoulder. 'Come on lazy bones, we are all waiting for breakfast,' he cried merrily to the back of his friend's head. 'We should arrive in London today with any luck.' His words caught in his throat as his efforts caused Lewis's form to turn, falling flat on his back, his sightless eyes staring up at the ceiling above him.

'Oh no. Not now, not when we are so close to home and success,' Simon cried, falling on his knees beside the bed, his arms stretched across the lifeless body. 'After all we have been through together, I thought you would hang in there until the end,' a sob choked him. He had acknowledged to himself how old and tired Lewis had grown in the last months, but it had never occurred to him that the old man would not be by his side when they cleared Rosie's name.

'Old friend,' he murmured softly, standing upright and brushing at his face with his hand. 'You are leaving behind many who have learned to love you greatly.' His head bowed he issued his own private prayer of farewell before carrying the sad news to his companions.

Simon stood, silent and erect in the doorway of the dining room, surveying the 'happy to be almost home' crowd busy with their breakfast, soldiers and civilians rubbing shoulders in the friendliest of manner. Little by little the room fell silent, each person turning expectant eyes his way.

'Trouble?' Captain Fisher asked, standing to attention, wiping crumbs from his moustache with his napkin then, reshaping it with his fingers.

His resolve crumbling his body shaking from shock, Simon muttered one word. 'Lewis!'

Rushing past him, several of his subordinates in pursuit, the Captain took the stairs to Lewis's bedroom two at a time, returning minutes later to lay a hand on Simon's shoulder.

'It is my unhappy duty,' he said with an embarrassed cough. 'To inform you that our friend, Lewis Maxwell, died in his sleep last night.' He listened for a moment to the murmur of shock that rippled through the room, then added. 'I did not know him, or his companions prior to my arrival here. My orders came from my superiors in London. I have to say that I was not exactly pleased with being given this assignment. I considered it a waste of effort and resources. But,' he held up his hand to stop the gasps of amazement his words were bringing. 'I was wrong. In the few short weeks I have been associated with these people I have learned a lot, a lot about love and respect. Today I feel like you, that I have lost a trusted friend whom I admired greatly.' Turning aside he assembled his men and issued quiet orders.

Simon went to Rosie's side, pulling up a chair he sat next to her. 'Are you all right?' he asked with concern.

She turned tear filled eyes to him. 'Would I be allowed to see him, one more time,' she requested.

Holding her chair Simon waited for her to rise then offered his arm, and escorted her slowly up the stairs.

A sheet had been placed over Lewis's face and Simon bent slowly forward to remove it, thankful when he noted that someone, presumably the Captain, had closed the sightless eyes.

'He looks so peaceful, younger,' Rosie said, gazing down. 'He was always so kind to me.' She looked steadily into Simon's face so close to her own. 'I feel sad for his loss, yet tears won't come. I know what he has done for me through

221

my life because everyone has told me of it, yet I am unaware of these things, therefore I can feel no pain.' Her tone full of regret, she lifted the sheet and replaced it gently over the kind face. 'I wish with all my heart I had known the Lewis that I have been told about,' she concluded softly.

Simon led her back to the room where she had spent the night. 'Would you like to rest? ' He asked tenderly, 'whilst, we make the necessary arrangements.' She nodded thankfully and left him.

Captain Fisher, with his usual efficiency spent the day organising. Lewis would accompany them to London, where he would be buried with due ceremony surrounded by his friends and extended family. A casket was ordered and provided within hours. A mortician was found to tend to the body, which was enclosed inside. A gun carriage appeared like magic, accompanied by more soldiers and Lewis's casket was secured to it for its safe transportation home.

Simon personally undertook the task of sorting his old friend's papers, surprised to find that Lewis had already tied up most of the loose ends usually left after death.

'He must have known he was in his last days,' he told Rosie later, when they sat together taking a quiet moment away from the hectic activity. 'He left a letter addressed to me and you.'

'How strange,' she murmured, thinking over the last couple of days and the travelling. 'He made no mention of feeling ill, though he was clearly a little uncomfortable.' She recalled how often he had mopped his brow and shuffled his position, stating without complaint that his old bones were not meant for the hard seating. Simon held her hand tenderly as she read. 'He wants to be buried next to his old friend Ninny,' she said softly, looking up from the page.

'She was a black woman, a friend of yours I believe,' he told her. She nodded.

'So I have been told.'

'The captain is aware of this,' Simon looked sad as he told her of the arrangements already considered. 'He is going to look after everything personally.'

'Why didn't he say he was feeling ill?' Rosie questioned, folding the letter in her lap. 'He said he was tired, and he found the air in the carriage stuffy.' She turned confused eyes to him. 'Am I responsible for all of this?'

'No,' Simon cried, drawing her frail frame to his chest. 'Lewis lived to find you. It was the finest triumph of his life that we did. He never lost hope, then or now, we will make his efforts worthwhile. You wait and see. We will clear your name and set you free. You will remember everything one day. I promise,' he whispered into her hair.

Allowing him to hold her in his strong, but gentle embrace, Rosie relaxed against his chest content to believe his words of comfort.

Later, after Rosie had retired for the night, Simon and the Captain had a well-earned drink together and discussed the events of the day.

'Rosie?' the Captain queried.

'Her sorrow is for the fact she has seen the death of someone she hardly knew, and wished she had know better. Her wish would have been for him to live long enough for her to learn to love him the way he so clearly loved her.' Simon told him bluntly.

The Captain nodded his understanding. 'I know another young lady who will feel heart broken at his passing. Have you sent word, or shall I see to it?' he asked.

'Tildy,' Simon cried. 'Oh lord I had forgotten about her. I have sent on to Jake and Molly.'

Swirling the red liquid round in his glass, the Captain promised. 'I will despatch one of my men first thing in the morning. If you would like to write a personal note, I'm sure she will always keep him dear to her heart,' he concluded.

'Thank you, ' Simon raised his glass in salute. 'I've been too worried about Rosie and neglected my duties,' he admonished himself.

'Maybe one day she will remember, then she can mourn properly,' the Captain replied sympathetically.

Taking Lewis's place inside the carriage, Simon sat with his arm around Rosie's shoulder allowing her to lean against his chest as they whiled away the hours to the end of their journey.

'By the look on your face you are happy to be inside the carriage, rather than on your horse,' The Captain muttered in his ear, during a brief stop.

'I am praying the hours would stretch longer,' he responded guiltily. 'I am so happy it feels traitorous to my old friend's memory,' he admitted.

'Don't,' the captain said bluntly. 'It's exactly what Lewis would have wanted to see.'

'This is the last leg of the journey we are approaching the outskirts of London,' Simon murmured tenderly into Rosie's hair watching the afternoon draw to an end.

'You have told, Tildy?' Rosie questioned raising her head, her thoughts suddenly turning to her friend.

'Yes,' he admitted. 'It was the hardest letter I have ever had to write.' With gentle hands he pulled her back to her place against him.

THIRTY ONE

Captain Fisher saluted, then spoke. 'I'm so sorry that it is my unhappy duty to deliver you here, instead of taking you home to your family.' He smiled kindly, his fingers smoothing at his moustache a little nervously. He cast his eyes around the prison hospital before looking back at her. 'You do understand why, don't you?'

'I have a trial to face,' Rosie smiled back at him. 'I'm still in custody after all,' she acknowledged. 'Thank you for making my imprisonment so comfortable,' she studied the floor, then added. 'You have been the perfect jailor.' Standing on tiptoe she reached up and pecked his cheek with her lips, laughing at him when his face turned bright red in front of her.

'I am leaving you in good hands,' he stammered. 'I have a personal acquaintance with this good doctor. You have nothing to fear from him.' He shook the hand of the man that walked up and joined them. 'Ronald Graham,' he said loudly, 'let me introduce you to Rosie Saunderman.' Again he clicked his heels in salute.

'My life has been nothing but doctors lately,' Rosie said with a wry smile as the doctor took her hand. 'How do you do doctor,' she said politely and waited whilst the two men exchanged pleasantries, the doctor turning his attention back to her with a short sigh.

'Somehow I think we are going to be spending a lot of time together, so how about you call me Ron, and I call you Rosie,' he told her grinning.

'I'm not sure I could do that,' she said honestly. 'What if I call you Doctor Ron,' she laughed.

He nodded agreement. 'We have never met young lady,' he told her thoughtfully his buttock resting on the back of a solid wooden chair. 'But I know a great deal about you. Years ago I treated a friend of yours,' His eyes twinkled and his lips twitched with humour. 'As I remember, she drove me mad telling me all about you. She spent most of her recovery badgering me to allow you to come and see her.'

Rosie stared wide, eyed at him. How could she have been so nervous about meeting such a good looking, friendly man, 'you must mean, Molly,' she chuckled thankfully, her pent up muscles relaxing in his presence.

'Well, I can see you two are going to get along famously,' Captain Fisher said with a smile. 'I must take my leave, farewell, I'm sure we will meet again.' He nodded briefly then, turned stiffly and walked away without a backward glance.

'Nice man,' Ron Graham murmured as he led her in the opposite direction. 'Yes I do indeed mean, Molly. The loveliest young woman I have ever had the pleasure of giving away at a wedding. I hope your reunion was worth all those hours of listening?' he dropped a deep wink at her.

Rosie shook her head, noting the laughter creases around the corners of his eyes, somehow she could not think of this man as a doctor. He lacked the officialdom she had learned to expect. 'There never was a reunion,' she confessed sadly, wishing she could remember these things the way he could. 'By the time Molly was released I had been abducted. I have no memory of those days, or these people. I'm afraid I only know Molly by what I have been told of her.'

The doctor paused his walk rubbing at his chin he studied her. 'Come to think of it I already know that someone had run off with you. I seem to remember it was being kept a secret from her. But I wasn't aware of any mind problem at that time.' He pulled papers from the pocket of his hospital coat, and flipped through them.

226

'Not then' Rosie corrected him. 'It is now I have a problem.'

'I'm sorry,' he apologised sincerely. 'I have been so busy I only read the top page. Yes, it's all here.' He took Rosie's arm and began to walk again. 'We will have to ensure your time inside these walls is as productive as possible. I will look into it,' he promised her.

'Thank you, Doctor Ron,' she replied allowing herself to be escorted without fear.

'You have a visitor waiting for you already,' he told her confidentially. 'A very professional man, I am impressed,' he said seriously pulling a wry face, ' Mr Alexander Howell. I hope he does as good a job for you as Lewis Maxwell did for Molly.' He pushed open a door and ushered her into a square visitors room.

Plain and rather austere, the room contained a spindly table and two chairs. Two windows clung to the ceiling, high up the unadorned walls. At the table sat an elegantly dressed man, his stance official, his, welcoming smile kind. Rising he held out his hand. 'Hello, I'm Alex Howell and I'm here to clear your name,' he told her without preamble.

Rosie was also impressed, his personality not only filled the room it had taken command of it. This was a man who would not take guilty as an answer, she felt sure. She smiled and sat opposite him.

'As a start,' the lawyer said in a stern tone. 'If we are to be friends, you will call me Alex.' He looked up at the doctor smiling. 'Don't you agree?'

The doctor laughed and nodded about to take his leave. 'She is a young lady with her own ideas,' he quipped. 'Don't ask me, ask her.'

'I have talked at length with a Doctor Phipps on your behalf,' Alex told her. 'I warn you he specialises in a very new field, psycho analysis, but if anyone can sort out your memory problem he can.' He paused waiting for a response.

Her head held at a tilt she studied him. 'This man, this Dr Phipps, is he part of my defence?' she questioned, there seemed to be so many doctors. 'Why do I need another doctor? What about doctor Ron does he agree with it?' she asked confused. 'He said he knew nothing about my case. Was he jesting?'

'Relaxing you I think,' Alex replied gently. 'He is the prison doctor here to oversee your general health, and it has been deemed that the hospital will be a safer place of custody, than a prison cell. Yes,' he added, 'he agrees. I warn you this new treatment is much ridiculed by conventional medical men. The workings of the mind are still very frightening to many people. He is blunt to the point of rudeness. If he thinks there is something really wrong with your mind he will tell you and recommend an Asylum. But, if on the other hand, he thinks your mind has been tampered with by something outside your control. He's the man to put it right. It's up to you Rosie,' he informed her bluntly. 'If you are prepared to be assessed in that manner, he is prepared to meet you.'

Nervousness filled her innards again as she mulled his words in her mind. 'I don't understand this psycho what-ever, all I do know is I don't want him to use a lot of untried drugs on me. I believe I have suffered enough from that quarter,' she replied tentatively, recalling her experiences of the last weeks. 'But if you believe in him.'

'I believe that he believes everything he says,' Alex answered. 'I can't pretend to understand these things myself. But he does know all that you have already been through at the hands of the clinic. I have explained all about you life with the man you thought was your brother. He has been told how your mind has been juggled with. I trust him. Other than that, I can give you no guarantees,' he said honestly.

Rosie smiled widely. 'In that case I will be happy to see him, Alex. Thank you.'

Alex stood and gazed down at her thoughtfully. 'I will leave you to get some rest. Tomorrow I will return with

William Phipps and we will begin to make a defence for you. Now,' he grimaced comically, 'I will go home to my long-suffering wife. Good night.' He left, walking quietly away down the long hall.

Later, settled in her high-sided bed Rosie closed her eyes and allowed herself to drift. London was proving so much different from the sea and the country and she had not seen any of it yet.

'Was Molly in a room like this?' she asked Ron Graham when he came to check on her night medication.

'Exactly,' he replied, rattling at the plain iron railings, which formed the framework of her bed. 'Sorry about these,' he muttered. 'Rules.'

She shrugged. 'What else would you expect in a prison hospital,' she replied kindly. If Molly had survived it for all the months that she was in custody, so would she.

'Will I be allowed visitors,' she asked quietly as he busied himself about the room, her mind drifting to thoughts of Simon.

The doctor turned, the gas lighting making his face shine and his eyes glitter, he gazed at her. 'If it's a favoured young man then the answers no,' he replied, pulling a woe bygone face. 'I get very jealous of my patients, especially when they are young and pretty,' he joked.

Rosie laughed heartily. She suddenly felt so much better, she was sure she should not feel this happy to be in custody, but she could not help herself. 'Everyone is so kind,' she told him. I am beginning to hold a little hope for my future after all.'

THIRTY TWO

Trumpets blared in a short fanfare. The tall, thin minister took his place at the graveside, indicating with the smallest gesture that he was ready. On his command, Captain Fisher's men lifted Lewis's coffin and shouldered it from the gun carriage to the open grave.

The air was humid and heavy and the small group of doleful mourners stood beside the yawning grave that had once held Ninny alone. Molly wept openly and Jake held her hand silently, his own grief robbing him of words.

The soldiers, resplendent in their scarlet tunics, gently lowered the coffin to the course hessian sacking that would eventually be used to ease it into the ground, already waiting at the graveside. A pure white cloth covered the cask, its edges fluttering with the movement.

The minister intoned the service, adding his own unexpected eulogy to a man none of them had been aware he knew personally. The poignant farewell was a touching time, bringing tears to each and every eye.

'Lewis would have been proud,' Molly whispered. 'It was as well planned as any he could have arranged himself,' she added, blowing her nose and wiping at her wet face.

'He respected the good Captain, and Fisher respected him in return,' Simon responded quietly. 'I for one, appreciate all he has done for us above and beyond the call of duty. He has more than upheld that respect.'

Jake and Molly nodded together.

'Ere, are they going away,' Dora cried,' watching the soldiers march back to the horses patiently waiting beside the empty carriage. 'I wanted to talk to them.' She pouted petulantly, her arms flapping at her sides childishly.

Captain Fisher's barked orders rang about the church-yard. As one the men mounted, turned, and with a clatter of hooves began to retrace their steps along the road. Offering a smart salute and a brief smile, the Captain took his leave and hurried after them.

'They made a few eyes goggle,' Lenny chuckled as he watched the retreat.

'It was fittingly colourful,' Jake agreed, gently pushing Dora in the direction of home. 'Lets get back now,' he told her, 'Lizzie's waiting.'

Grinning briefly Dora did as she was told, linking arms with Lenny to help her along.

'What a pair,' Molly mumbled watching them walk ahead. 'Dora's senility is getting worse, Lizzy is about the only person who can raise anything more than a blank look, and Lenny's leg must be more painful these days, do you see how he's limping?'

Jake and Simon studied the two people ahead of them for a long minute, before Jake replied.

'After all those years of tying his leg up behind him, I'm surprised it hasn't given up on him completely.'

'Listen to me,' Molly half laughed, nudging Simon in the ribs with faint embarrassment. 'I'm a fine one to talk about anyone else limping, when I limp so badly myself.'

'Jake told me why,' Simon replied, his face serious. 'I don't think anyone will ever laugh at your imperfection. And,' he added with a note of reprimand. 'You are only voicing concern for those who are dear to you. If you think Lenny requires medical treatment?'

'Oh no. No, thank you,' Molly cried now completely nonplussed at the turn the conversation was taking. 'We have a very good local doctor. Lenny would not appreciate any of us interfering.'

'That place is rapidly filling with our old friends,' Jake said. Though he had been walking beside his wife and Simon he had taken no note of the conversation. 'Old Sam, Ninny and now Lewis.' He stuck his hands deep in his pockets and strode on, concentrating on his own thoughts.

'Is there anything I can do?' Simon asked Molly, nodding towards Jake.

'No,' she replied smiling sadly. 'Sam, was a very dear friend him and Jake were very close. They had a special understanding that even I will never match. Then Ninny, she began as my friend and companion, but we all loved her dearly, and now Lewis,' she looked up at her earnest young friend, her own pain at their loss written on her face. 'Lewis was like a father to Jake, he not only loved him, he respected him greatly. There will never be another man like him in our lives.'

'When we get back to the Refuge,' Simon said softly. 'Perhaps you would arrange for everyone to gather together. I have Lewis's last wishes and I think it would be better if I read them to everyone at once.'

Molly nodded. 'Give me an hour.'

The private quarters of the Refuge felt crowded, they all sat in silence, each contemplating what they were about to hear. Simon stood, rocking gently on his heels in his hand a sheaf of papers, at his side resting on a tabletop a thick, leather bound tome. He coughed lightly and patted his chest all eyes turned to him, waiting for him to begin.

'These papers represent the final wishes of our friend, Lewis Maxwell. Written during the hours he spent with Rosie on the journey home from the West Country.' He paused and swallowed to clear his throat. 'I believe he knew he was near his end, and typical of the man we all loved, he saw to it that there would be no untidy ends, he has not forgotten any of us.'

Reading the notes diligently he went on. 'He begins by saying how he could never have imagined, that day so long ago, when Molly appeared on his doorstep and offered to return Jacob Ebson to the fold how the two of them would change his life. He will always be grateful to you, my dear,' Simon told her with a smile. 'Grateful for the abundance of love you brought with you, for Jake's return, and for Rosie. He is so proud of what you have achieved, here at the Refuge, and hopes you will continue to grow and prosper with it.'

He turned away from Molly's upturned face, her eyes bright with unshed tears, and looked at Lenny, Dora and Lizzy. 'You my friends,' he said, reading a separate sheet of paper to them. 'Have always shown him warmth and friendship, in return he asks me to see that you have your pick of items in his home. Something personal to remember him, is how he has put it.'

'I've been in his home,' Lenny protested. 'It's full of expensive furnishings and the like. We couldn't take any of those things.'

'You could and you will,' Jake insisted quietly, leaning towards the older man. 'It's Lewis's wish, he wants you too.'

'Ohh...' Dora giggled, and Lizzy smiled, putting out a restraining hand to quieten her down.

'The house itself,' Simon continued. 'Is to go to Rosie. I know, he says, she is a lady of substance now, but he feels it will be a long time before she will be capable of entering that new and strange life. He wishes for her to have enough independence to see her through the months until she can face what is expected of her. There is also a small sum to be administered independently for the twins.' Simon licked his lips. 'In case she never finds herself able to trust again, and can't, or won't, take up her position as regent.'

A murmur rippled around the room then settled again.

'His small country cottage, the home that contained his happiest memories of the short period of time that constituted his marriage, he has left to his latest ally, Tildy. A young woman who proved strong in adversity, a young lady he would have been proud to call a daughter.' He paused expectantly, and looked from face to face. 'If she does not wish to keep it he has asked that I arrange its sale, and advise her on the best investment for the money. First though he would like Tildy, Donald, and little Bethany, to visit and stay a few days there. He adds, they deserve it.'

'You will let her know immediately?' Jake asked, receiving a nod of reply. 'We would also be happy to see her here, at Battersea. Please communicate that to her.'

Simon let out the breath he had not been aware of holding. Thankful that there had been no objections to the proposal.

'Finally,' he turned to Molly. 'The bulk of Lewis's money is to go to the furtherance of the Refuge. He wants to ensure he has a little part of its continuance.' He grinned at the two stunned faces staring at him.

'It's too much,' Molly gasped. 'After all he has already done for us.'

Ignoring her Simon continued with a smirk. 'To my dearest, Molly,' he read. 'I have left a few personal items of my wife's. I have treasured them for years and I know you will too. I can think of no finer neck or arm to grace them, than yours.' Simon leaned down and handed her the note along with his own handkerchief to mop up her silent tears.

'What has he left you, Simon?' Jake asked with concern. 'You were closer to him than any of us in the last couple of years.'

'He knew I had no need of his fortune,' Simon replied softly. 'What he has left me is far more precious. Firstly he has bequeathed me his laboriously scripted notes on our quest.' He placed a hand on the volume on the table. 'If I do no more than look at his copper plate handwriting once in a while, it will give me the greatest pleasure. He has also left me his pocket watch. I'm afraid I teased him every day about its immense proportions and his unconscious habit of looking at it continuously without really seeing it at all.' He sat down quietly waiting for the comments.

'What he has left us is not important,' Molly said with a sniff. 'He was a dear man who will always remain close to our hearts.'

'Well Lizzy, we don't need to worry about going to the market tomorrow, we can afford to feed the hoards again,' Jake quipped, then rose abruptly and left the room.

'Ignore him,' Lenny advised. 'Whenever he gets emotional he always falls back on the old clown humour.'

'I think we all feel the same,' Lizzy remarked gently, rising and taking Dora by the hand prepared to return to her duties. 'He was a lovely man, kind and gentle, and so full of remorse over Rosie. I hope he has found peace at last.'

'Amen,' Simon said softly as he watched them leave the room.

THIRTY THREE

He was not at all what Rosie expected. Her imagination had conjured a man of stature, an impeccably dressed person, who knew his own place in society, and expected everyone else to defer to it. Instead she was confronted by a pleasant enough looking man, who's appearance was nothing less than dishevelled. His clothes so crumpled, she was sure he had slept in them, not once, but regularly.

'Well young woman! What exactly do you think is wrong with you?' His tone was brusque, his manner condescending.

Dr Phipps leaned his hands on the table between them, his body unfolding and elongating, he stretched across to where she sat, his stooped shoulders, hunching in line with her eyes. At this angle his hooked nose looked sharper, and, his pointed chin, which was inches from her face, looked longer. He hissed a string of sharp questions at her.

Bristling at his attitude, Rosie stood up. 'Surely, sir,' she stated curtly. 'You are the person to answer these questions. As far as I am concerned, I am now in good health, with the exception of my memory.'

'Hmm, minds are funny things,' he replied, ignoring her indignant outburst. 'They often imagine things that don't exist.' He muttered whist he walked the small room. 'What do you think your mind is imagining?' he asked suddenly, cavorting and turning to her, his arms waving as though to conjure thoughts from mid-air.

Her eyes fixed firmly on the roll of trouser bunched over his scruffy footwear, Rosie tried to remain calm. 'I have no memory of my childhood, and I am led to believe what memory I have has been falsely planted, is that the information you require?' She sat down again.

'So your mind is imagining nothing?' he persisted, facing her, his hands clasped behind his back, his eyebrow raised in query.

Her voice trembled and she began to doubt herself. Rosie stood again and almost shouted at him. 'If you think I wish to be here facing murder charges. Then you are wrong.' Emotional anger shook her body.

Waving her back into her seat he sat opposite and spoke more gently. 'Don't get upset. For me to unlock your brain I am going to have to ask many questions you will not like. Have you heard of hypnosis?'

Rosie shook a helpless head, looking across the room at Doctor Ron sitting quietly in the corner. He stood and came to her side, patting her hand.

'You will come to no harm,' he said softly. 'Just answer as best you can, I will always be here to monitor the visits.'

Vaguely thinking how often people absently patted her hand in the manner of a helpless child, Rosie briefly smiled her thanks.

The first meeting of the eminent Dr Phipps and his young patient ended abruptly, as it had begun. With a terse promise to return the next day, he left her a little bewildered, and somewhat frightened.

'Will he always be like that?' she asked nervously.

'I'm sure you will get used to him,' Doctor Ron promised. 'The first meeting is always the worst.'

Rosie was not so sure.

So began a regular routine that made the days fly by. Alex, busy with his delaying tactics for her trial. Dr Ron overseeing her general state of health and Dr Phipps badgering her to recall the tiniest detail. The only light relief a weekly visit from Jake.

He always arrived with long, chatty letters from Molly and Harriett holding news of her children's progress.

'I miss them so much,' she told him after they had laughed about Nancy's wobbly efforts to stand. 'I miss you all. How is Simon?'

'He's fine, and just like the rest of us misses you. He would love to visit, but.' Jake shrugged he had been warned, one visitor only for thirty minutes, once a week, classed as a dangerous prisoner Rosie was allowed few privileges.

'How is your treatment progressing?' he asked eager to know every detail.

Rosie laughed. 'Doctor Ron knows more about my childhood than I do. Molly must have almost talked him to death about me.'

'They got on very well,' Jake recalled, a cloud passing over his face. 'We are all praying that everything will turn out as well, for you.'

'I am improving,' she assured him. 'And Dr Phipps no longer frightens me with his harsh manner. In fact, I have quite warmed to him. If he weren't such a dedicated man, he would make a wonderful husband and father.'

'For whom?' Jake queried cocking his head to one side.

'Oh, not me,' Rosie laughed.

'So what have you remembered this week?' he asked seriously.

'I remember Raymond,' she told him softly. 'It's funny, although I know the truth, I still feel that I had a brother. I know Robert was no such thing, and now I recall knowing him as Raymond it's even more confusing. I remember him taking me out to tea, in a little old world teashop when I was very young. Its all mixed up in my head, but I am assured it will sort itself out.'

Jake jumped up and hugged her. 'Darling I'm so pleased,' he gushed over her. 'Just wait until I tell Molly.'

'I used to have a sort of waking dream,' she told him in a far away voice, her eyes misting with memory. 'I used to see a little girl dancing, in a bonnet with long blue ribbons. It often came to me when I looked in a mirror. Now I know it was, me. We lived by the river,' she reached out and took Jake's hand. 'You and Molly bought me the bonnet. Sam said I looked like a princess. I loved Sam,' she stated innocently, with conviction.

Jake almost whooped with joy.

'Dr Phipps has also explained about Robert,' she added, a frown creasing her brow.

'Robert?' Jake questioned. 'Oh Edward.'

'Yes, I have been unable to understand why, if he was so rich, did he choose to live in squalor. Why did he tell me those awful stories about our parents being killed.' She traced a pattern on the table with her fingertip. 'All those things he told me we owned he really did have. Rich parents, a big mansion and his mother did die. The doctor explained he could manipulate my mind, but could not control his own, he was two people, inside one body. One got real pleasure from inflicting pain on others, the other wanted his rich lifestyle desperately, but thought that by turning his back on it he was punishing those that loved him.' She smiled regretfully. 'He probably felt they had all let him down in his lifetime. However much love he got, it was never enough.'

'And that's why he took you,' Jake replied sadly, her air of vulnerability touching him deeply. 'He saw a mind that could be manipulated to animal like devotion. Someone who would allow herself to be treated however he wanted, and still love him to distraction.'

'I certainly did that,' Rosie replied with a long, heart felt sigh.

'True,' Jake admitted. 'But not by choice.'

Rosie nodded slowly. 'No that was his biggest problem, he had to work hard to make it happen at all,' she informed him with pride at her new found confidence. 'Then, the doctor believes, I would confound him by recalling something I should not, he would have to back track and

239

criss-cross, to achieve his goal. That's why it has been so difficult to recover any part of my memory. It must have frustrated his own mind too, and coloured his behaviour.'

'Was that why he wanted to have children,' Jake mused. 'So they would love him naturally without his help.'

'Maybe,' she answered, with a downward curve of her lips. 'Though, I'm not convinced that children were ever part of his plan.'

'So that's why he rejected them?' Jake wondered.

'Possibly, the good half of him knew he had committed a sin his own mind was doing battle with itself. It was easier for him to make out they belonged to someone else.'

Jake whistled low. 'You have improved. I'm impressed.

THIRTY FOUR

Trial day dawned bright and fresh. The hopeful members of Rosie's extended family huddled together in a little block, dwarfed by the imposingly high domed hallway of the London Court House.

Tildy, Donald her husband and little Bethany had arrived the previous week. Simon had taken them at once to the timber- framed cottage in its serene setting, on the outskirts of London. As Lewis had hoped they had fallen in love with it on sight. Neither felt inclined to dispose of the property.

'I'm so glad you are not going to sell the cottage,' Molly murmured in a near whisper, her words echoing above her head. 'Lewis would be so pleased.'

Tildy, who's arm linked Molly's, whispered back. 'Simon is going to find us a suitable tenant for a year or two, after that maybe we will decide to live in it ourselves. We are people of substance now.' Her words brought a smile then, she added a little more seriously. 'I couldn't consider doing so whilst my mother is alive.'

'Quite,' Molly replied, watching Alex Howell stride confidently to their sides.

'I'm glad you are all here in good time.' He spoke in normal tones ignoring the echo as he continued. 'There are a few points I wish to run over with you.' Leading them off to a sizeable anti-room he introduced a man already waiting inside.

'Everyone, please meet Dr Phipps.' He stood back allowing the main members to shake hands with the doctor.

241

Dr Phipps looked no less crumpled for his day in court than he did when he attended Rosie at the prison hospital.

'How is Rosie?' Molly asked, her eyes ranging over the manic figure before her.

'Much improved from those early days,' he replied, running a hand through his unruly mop of hair, which he had clearly endeavoured to grease into place. Removing his hand from his head he studied his palm, now slick and shiny with oil. After a second or two of deliberation he carelessly wiped the hand down the side of his trousers.

'Does that mean she is cured?' Tildy asked.

'Not at all,' he barked his reply. 'I said she is improved. You will no doubt notice a difference. ' His look reproved her as though she were a silly child.

'How do you expect your testimony to be received?' Jake asked impatiently, recalling many of the things Rosie had said about him. If he were not impressed with the man's manner, how would the court feel?

Absently the doctor ran his hand through his hair again. 'Maybe not well,' he admitted studying his palm again. 'I have no idea how modern judges feel. The very idea of mind control or the mind acting as two people frightens others. Mostly they don't wish to believe such things, so denial comes easy.' He wiped his hand on his clothing once more. 'We can only put forward our ideas and hope.'

Jake and Simon looked at each other, they both looked at Alexander. Reading their minds he replied.

'We have a long line up of witnesses that will come first. Hopefully the jury will already be convinced of her innocence early in the proceedings. The doctor here, will be putting the finer points on what will have already been heard.'

'We must trust you, you're the expert,' Simon said, if his tone sounded dubious nobody commented on it.

The courthouse was cool and quiet. Several of the court dignitary's were in place prior to the general public being allowed to file in, which they did in an orderly manner.

242

'It's a far cry from the Dartmouth court I attended with Lewis,' Tildy whispered to anyone that could hear her. 'This room feels almost sacred,' she added thankfully.

The shuffle of feet, the occasional scrape of a chair here and there a cough, were the only noises to be heard. At last the gavel was banged and everyone stood to watch the judge in his snowy white wig, emerge from a side door. Before they sat, another door opened and Rosie was led in flanked by two officers, this time she was well dressed and looked wide awake and alert.

A flicker of a smile crossed her face when she saw the people she knew gathered together, sitting in the centre of the court.

Formalities were observed, a couple of the juror's question, then with a nod from each legal representative the trial began.

What followed for the rest of the day was a prosecution parade of one witness after another, it became tedious repetition. It also caused more than a little concern to the family waiting patiently for Alexander to begin his defence.

Choosing not to take up the option of cross questioning any of the witnesses that had so far described in lurid detail, many of the murders on the list against Rosie. Simon began to wonder if indeed they had secured themselves the right man. In undertones he said as much to Jake.

'He will hear exactly how we feel as soon as this days proceeding are over,' Jake hissed in return.

'We have listened all day to a lot of people talking of death and destruction,' Jake almost shouted at the lawyer, when they pushed their way out of the court. ' None of which bodes well for Rosie.'

'When, are you going to say something in her defence?' Simon joined the argument.

Placing a hand on a shoulder of each man, Alexander replied quietly. 'Be patient. Wait, it will change.'

'We must trust the man,' Molly begged her husband.

243

'Yes,' Tildy added. 'Give him a day or two before you think of dismissing him.'

The following morning brought more of the same. Not only Jake and the family the court itself was getting restless. Descriptions of brutal killing no longer wrought absolute silence. Coughs, shuffles and mutterings now interrupted the proceedings.

Rosie sat demurely throughout the day. Twice the judge asked if she felt well enough to continue. She had politely declined his offer to recess and allow her to rest. A small smile could be seen playing on Alexander's lips.

'She is having a greater affect on everyone in this court than all the tawdry evidence they can produce,' he assured them during a break in proceedings. 'Look at her, poised and polite, showing just the merest hint of fear, not a soul in this room would believe her capable of the smallest of these crimes.'

The day ended and Rosie was led away. Again Jake rounded on their legal representative. 'Why have you allowed another day to go by in this fashion,' he cried.

'Tomorrow' Alexander promised. 'I have purposely allowed them to bore the jury with the tedium of the case. Now they have the official version clearly imprinted on their minds. We can start overlaying it with impossibilities. Did you not notice each and every one of those good men, studying Rosie's small frame as some of the details were described. They already doubt she could have taken any active part in any of it.'

'I appreciate what you are saying,' Tildy acknowledged. 'I too have been watching the men of the jury. But surely it would have been better to take each case one at a time.'

'The witnesses will still be here tomorrow for Alex to recall,' Simon cried, seeing the light at last. 'Clever strategy old boy.'

Turning to join a colleague, Alexander spoke directly to Tildy. 'We will have plenty of time and opportunity, you see.' Raising an arm in salute he left them.

The prosecution rested its case at the beginning of the third day the lawyer parading about the courtroom in a most unseemly manner whilst he gave a brief summing up of details. Then Alexander stood, still and erect, he studied the court in silence giving them time to observe his confident air, giving them unspoken assurance that he would not be strutting about the room waving his arms melodramatically in the air before them, as his predecessor had done. Then he began.

'I call Molly Ebson.'

Molly nervously took her place and went through the ritual of allegiance to her Monarch.

'Molly, I know my colleague has already asked you, but can I take you back again to the days in Jerome Benson's mansion. You have told us how you worked there and what you did.' He gazed at the jurors almost daring them to deny the fact that they, had never thought about, if not actually used a whorehouse at some time in their lives. 'Could you just give us again your description of the young gallant you say this Benson fellow sold the child that was murdered too.'

Molly swallowed nervously. She had never stood trial for the murder of Jerome Benson, and feared openly that it would all come to light again. It was so long ago and it had all been so tragic. This was the first crime that Rosie was charged with, not the child's murder, but collusion too it. In a small voice she repeated her description of the young nobleman.

'How long before this night of the child's murder had Rosie and her companion Nancy, left the Mansion?'

'About two years sir,' she replied her voice trembling dangerously.

'Did she ever return to the Mansion?' Alex barked at her.

'No sir.'

'How old was she when she left?'

'About five years old sir,'

'So on the night of the murder, she would have been about seven years of age?'

A titter ran round the court almost drowning Molly's 'Yes sir,'

'The night of the child's murder was also the night that Jerome Benson was stabbed to death, was it not.'

Molly's hands twisted in her lap. Jerome Benson was the second murder on Rosie's list. 'Yes sir.' Molly had offered to admit to the crime if it would save Rosie, Alex had scoffed in return, telling her to keep quiet.

'Would Rosie here,' he extended his arm to his client, 'have grown any older between these two murders.'

'No sir.'

This time the court laughed openly.

'Thank you Molly, no more questions,' Alex smiled warmly as she retreated from the room. 'I would like to call my second witness, Mrs Abel Gimlet.'

A much older, more stooped woman, than Simon remembered came and took her seat, responding to the legalities of the court in a quiet voice.

'Mrs Gimlet, do you recognise this young lady,' again he pointed to Rosie.

Mrs Gee peered across the room and smiled widely, receiving a similar smile of recognition from Rosie.

'I do sir, that there's Rosemary. I knew her well when she was a young girl.'

'Tell us a little about her, be brief,' he warned as the judge eyed him. 'Just let the court know what you knew.'

Doing as she was told, Mrs Gee gave a short, succinct speech about Rosemary and her brother Robert, and all she had been led to believe about them.'

'Do you still believe the story of her upbringing?' Alexander asked.

'No sir, I never believed it then. I knew he were covering up something.'

'At that time in your town a prostitute and her child died, is that correct?'

'Yes sir, but it weren't Rosemary that did it, her were only about ten or eleven years old then. Added to which, all the time she lived with me an' my Abel she were poorly, and I never let her out o' me sight.'

Again the court chuckled.

'In what way poorly?'

'Her mind sir,' the good woman repeated. 'Like I said when she arrived she had lost her memory, and it had gone again just before she left.'

'How long before she left?'

'Two or three weeks as I recalls,' she told him.

'One last question,' Alexander said firmly. 'In your opinion, who did commit these murders?' He knew well that these were two more on Rosie's list.

'Oh he did, sir. Him that called himself Robert.'

The prosecution lawyer jumped up crying his objections and waving his arms like a demented creature.

'Sit down.' The voice of the judge boomed through the room. 'Thank you,' he said, turning to Mrs Gee. 'If there are no further questions,' he looked at Alex, who shook his head. 'You may leave,' the judge told her kindly.

At a wave from Simon she joined the group and sat stiffly beside him.

The afternoon came to an end all too soon, Alexander cross examined many of the previous witnesses, cutting much of their evidence to shreds with his insistent questioning. The vital points he was scoring all adding up to an impressive total.

'Mrs Gimlet, I'm so happy to see you again,' Simon cried as they left the court and he hugged the frail figure. 'Why wasn't I told you were coming. I could have made arrangements for your journey. How is Abel?'

'He passed over sir, a blessed relief from his suffering,' she said in a quiet voice. 'He never got over the loss of the bairn. He would be so happy to see her all grown up, and so lovely.'

Simon introduced her to each of them in turn. His last communication with the Gimlets had been to tell them of Lewis's death, he had not received, or expected a reply.

'I only arrived this morning,' she told everyone in answer to the questions fired at her.

'You must at least be my personal guest for the duration of your stay,' Simon insisted, refusing to take no for an answer.

Molly clutched at the woman's weathered old hand. 'You must come to Battersea and tell us all about the time that Rosie spent with you. Please,' she turned to Simon for his help.

'I will bring her along this evening, if you're not too tired?' he questioned, turning to his guest.

'I would love too,' Mrs Gee, replied with feeling.

After an evening of emotional news on all sides, everyone felt much happier about the way the trial, was proceeding.

Tildy was called as first witness the following morning.

'You knew the defendant as a work colleague I believe,' Alex asked for his opening question.

'Yes,' Tildy nodded. 'We were seamstresses together, at Madame Mildred's. Rosemary, as I knew her then, lived in the apartment about the workshop.'

'You became firm friends?'

'We did. I liked her and felt her to be poorly treated by the man known as her brother.'

'Did you like this man?'

'No sir.'

Alexander led her through a series of questions designed to highlight the mans worse points, asking about the times when Rosie told her of Roberts fighting. The times when he came home with torn, or blood stained clothing.

'Why did you never encourage your friend to go to the police about her brothers behaviour?'

'We often discussed him, but neither of us thought it to be any more than his bad temper getting him into fights,' she replied honestly.

'The last time you saw this young woman during that period of time, she had been the victim of his temper, is that correct?'

'Yes sir.'

'Would you tell this court, in your own words, what happened that morning?'

Quietly and clearly Tildy did as she was told, noting the understanding smiles around the room as she told her tale.

'Would you say this man was of exceptional build, he seems to have been capable of many unexpected deeds?'

'No sir, in fact his stature was not particularly large at all. It was his temper that leant him his strength, at those times he was capable of anything.'

Dr Phipps followed her to the seat and took his oath.

Alexander wasted no time on frivolities with the doctor, keeping his questioning to medical matters only. Dispensing with the years served in general practice he went on to ask about his present chosen field.

'I specialise in the vagaries of the mind.'

'Tell us exactly what that means?' Alexander requested.

'I deal with people who have troubles that range from simple loss of memory, an accident, bump on the head, that sort of thing, to serious head injury that require them to relearn the everyday skills of living.' He nodded about the room, stroking his chin in his cupped hand. 'People who have unexplained noises in their heads, or those with a double personality.' He shrugged as he heard the low rumble of noise that met his words. It was an everyday thing to him. He did not understand the gasp that rippled around the room.

'Double personality?' the judge queried, looking sceptically at the witness.

'People who battle inwardly with two selves,' he told the judge calmly and evenly. 'A mild mannered person who is given to sudden and unexpected bursts of temper. Maybe someone that has led an honest and blameless life, then suddenly does something shocking to bring shame on the family. That's what I mean.'

The judge's, 'ahh…' was heart felt.

'In the course of your work do you deal with hypnosis?' Alexander asked, taking the questioning back again.

'Many times,' the doctor replied curtly.

'You are both familiar and comfortable with it?'

The doctor nodded and stated a simple 'yes.'

'Perhaps you would tell us if you have examined the defendant, and what the medical finding were?'

The doctor looked from Alex to the judge, who nodded affably for him to continue.

'In the beginning her health was poor, her body physically exhausted from many years of under nourishment and scared from years of mistreatment.' He intoned these facts, which he had learned from her other medical advisor. 'She had spent several months being treated with drugs, known and unknown.' He went on to describe some of the horrors she would have suffered at the hands of the Dartmouth Clinic, his anger visibly heightening as his tale unfolded.

'When, in your opinion was she last in full health?' the judge intervened, again waving aside the prosecutions objections.

'She was thin, underweight for her height and framework, undernourished and overworked, three to four years in my opinion.' He looked squarely at the judge as he spoke. 'Her body bears scares some of which she can not account for, others, the explanation is to say the least disturbing.'

All eyes had turned to Rosie, who cast her eyes to the ground in embarrassment, memories of what happened to her making it impossible to look anyone in the face.

'How has her mental state held up under all this?' the judge asked sympathetically.

'Mentally she has always been quite alert. What has been done to her mind is from outside sources, not of her making,' the doctor stated bluntly.

Looking about him the judge asked a court official if the scars mentioned had been documented. Walking slowly across the room, Alexander handed a separate sheaf of papers directly into the judge's hand, making his slow return to his place and waiting in silence as they were read. Finally a brief nod restarted the proceedings.

'In your opinion doctor, was the defendant mentally disturbed when you first met her?' Alex stared at the jury as he asked the question.

'Not at all.' Dr Phipps replied in a firm tone.

'Is she mentally disturbed now?'

'No, perplexed at her lack of memory from her child-hood, otherwise she has no difficulty with her everyday living,' the doctor replied confidently.

'Does the defendant have a memory now?'

'Some,' he replied, flashing a smile in Rosie's direction, and nodding insistently. 'She is slowly putting the missing parts of her life back together.'

'What explanation do you have for her memory loss?'

'Her mind had been manipulated by an inexpert showman. Someone, who's, skills have been learned from a stage artist. He could place his victim in a trance, the difficulty being the instruction then given to the mind. They have not been clear or concise, causing extra conflict to the brain.'

'Pray give us an example?' the judge requested.

'In a stage show,' the doctor began, turning directly to the judge. 'It is simple directions, crawl like an animal, bark like a dog, simple and clear. In the defendants case the requirement has been lengthy and complicated. Old beliefs would have to be overlaid with new instruction. Therefore he would have criss-crossed himself with many confusing suggestions. Rather like walking in a maze,' he said with sudden inspiration. 'Each avenue would have to be successfully blocked before another could be created. In this he failed miserably.'

'Who, in your opinion, did all this mind juggling?' Alexander asked pointedly.

'Oh without a doubt, the man she believed to be her brother. Edward Saunderman.'

'Would he have found it necessary to keep topping up this procedure?' Alexander asked, turning his back on the doctor and gazing intently at the jury.

'I believe he found it necessary to exert his will over her at every opportunity. He would have too plug the holes that appeared constantly.' The doctor gave a satisfied lift of his shoulders and nodded his head enthusiastically.

'So,' Alexander went on, his eyes still on the jury. 'Any action at all, even her everyday chores, would have been manipulated by this person. The defendant would never have been responsible for her own actions?'

'I believe she would have been responsible for nothing,' the doctor replied confidently.

Uproar suddenly broke out in the court. Chairs scraped as people stood and shouted at the officials. The gavel banged again and again slowly quieting the hubbub. Standing, the judge called both lawyers to his side. Instructing that the jury be led from court, he turned and followed. The two bemused lawyers in his wake.

Rosie remained between her jailors, stoically sitting as upright as possible, her eyes seeking and exchanging brief messages with her family. Bouts of coughing overtook the waiting crowd, they shuffled in their seats, the murmur of voices rising and falling in undertones. The doors opened and the jurors were led back to their places.

The gavel banged, judge and lawyers returned to their places. The judge began to speak.

'I have sat here for almost a week listening to the evidence. It has, during that time, become abundantly clear to me, that there is in fact no case to answer.'

Stunned silence shrouded the room. No breath could be heard as he continued.

'What say you members of the jury?'

Standing the man selected to speak for them all, nodded his agreement.

The judge spoke again. 'It seems this young lady would have required to start her life of crime at the tender age of six or seven years, continuing a stream of brutal murders which, neither her physical capabilities nor, her mental state would have allowed. I am not conversant with the matter of the mind, but I have taken up other opinions on what the doctor has said in this room. I agree, the defendant has been subjected to unhealthy manipulation, for which, she should be made to suffer no more.'

Pandemonium greeted his words. Wave after wave of cheering rang through the room as order was again restored, with difficulty.

'Young lady,' the judge said turning to speak to Rosie direct. 'I believe you have already suffered greatly at the hands of others. Not only Edward Saunderman, but at our hands in the name of justice. I cannot make reparation for that fact, I can only give you your freedom and pray to God on your behalf, that you never again suffer this way.' The gavel banged once more, the judge rose and left the room.

Simon leapt a chair to reach Rosie's side, as she sat, totally bewildered by the proceedings. Suddenly she found herself surrounded by so many people, all hugging and kissing her, laughing and crying in equal measure.

Simon grabbed Alexander's hand and enthusiastically shook his arm up and down. 'You did it, you did it,' he cried beside himself with joy.

Separating herself from the group, Rosie clasped Mrs Gee. 'Is the sea still as beautiful in the summer? Does the wind still howl in the winter?' then added more softly. 'I'm so sorry about Abel. I loved him too, you know. Alex told me,' she added in response to the woman's raised eyebrow.

'The bairn, the bairn, she remembers,' Mrs Gee laughed and cried as she hugged her back.

'Tildy it's so lovely to see you again,' Rosie said smiling at her friend, Then placing her arms around Molly's neck she cried hot tears.

'I'm so sorry Molly, sorry that I caused you so much pain. Thank you for sticking by me all these years,' she sobbed.

Prying them apart Simon led them outside into the fresh air.

'You have worked miracles,' Molly told Dr Phipps, as she mopped at her eyes.

Shaking his long head, he replied in his usual manner. 'It's only a question of finding the right key. We are not completed yet.' He looked at Rosie enquiringly. 'I trust that we still have a lot of work to do.'

Nodding, speechless, Rosie agreed.

'Good,' he said and stomped away.

All talking at once the group gathered together to make their way back to Battersea. Simon with his usual diplomacy made the travelling arrangement, for what he knew would be the start of the finest celebration Battersea had ever seen.

Rosie Again

THIRTY FIVE

Dora sat like a shapeless, sack of potatoes a guileless smile adorning her toothless face, her hand clutching Rosie's, they watched the children at play.

'Emily is such a bossy one,' Molly chuckled, 'I'm sure I don't know who she takes after.'

Rosie did not reply, instead she continued to feast her eyes on the sight of her twins. A sight she never seemed to get enough of. They toddled and played, happily accepting Emily's bossy organisation.

'I knew this garden,' she said softly. 'Back on the moor, every time I looked at the back yard it reminded me of a similar, enclosed area that was being turned into a garden. It was here.' She looked at Molly for understanding. 'My memory was there all the time just hidden.'

Molly nodded absently. 'I can't understand all that happened to you,' she replied quietly. 'But I do remember those early days, here at the Refuge, when you were only a girl. You, and Lenny and Dora did most of the work out here. Jake said it was good therapy for all of you, after Sam died. Now it all grows on its own we put in very little effort to keep it looking colourful.'

Rosie looked from her children to Dora and listened to the old woman's breathing as it wheezed and whistled in her chest. 'When I first came to Jake, Dora was like a mother to me,' she said tenderly, chaffing at the old hand gripping her fingers so tightly. 'I fell asleep almost every night with my head on her knee. It's such a shame to see her this way.' Her face clouded with sorrow. 'She seemed so old to me then, yet after all this time her body has not changed so much.'

'Unfortunately,' Molly acknowledged. 'Her brain has let her down, she has gone backwards and become childlike, harmless, loving and incapable of serious thought.'

'The children don't seem to mind,' Rosie said, laughing at Daniel's antics as he chased his sister. 'They treat her better than we do, they include her in most of their games.'

'Children don't judge others they accept.' Molly replied. 'To them Dora is a child, simply larger than they are.'

Dora giggled as though she knew she were the subject of the conversation. 'You ain't half quiet,' she mumbled looking at Rosie, her eyes suddenly clear and lucid. 'Are yer' going to marry that young man?'

Shocked Rosie tore her face away from Dora and looked at Molly her mouth opening emitting no sound. 'Do you mean Simon?' she questioned with difficulty. 'He's only a friend.'

'He loves yer' though,' Dora replied with a brief smile before her features slid back to they're normal vacant state.

Stunned, Molly leaned forward and waved a hand in front of the old woman's face. Dora looked blankly past her. 'I've never known her do anything like that before,' she stated in disbelief. 'How strange.'

Rosie shivered she felt that Dora must have been reading her mind, which had been thinking of Simon at the time. She herself, was not aware of any love from him, though he was a constant companion whom she had come to rely on greatly, and she was still pondering her own feelings. Staring stupidly at the woman's fat, slack face she began to wonder if they had imagined the incident.

'You've blushed a pretty pink,' Molly informed her. 'And I do agree Simon is madly in love with you. How do you feel about him?'

Again Rosie opened and closed her mouth, the heat from the blush deepening. 'I don't know,' she admitted. 'Maybe

257

what I feel is love, but I'm not capable of placing my trust in anyone, not yet. Then again the thought of not seeing him,' she allowed her words to trail away, her shoulders lifting in a tiny shrug.

'He's a patient man, let things take their course,' Molly advised, looking up as Harriett arrived to supervise the children.

'Are you feeling ill?' she questioned Rosie, looking at her with concern. 'You're very flushed.'

Laughing, the tension easing instantly, Rosie turned and hugged the old figure of Dora next to her. 'Yes,' she replied gaily. 'It's our Dora she's been making improper suggestions.'

'She understands more than most of us think,' Harriett said softly, touching the woman's hand lightly. 'You're not as stupid as they make out, are you?' she said, stroking a finger down the side of Dora's face receiving a beaming smile in reply.

Rosie watched as the red headed girl walked away, a twin held firmly in each hand, Emily skipping by her side. 'I'm so glad she has no urge to return home,' she said more to herself than Molly.

'I can understand that,' Molly replied with feeling. 'She is wonderful with everyone, not only the children, she keeps a few adults in their place as well.'

They laughed and Molly rose to go about her own duties raising a silent eyebrow to question Rosie on her intentions.

'I'll sit her with Dora a few more minutes,' she replied, looking kindly at her old friend. 'I'll join you shortly.'

Silence fell and Rosie turned her thoughts to her children again. Nancy was so bonny and sweet natured. It was Daniel that she worried about most. He was inclined to be truculent, hard to please, always tearful, requiring more attention than he was due. No, she corrected herself, not requiring, demanding was more the right word. She worried about him, tried to shut her mind to how much he reminded her of Robert. He could also be charmed out of his sullen moods in much the same way his father could. Yes, she had to acknowledge, even in his best of tempers he was never as sunny as his sister.

Rising and helping Dora to her feet she walked slowly at the old woman's pace, to the corner of the garden set aside in memory of Ninny and Lewis. The wooden bench, which the pair had sat on so often, was now rose covered. The flowers being encouraged to twine their stems between the latticework of the wood, the small plaque placed at Lewis's request in memory of Ninny, now joined by one that Molly had commissioned in his memory. He would never see either of them.

With difficulty Rosie tried to picture them. She could vaguely recall Ninny, a plump black woman, with a strange lilting speech. She had apparently grown so thin in her old age she could not imagine that. Lewis she knew as the loving, friendly face that spent so long at her bedside.

'Yer' knows yer' should be leaving,' Dora stated, in matter of fact tones that rooted Rosie to the spot.

'Yer' need a fresh start.'

Rosie turned to look at her friend only to see the empty gaze of the old woman staring at the rose covered seat.

'Dora,' she said softly, placing her hands on the old shoulders and turning her so they faced each other. 'Speak to me, repeat what you have just said, please?'

Dora's mouth stretched in a toothless grin her expression unchanged, 'dinner,' was all she said.

'Yes dear, it's dinner time,' Rosie replied with a sigh of resignation. She would ask the doctor about these flashes of clarity that Dora seemed to suffer, on their next weekly meeting. He would help her to understand.

Deep in thought she led the way back inside, and sat Dora's plump body in a chair at the table. Suddenly she felt she had a lot to think about. She would contact Simon he would discuss the problem with her. Maybe, he would take her to look at Lewis's town house, which was now hers.

Perhaps Dora was right perhaps it was time she considered making the property her own.

Her mind slipped back to the day only weeks before when Simon had taken her to see the country cottage that had been left to Tildy. It had been a lovely warm sunny day they had laughed so much. She breathed deeply and could almost smell the honey-suckle, which graced the cottage door. They had gone there to welcome the middle aged couple that had agreed to take the tenancy, and would be moving in almost immediately. She had liked the people a Mr and Mrs Loveday and written at length to tell Tildy all about them. The timber-framed cottage, nestling in front of a small copse, had left a lasting memory with her. Suddenly she could not wait to move her life onwards. She wanted the town house to be as warm and welcoming as that cottage had been.

She had delighted in painting a pen portrait of the cottage the way it looked in the early autumn sun, and promised Tildy she would visit again each season to let her know of the changes. Tildy was so happy to be, as Simon had termed it, a woman of substance, especially now that Bethany had a new baby brother, Michael. We must never loose touch Rosie had written and meant it. For now that meant letters, lots and lots of them, but one day when Tildy was free to move, they would live in close proximity to each other then they could renew all their old ties personally.

THIRTY SIX

Gazing upwards, Rosie studied the gas lamp hanging from the ceiling. 'When I was a child I thought that to be enormous,' she said pointing it out to Simon. 'I used to worry that it would fall off the ceiling on top of us,' she confided with a chuckle.

'Well, how do you feel about this as your new home?' Simon asked tentatively. 'You know you could move straight into the Berwick estate, it is all waiting for you.'

Her eyes wide with horror at the thought, Rosie shook her head. 'I'm not ready for that. I'm not entirely sure I'm ready to move in here, but I know I must start making a new life, and this is as good a start as any,' she assured him.

'Is Harriett moving with you, or do you need a new nurse?' he questioned, his disappointment showing despite his efforts to smother it.

'Thankfully, yes,' Rosie told him, as she wandered from room to room. 'I will need other staff, but the house is not large, they will have to live out.'

'I trust you will allow me to be of service,' he requested, following close at her heels. 'What about refurbishments?'

She picked an ornament from the wide mantle over the open fireplace, turning it in her fingers as she spoke. 'Lewis had excellent taste, there is very little I wish to change.'

'So when will you move in?' he questioned.

'At once,' she replied grinning.

The days flew by as moving arrangements were made. Despite her earlier protestations that little or nothing was needed for her new home, Rosie found herself in a flurry of shopping sprees. Once Molly had taken charge of the organisation there had been no stopping her. Looking round her home as she waited for her guests to arrive Rosie had to agree, Molly had been right. The décor had been too masculine. It was so much softer now, charming and welcoming.

Extending her hands to the blaze of the fire she shivered a little, this would be her first attempt at entertaining, though she knew her guests all loved her dearly she still felt nervous about the outcome. If it went well she had plans to entertain on a regular basis. There were lots of people she still knew she owed that personal thank you, and now she was stronger in mind and body it was time she did something about it.

'You should be congratulated on your choice of cook,' Jake said with satisfaction, his hand patting his expanding waistline, his feet extended to the flickering flames of the fire as he relaxed in the armchair.

Rosie laughed at him. 'You know well the choice of my cook was nothing to do with me. It was all your wife's doing,' she chuckled, pleased that the meal had been such a success.

'Well.' Simon lifted his freshly made coffee to his lips and sipped before making his comment. 'Whoever is responsible for the cook, I haven't enjoyed such a good meal for a long time.'

'This move has been good for you,' Molly told her. 'I wasn't sure you were ready but you look so well and happy.'

Rosie nodded she did feel in good spirit. 'It's thanks to Dora really,' she told them, laughing as their collective voices questioned her words. She went on to tell them of her afternoon in the Refuge garden, only leaving out the reference to Simon and love.

'Blow me,' Jake responded. 'There's more to that old woman than we know.'

'I believe you made a visit to Daniel's family home,' Molly said, changing the subject and looking from her hostess to Simon, and back again. 'What did you think of it?'

'Huge,' Rosie replied with awe. 'There is so much of it. The house is so large I would never find my way around it, or the grounds. They go on for as far as the eye could see.' She turned a flushed excited face to Simon. 'It was a wonderful day out and one day Daniel is going to be so lucky to live there, but.'

Simon nodded understandingly. 'It does take your breath away the first time you see it. Unfortunately,' he added, his cheerful look changing, his tone falling serious. 'I have some news that you may not consider good.' He turned to Jake. 'I was hoping Rosie would fall in love with the place when she saw it and want to move straight in, unfortunately not so.'

'Good God, man, what are you waffling about?' Jake cried. 'I'm getting worried, say what you have to say, put us out of our misery.'

'Estate affairs require me to take ship to Spain. If Rosie had moved to the estate, we could have made the trip together.' He looked at his feet, which, shuffled on the carpet. 'I will be leaving in a couple of weeks,' he stated bluntly.

'Oh my,' Molly squeaked, her hand flying to her throat.

'How long will you be gone?' Jake questioned, amazement lighting up his face. 'Why Spain?'

'I'll be gone about a year. A long time ago my father acquired land and properties out there, apparently they have been neglected, the Spanish authorities require action to be taken.' Simon admitted looking at Rosie. 'I was going to ask you Jake, if you would oversee things again for me?'

'So your father was a traveller?' Molly queried.

Simon shook his head. 'Never left the estate,' he assured her. ' These properties were given through favours done for a royal personage.' He looked a little sheepishly at the assembled gathering making no further reference to what the favours incurred.

263

Warming to the subject, Jake launched into a question and answer conversation about what would be expected of him. Molly interrupted occasionally to glean her own news, only Rosie sat in silence her heart hammering at the thought of his leaving, her spirit deflated and crushed by the news.

'You will miss Simon,' Molly whispered, leaning towards Rosie and touching her arm, the two men deep in conversation about foreign affairs.

'I must admit to a genuine dismay. It was the last thing I expected to happen,' she admitted, turning from her reply when Harriett knocked, her head popping around the door.

'I'm off to bed,' she informed the two women in undertones. 'Nancy is fretful, teething I think. So I will stay with her. Good night.'

'She's a good girl,' Molly informed nobody, watching the red headed girl disappear upstairs to the nursery. 'I was so glad she decided to move with you.'

Anxious now for the evening to end Rosie played her role of dutiful hostess, glad when it was time to wave her guests goodbye at the doorstep. Extinguishing the lamps and damping down the fire she made her own way to bed, thoughts of a year without Simon revolving in her head as she drifted into an uneasy sleep.

Persistent knocking roused her from a dream, where she had been sailing the sea with Simon, her hair blowing behind her in the light wind, him so handsome in a seaman's uniform.

'What is it,' she called drowsily, shaking her head to clear her thoughts and trying to establish whether the noise came from inside, or out

'Rosie, Rosie come quick,' Harriett cried through the closed door.

Jumping from her bed and lighting her night light, she rushed to open the door and face a dishevelled Harriett, stood shivering in her night attire, her worried face shimmering in the guarded light from her candle, her red hair standing out from her head in a most unruly manner.

'It's Nancy,' the girl gasped. 'She's really ill. I think she needs a doctor.' Not waiting for a reply she turned and hurried back to the nursery.

One look at the red-hot child, bathed in perspiration that she tossed and turned in the cot, sent Rosie's senses reeling. The rasp of her daughters breathing grated on her ears. 'Run for the doctor,' she instructed Harriett who was already pulling on her clothing, preparing to do exactly that.

'Get a message to Molly and Jake,' Rosie called after the fleeing figure.

'But it's the middle of the night,' Harriett called back up the stairs. 'Shouldn't we wait until the morning?'

'No,' Rosie commanded. 'Molly would never forgive me for not sending for her immediately.'

Collecting cold water and cloth, Rosie set about bathing the child's over heated skin, then tucking the covers more securely around the small form when the girl was attacked by violent shivering. She prayed between her ministrations that this would prove to be no more than some childish infection and would disappear as quickly as it had arrived.

After what seemed like an eternity, Harriett returned, closely followed by a man who pushed Rosie aside without ceremony and proceeded to examine the patient.

'I have arranged for a message to go to Molly,' Harriett whispered, they stood together watching the doctor minister to Nancy, muttering to himself all the while.

The next hours went by in a haze, the arrival of Molly and Jake, Daniel waking, his demands for attention which, only satisfied him if given by his mother. Her son clutched in her arms, Rosie paced the room helplessly all the while Molly, Harriett and the doctor, carried out several unpleasant looking remedies, that he felt sure would alleviate the girl's suffering. The slow light of day was dawning when the doctor announced there was little more he could do.

'She's a very sick child,' he confirmed shaking his head. 'I have no idea what she is suffering from at this time. I will be back later when I have consulted with others.' With no more than a few cursory instructions he left.

Molly stood, propped against the door frame, her face pink, her hair stuck to her head with perspiration, wiping a weary arm across her temple she looked at Harriett.

'Harriett dear, can you clean up after the doctor, then you must get some rest you look worn out.' Taking Jake and Rosie by the arm she led them downstairs.

Settling Rosie into a chair she issued her orders. 'When Harriett has cleared everything away, I want you to sit with Nancy. Jake and I will go back to the Refuge for our things. We will return at once and stay as long as needed. 'She knelt awkwardly in front of the younger woman, her voice holding all the authority needed. 'You must move Daniel out of the nursery and leave him in Harriett's care. We, you and I, will look after Nancy. We will take it in turns.'

Staring at Molly's serious face Rosie shivered. She felt a cold hand, clasp at her innards, its clammy fingers taking charge all over again. Was fate going to take its revenge on her children, did she have to pay for her escape from the gallows. 'She will live, won't she?' Her voice was little more than a whisper, which Molly failed to answer.

The days that followed were a living nightmare for Rosie and her family. A trail of doctors, ordered by Simon, trooped in and out of the house. They all stood around the defenceless child shaking their heads and rubbing their chins.

Troublesome Daniel made Harriett's life a misery as she endeavoured to keep him out of the way.

Rosie and Molly sat by the cot day and night, Daniels cot had been removed to Harriett's room and a trundle bed put in its place. Here the two women took it in turns to grasp whatever sleep they could.

Jake made daily visits to the Refuge. At the doctors request he avoided contact with his own children as much as possible.   Simon delayed his trip and spent every spare moment at the town house doing his best to help, but mostly getting in the way. Taking every brief opportunity open to him he endeavoured to comfort Rosie with a word of encouragement, a swift hug, or a peck on the cheek.

Three days into Nancy's illness Daniel began to show signs of a rising temperature. Within twenty-four hours his cot was returned to the nursery and they were caring for two children. Daniel as expected, proved to be the noisier, more troublesome of the two patients.

'I'm so worried about Nancy,' Rosie sobbed against Simon's chest. 'She has grown so quiet she hardly makes a murmur and barely moves a muscle now, yet still they seem to have no idea what she is suffering from,' she wailed.

His lips against her hair he shushed her as he spoke soothing words of comfort to her. 'She's a strong little girl, she will get better, you see,' he promised. 'So will Daniel.'

'Are his actions because he is naturally more demanding in nature,' Molly asked the doctor when helping to change Daniel's sweat soaked clothing. 'Or is he more ill than his sister? She looks to be at death's door, if he is sicker,' she failed to complete her sentence.

The doctor shrugged. 'The infection, illness, whatever, it seems to affect their limbs in a most painful manner. I imagine he has less tolerance of pain than his sister. I do not think he is any worse than she is.' He patted Molly's twisting hands. 'You two ladies look as if you will both be ill soon if you don't get some proper rest.'

'I keep telling them that,' Simon chimed in the conversation. 'Look how pale and drawn they both are. I want to employ a nurse.'

Waving the comments away, Rosie turned back to her children. She could not think of allowing anyone else to nurse them other than herself, with the help of those she loved.

Simon said no more but left the house, returning later in the day with news. 'I've been to see Dr Phipps,' he informed them. 'We well know it's not his field, so he feels it would be of no benefit if he paid the children a visit. Instead, he spent time examining his own library of medical journals.'

'And,' Jake prompted.

'He thinks it's an infection of the spinal column affecting most of the bones and joints, in particular those of the lower part of the body.'

'We already know that,' Jake growled. 'Is it life threatening?'

'Usually it claims the life within the first few days. Now that Nancy is well past the period, he thinks she might be successful in fighting it.' He stopped speaking, licking his lips in nervous agitation.

'Go on man,' Jake urged. 'Whatever it is, we must know.'

'The rare survivors are often left with twisted limbs. In some cases it destroys vital sections of the bones altogether,' he replied, then, with an agonised cry he added. 'What's the use of having plenty of money when you can't stop something like this happening?'

'They could survive, but be left deformed,' Jake finished for him. 'Oh God,' he muttered harshly.

'At best,' Simon informed him. 'At worst they could lose the use of whole sections of their bodies.'

Both men stepped forward to offer what crumbs of comfort they could to the women who had been listening to the news in disbelief.

'Is this catching?' Rosie whispered, thinking of Emily and Samuel.

'Not in the way you mean,' Simon told her softly gathering her into his arms. 'It affects certain people with similar physical structures. Both children have been struck down because they are twins. Dr Phipps feels had they been simply brother and sister, they may not both have suffered.'

It was a further week before Nancy began to show signs of gradual improvement. Her trancelike sleep softened and became more natural. Her breathing lightened and her eyes fluttered from time to time.

'She's on the mend,' the doctors announced jubilantly.

Daily Molly and Rosie examined each child for signs of limb deformity insisting on moving the small arms and legs, despite any protest that may be offered. Rosie spent hours massaging each child in turn in a vain effort to counter any ill effects.

Each day brought fresh strength to Nancy, although Daniel's coma like state seemed to go on forever.

'The house seems so quite,' Harriett confessed as she sat by his cot gazing at his small, pale face.

'I think this young lady could do with a change of scenery,' the doctor told Rosie when he had completed his inspection of Nancy. 'Wrap her up and take her for a walk around the house. It will do her no end of good.' He smiled kindly watching the young mother do as she was told. Hugging the little girl to her chest, she walked slowly out of the room.

Taking the girl from Rosie's arms, Simon walked beside her. 'It will do Mummy good as well,' he confirmed with a smile. They walked sedately down the stairs and he dropped a kiss on the end of his nieces nose, raising the first small laugh the house had heard for weeks.

With tears swimming in their eyes, Harriett and Molly listened from the nursery doorway. 'They will both get well,' Molly said aloud.

Aided by the vitality of youth, Nancy's recovery galloped away, her limbs strengthening and retaining all the knowledge they had known before, showing no signs of mis-shaping or inability to perform naturally.

'She has been very lucky,' the doctor told the assembled gathering. 'You have done well,' his gaze encompassed the women. 'Your efforts to manipulate her limbs have proved successful.' His tone fell and the small smile slipped from his lips. 'Unfortunately, her brother has not fared so well. The lower bones of his spinal column are showing signs of deformity and some crumbling. We won't know immediately, but I fear you must prepare yourself for the fact that he may never walk again.'

Rosie wept for days on end.

'We must be thankful for his life,' Jake comforted her.

'I know, I know,' she moaned. 'But Daniel, I didn't want it to happen to either of them, he will never cope with it.'

Jake nodded, words defeating him.

Of her two children Rosie knew in her heart that Nancy, with her quieter nature, would have accepted disability with a greater understanding, she would have found it inside herself to count her blessings. Daniel never would. His eventual growth into adulthood was already beset by problems not of his making. She had imagined many times how she would tell him the facts of his father's crime ridden past. In many ways he was so like his father she doubted he would ever believe the truth. Now she could see it fraught with insurmountable difficulties.

THIRTY SEVEN

Molly and Jake returned to the Refuge, worn out both physically and emotionally. They delighted in the fact of the infection being contained and not passed on to their own children, revelling in the hugs and kisses that greeted their return.

To make up for her extended absence, Molly helped Lizzie prepare a special treat for the regulars, which gave the day a party atmosphere, something that Jake encouraged unashamedly.

'It will do us all good,' he told his family firmly. 'It will help to relieve our pent up tensions.'

Snuggled in their own bed, still feeling the warmth and love that had pervaded over their homecoming, Molly whispered.

'What do you think Rosie will do with her future now?'

Lying still for a long moment Jake made no response immediately. 'That's something I've been asking myself for days now. I don't know. It's unfair that she should be made to suffer so much. I would like to see her marry Simon and go off to Spain with him. But I fear she won't.'

'Has he said he intends to propose?' Molly cried, sitting up prepared to hit her husband if he knew something he had failed to tell her.

'Not in so many words,' Jake laughed. 'But it's written all over his face.'

'Rosie loves him,' Molly said more quietly. 'She's just afraid to trust yet. Her being the mother of Edwards children

271

and having stood trial for murder, well, she feels that the scandal would be far too great anyway.'

'That's ridiculous,' Jake snorted. 'My God there was enough publicity the news sheets couldn't get enough of the details, everyone knows she wasn't responsible for any of it.'

'She's a woman,' Molly replied softly, nibbling at her husband's ear. 'Women have idea's of their own.'

Succumbing to his wife's actions, Jake allowed the conversation to peter out, their loving gestures proving how much they still cared for one another.

'Rosie doesn't know what she's missing,' Jake whispered against Molly's hair passion taking a firmer grip of his actions. Abandoning themselves to each other they silently agreed to think more about the problem, tomorrow.

THIRTY EIGHT

In Harriett's mind the only draw back to the town house was the garden, it did not leave much room for play. Watching Nancy potter about and Daniel sulk in his specially made seat, she thought about her own childhood. How she had run barefoot across the open countryside, chasing rabbits in the fields, picnicking on bright sunny afternoons, paddling freely in the cold streams that abound in her part of the country. Sometimes she missed it. The clean fresh air, the solitary walks to get away from the family hustle and bustle, but not often.

Mostly her life here in London, was as near perfection as she ever dreamed of. She had willingly left her family and few friends behind.

'Are you sure you don't want to go home, not even for a visit,' Rosie asked regularly. 'You deserve some time off.'

Harriett had answered a polite, 'no thank you,' and meant it. She found more affection here in this small house than she had ever known at home amidst all her brothers and sisters.

'Maybe one day when I'm married and have plenty to show for my life, then perhaps I will,' she assured her employer.

'Does that include the delivery boy?' Rosie had asked with a sly smile.

Now Harriett turned her thoughts to him herself. He came to the house twice a week. They had become quite chatty of late. He had red hair, redder than hers. Whatever would their children look like? She asked herself, blushing at the thought, stopping herself before her imagination went any further.

Daniel began to cry and she sighed inwardly. His illness had changed him so, and for the worse. Never happy by nature he was now morose and sullen to the extreme. His face never lightened to brighter than a frown, his usual expression being a deep scowl. Rising she picked him out of his chair knowing full well that if she ignored his cries, as she would like to, they would soon become ear splitting screams. Plonking him on her hip she gave him the attention he craved.

'I hope he will grow out of these bouts when his brain becomes more agile,' Rosie had confided.

'It's Nancy I feel sorry for,' Harriett told her. 'She behaves as though she's his personal slave.

'I swear she reads his mind,' Rosie replied. 'She almost anticipates his needs. Probably because they are twins,' she added, in a tone that told Harriett she was trying to convince herself. 'Emotionally tied together.'

Harriett ushered her charges into the house, food would placate him it always did. She was not so sure that Rosie was correct about her son. She felt that well, or ill, Daniel would have such a dominating nature he would always have people waiting on him.

EPILOGUE

Rosie had taken to dining quietly on her own. She missed Simon. He had delayed his business trip for a full two months because of the twin's illness. She thought about the last time they had dined together, here in this house, the evening before he set sail. She had not been at her best, unable to hide her feelings. They had eaten the meal in near silence all attempts at small talk failing miserably. Then they had sat side by side on this sofa.

Putting out a hand she smoothed the fabric on the portion of seat that Simon had occupied before his declaration. She smiled as she thought of him falling to his knees in front of her.

'Rosie, you must know that I am hopelessly in love with you. I have dared to presume that you have some small amount of feeling for me,' he declared.

Her heart pounding she had falteringly told him she had.

'Enough to marry me?' he asked, that little boy lost look that she loved so much on his face.

She had nodded, not vigorously merely inclining her head a couple of times.

'Marry me and accompany me to Spain?' he persisted.

That was when it had all gone wrong. Agreeing to marry him at some time in the future was one thing. Marrying now and leaving the country, that was something else again.

'I thought you meant when you get back,' she told him plaintively.

275

'Why not now? Is there a reason why you can't join me on this trip?' His tone held an urgency that almost destroyed her resolve.

'The children,' she had stammered stupidly. 'Daniel is still so weak.'

'The sea air will do him good. I will employ the best nurses,' he promised earnestly.

'It is too soon,' she prevaricated. 'The notoriety will do you no good. I have only recently been cleared of murder. It will destroy your good name.'

'Your son bears the same name, are you not worried for him?' he challenged.

'Go. Get your business settled, then when you return we will marry. I promise,' she had told him sorrowfully. Positive she could never undertake such a gigantic step at such short notice.

He had been distraught, begging her to change her mind, pleading that if she loved him as he loved her she could not face the separation. She had not replied her heart cracking inside her ribcage at the thought of one whole year without him, but determined that what he wanted was not the way it should be done. In the end she had pleaded her own case.

'I can't, it's too soon,' she had told him regretfully. 'I love you, that won't change, but I would not make you a good wife, not yet. I have not yet got used to everything that happened in the past I still have nightmares about Robert, and I am still meeting with Dr Phipps to work on my memory.'

Simon had risen from his knee and sat back beside her. 'Your visits with the doctor are monthly now, I'm sure if I spoke to him he would agree you are as well as you are going to be.'

'Maybe,' she replied then, placing a hand on her breast she had said softly. 'But in here I still have demons that I have to lay to rest. Please be patient. I will count the days until you return.'

He had not persisted. 'I will take Albert with me and should be able to get word back to you in two or three months. I will hurry my business as quickly as I can. Albert will return and tell you how long before you can expect me.'

'At which time,' she replied with a happy smile. 'I will immediately recruit Molly and Jake they will help to make arrangements. Be prepared'. She smiled again the way she had that night. 'You will return to find the wedding ready to take place the moment you set foot on dry land.'

They had embraced passionately.

'Whilst I'm away,' he begged. You will think hard about taking up your rightful place in life. As the mother of an Earl.'

She had promised and meant it, and still did. Though now, four months on with no news, she daily regretted her inability to accept his proposal and rush off to Spain with him. She went to bed each night, as she was about to do now, a prayer on her lips that news would come the next day.

Late winter was in full flow, the wind howling rain blowing in sharp gusts against the windows when Harriett hurried to answer the intrusive knocking at the door.

'It's Jake.' She cried. He swept past her, pushing his way into the main living room where Rosie sat sewing.

'Jake, you look windswept,' she said putting her needle and thread to one side. ' Come and sit by me before the fire and get a warm.'

Jake stood in front of her unmoving, his jaw twitching. He looked down, his, eyes full of sorrow.

'What is it,' Rosie cried, sensing his news was not good. 'Is it Molly. I'll get my cape.' She stood making a move towards the door.

Jake's arms enfolded her a sob escaped his throat stunning Rosie, and Harriett, who still stood in the doorway.

'Darling I'm so sorry,' he muttered into her neck, his tears wetting her skin. 'After all that you have suffered, I am the bearer of terrible news.'

Harriett moved forward and pulled him away from her employer. Looking him straight in the eyes she demanded. 'Tell us, Jake. Just tell us, what on earth is it.'

Both women stared at each other lost for words at Jakes distraught state.

'It must be Molly,' Rosie whispered, 'he would never get this upset over anyone else.'

'Except you,' Harriett corrected her. 'Jake you have news of Simon, don't you?'

Jake nodded rubbing his fists in his eyes he drew a deep breath before speaking. 'Simon's ship, it went down. It floundered in a storm off the Spanish coast.'

Harriett kept calm. 'And Simon?'

'All hands were lost. Nobody survived,' he moaned, tears again wetting his cheek.

Rosie stood, bemused she gazed at each of them in turn. 'When?' She asked in a small voice.

'Two weeks after he left,' Jake told her wretchedly. 'The news has just been sent back to the estate. I've come straight here, from there.' His arms went out to embrace Rosie again she stepped backwards, out of his reach.

'Go home, Jake,' Harriett told him kindly. 'Go and tell Molly. I will take care of Rosie. Give her time to get used to the news.' She accompanied him to the door gently pushing him out into the rain. 'Come back later,' she advised wisely.

Rosie was seated again when she returned. Harriett sat quietly beside her and said nothing. The silence went on for a long time.

'What will I do now?' Rosie asked her voice strangled. Her breath coming in short, sharp pants as she tried to still the turmoil inside her. Her eye casting here and there about the room searching for something, she knew not what.

'I loved him so.' She whispered, clutching the hand holding hers. 'I promised to marry him and move into Daniels rightful home. How will I face life without him?' She turned a stricken face to the girl who shared her world, these days.

Harriett said nothing, the pity and sorrow she felt written on her features.

'Tell me,' Rosie cried, her throat constricted with unshed tears. 'How will I ever be able to give Daniel his rightful place? How could I ever conceive of moving into the family estate without Simon's strength beside me?'

REWARDING HARVEST

Rosie's heart pounded in her breast as she watched him appear from the shadows, a dark, faceless, figure. The apparition trembled in the shadowy darkness, gliding towards her on silent feet. The candle at the bedside flickered in the small breeze stirred by his long, black cloak.

Frightened, yet exhilarated, she shuffled back pushing into the safety of the bedding, bumping against the hard, rail, of the cast iron bedstead, which bit into her neck. The pressure serving to remind her, this was not a dream.

The figure continued to glide towards her. Mouth open in a soundless scream, fear drying her saliva and restricting her throat, Rosie felt the cold trickles of perspiration snake down her spine, wetting her soft, lawn, night attire.

The figure drew level with the bedside, the candle finally guttered, and expired, plunging the room into the starless blackness of deepest night. Arms reached out for her as her scream found its voice, only to be stopped by the delicious pressure placed on her mouth.

Extract from Rosie, part three.